AN UNFORTUNATE SITUATION

by
Caroline Blake

"I pray you, in your letters,
When you shall these unlucky deeds relate,
Speak of me as I am; nothing extenuate,
Nor set down aught in malice. Then must you speak
Of one that loved not wisely but too well;
Of one not easily jealous, but being wrought,
Perplexed in the extreme. . ."

— **William Shakespeare, <u>Othello</u>**

Other Books by Caroline Blake

Just Breathe

Forever Hold Your Peace

Unexpected Storm

The Brief

Chapter One
September 1908 - Violet

I am standing in front of the mistress in the drawing room, with a racing heart and sweaty palms, while she sips her tea. I can sense that within the next few minutes, I am going to be dismissed, sent away from Compton Hall in disgrace.

'Sit down, Violet,' she says.

I perch on the edge of the opposite sofa, thankful for the barrier of the low table between us. I put my hands underneath my thighs for a moment, but withdraw them quickly and place them on my lap. My right hand clings onto my left thumb, as I learned to do in school when Sister Beatrice would walk slowly between the small wooden desks and rap any child sharply on the knuckles if they were judged to be fidgeting.

Mrs Compton raises her eyes from her cup and stares into the fire. The black hearth that I had scrubbed on my hands and knees at six o'clock this morning gleams like polished obsidian and the fire is perfectly lit. Not too many logs have been used. I know that the mistress doesn't like the room to be too hot during the day, September being such an unpredictable month.

'Something has come to my attention,' she says. She hasn't yet looked me in the eyes and continues to examine the dancing flames in the grate. I follow her gaze and wait for her to continue. 'I understand that you are in an unfortunate situation…'

We are interrupted by the intrusion of Mr Compton. I shouldn't call it an intrusion; in all fairness, this is his house. But he is so seldom around that when he is, it feels alien. When he is at home, he moves about the house in a cloud of cigar smoke, which follows him to his study, where he shuts himself in for long periods of time. Often he is alone, but sometimes male visitors in black suits and bowler hats accompany him. Raised voices can be heard through the door and whichever maid delivers their refreshments, does so cautiously and with anticipation.

I jump up as soon as he appears, as though my legs are burnt by the rich velvet fabric of the sofa.

'Where are we up to?' barks Mr Compton.

He reaches the fireplace in a few long strides and stands with his back to it. The cigar smoke swirls behind him before it finally catches him up. He blows it away and Mrs Compton coughs gently. He rolls his eyes and waves his hand in front of him until the smoke dissipates. I watch as a slurry of ash falls from his cigar and lands on the rug. It isn't my rug. What do I care if it's ruined? But the careless act, the act of a privileged man who has never had to count his pennies, or watch his tired wife beating the dust from the rug, annoys me and I concentrate hard to keep a neutral countenance.

'We haven't yet started,' says Mrs Compton. 'Sit down, Violet, please.' She finally looks at me.

I look over to Mr Compton, who is examining the burning end of his cigar, concentrating on blowing onto it to fuel the ember. As he shows no objection, I sit down again and wait for my employers to decide my fate.

'I was just explaining to Violet that we are aware of her unfortunate situation,' says Mrs Compton.

Mr Compton doesn't look at me but nods and takes another puff of his cigar. 'Has the girl seen a doctor yet?'

'I don't know, dear, I haven't had the chance to ask her yet,' answers Mrs Compton. 'Well?'

'No, ma'am,' I reply. I can feel a blush rising from my neck into my cheeks. I'm not sure what I was expecting, but I certainly wasn't expecting the conversation to begin in such a personal manner.

'So you might be wrong then?' asks Mr Compton. He lifts his chin and peers down his nose at me as he awaits the reply, willing me to defy him. But defy him I must.

'No, sir, there's no mistake.' I have missed four of my monthlies, but I keep this private information to myself.

'I would call it a huge mistake,' he bellows. 'And are you sure that the baby is Ernest's?'

I have heard Mr Compton's loud voice many times reverberating through the walls of the house but I have never personally been on the receiving end, and the shock of his accusation brings tears to my eyes. I assure him that the baby may be a mistake, in that it was unintended, but there is no mistake as to the father. It most definitely belongs to his son. I want to tell him that Ernest is happy, that he loves me, and that I love him, but I bite my tongue.

Mr Compton storms over to the window and looks out onto the garden. He straightens the long curtain and I wait for another outburst in which he tells me that my work is shoddy. He has been known to walk into a room that has just been cleaned and run his fingers along the woodwork and the mantelpiece, searching for dust.

'Darling, I'm sure you have better things to do,' says Mrs Compton. 'Why don't you finish your work in your study and I shall speak to Violet. I'll ring for Cook to bring you some tea and cake, shall I?'

Mr Compton hovers on the edge of acquiescence before he finally agrees and leaves the room.

'Now then,' says Mrs Compton. 'Shall we begin again?'

'Yes, ma'am,' I manage to say between sobs that have suddenly overtaken my capacity to speak.

'Now, now, Violet,' says Mrs Compton. 'You must dry your eyes.'

I take out a clean handkerchief from my pocket and wipe my eyes and my nose. I take deep breaths and ready myself, for by now I am pretty sure that Mr and Mrs Compton are not going to welcome me into the bosom of their family as their future daughter-in-law. I wait for Mrs Compton to dismiss me and wonder whether it would be impertinent to ask her for a reference. I look towards the window and thank the Lord that the threatening clouds haven't yet dropped any rain. I might be able to make it to the train station before the storm which is inevitably coming.

'Violet, we need to have a serious conversation,' says Mrs Compton.

'Yes, ma'am,' I reply.

Since that evening in early Spring when Philip caught me and Ernest in the downstairs kitchen together, I have been anxiously waiting for this moment. Philip had seen Ernest's lips on my neck and his hands on my breasts as he pushed me up against the wall. He may have been forgiven for thinking that Master Compton was taking advantage of a young housemaid - as I'm sure in some houses such instances are not unknown - were it not for the giggle that escaped my lips and the fact that my fingers were wrapped around Ernest's hair as I pulled him closer towards me.

I didn't hear the kitchen door open, but I heard Philip's sharp intake of breath and I heard him slam the door shut behind him. I pushed Ernest away and rushed across the kitchen to open it, to call out to Philip, to plead with him for his discretion. But all I saw was the retreating back of the chauffeur as he scuttled down the narrow corridor, his tailcoat swishing angrily, a lamp held aloft in front of him.

'Father must be home,' said Ernest calmly, peering over my shoulder.

I turned and looked up at his face and couldn't see any traces of concern. But then again, he wouldn't be the one who would be punished for fraternising with one of the servants. He wouldn't be the one who would be dismissed from the house with no reference. I burst into tears, closed the kitchen door, and sank in despair onto one of the wooden dining chairs around the old kitchen table.

'Don't cry,' said Ernest, sitting down next to me and stroking my hand. 'You're not worried, are you? Philip won't say anything. I'll have a word with him and make sure of it.'

I couldn't speak for a moment. The thought of Ernest taking Philip to one side and pleading for his silence was abhorrent. Philip's allegiance was to Mr Compton and he alone. Everyone knew that. I snatched my hand away, lifted my apron to my face, and wiped my eyes. 'You shouldn't be down here,' I said. 'Your father will be looking for you.'

'I doubt it,' said Ernest. 'He will be drunk and he will fall into his bed within a few minutes.'

'That's where I need to be,' I said. 'I have to be up early and it's almost midnight already.'

'Then I shall accompany you,' Ernest whispered.

His words were followed by a gentle kiss on my hand. I rose to my feet and we tiptoed up the servants' stairs together, hand in hand, and silently into my bedroom at the top of the house.

Neither of us had much sleep that night, but as he curled around me in my tiny single bed, I must have drifted off to sleep at some point because I remember waking to the sound of the cockerel; a sound which ordinarily I would have cursed for waking me too early, but for which sound that day I was extremely grateful. I nudged Ernest awake and urged him to dress quickly and go back to his own room before anyone saw him.

I remember that I went about that day in a daze, daydreaming of what might be, had I been born into a different family; had I been destined to be a lady, instead of a lady's maid, or had Ernest been destined to be a gentleman's valet, instead of a gentleman. I dreamed that Ernest would tell his parents of our blossoming romance and that his parents, being the modern liberal thinkers that they were, would tell him that they could not have chosen anyone better for him. Mr Compton in an avuncular manner would say that I was intelligent and kind and pretty, and I would make the perfect wife for his young son. My years in service would not count against me, Mrs Compton would add. Quite the contrary, in fact; my skills would no doubt be useful, as I could teach my own servants how things should be done. My experience would be invaluable to the running of a household.

In reality, I know it will never be so and I constantly tell myself that, despite my intelligence and good education, I need to look for my husband elsewhere. Ernest isn't the one for me and wishing will never make it so. I need to choose someone else. Philip will make someone a fine husband one day. Being a chauffeur is a good job. He isn't much older than me and he isn't bad looking. He can be surly and grumpy, but we all have our faults. Arthur, the butcher's apprentice, who delivers fresh meat twice a week, wouldn't be a bad choice for me either. He has had an eye on me for a long time. I can tell by the way he winks at me and lingers by the door if I happen to be in the kitchen at the time of the deliveries. Cook had to shoo him away last week, telling him that he would be missed very soon by his boss if he didn't get a move on and she had lunch to make.

'Get out of the road, lad,' she had said, wafting her tea towel at him until he retreated out of the kitchen and into the yard.

But I don't want Philip or Arthur. I want Ernest.

The morning after that first night, I should have told myself that it was a once-in-a-lifetime circumstance and I should forget that it had ever happened. I had been foolish and reckless and should never have allowed a man to spend the night in my bed. I should have told myself that Ernest would undoubtedly forget it and he would move on to his next conquest, as sure as eggs are eggs. But that choice wasn't mine to make, it seemed. Ernest made sure that I didn't forget it, by seeking me out the next night after dinner and kissing me again, this time in the yard by the kitchen door. And the night after that, and the night after that.

As I sit here now, I wonder how much Mrs Compton knows about what has happened between me and her son. She knows that I am carrying his child – I told Ernest a few days ago – but does she know that we are in love? He must have told her. He must have explained that when I told him the news, he was overjoyed.

Mrs Compton had sent me to Skipton to collect a pair of her shoes from the cobblers that day, and I was prepared to walk, it being a beautiful and dry Autumn day, but Ernest had offered to drive me, telling his mother about some non-existent errand that he also had in the town. She was distracted by her letter writing and didn't pay either of us too much notice. If she had, she would have seen the conspiratorial wink he gave me and my uncontrollable blushes.

Once I had collected the mistress's shoes, Ernest persuaded me to take a walk with him in the Castle Woods, and for an hour or so, I forgot that our relationship was doomed, so wrapped up was I in the moment. We held hands and I pretended that this could last forever. When finally I had to face the truth, I stopped under an old oak tree and told him that I had some important news to tell him. The leaves on the trees were the colour of dying embers. The late afternoon sun struggled bravely through the canopy but, despite its efforts, it failed to warm me and I shivered as I leaned against the trunk, despite the fact that I was wearing my overcoat.

'There's no easy way to break this news,' I said. 'So, I'll just come out and say it.'

'What is it?' said Ernest. 'You're not leaving Compton Hall, are you?'

'I'm having a baby.' I blurted out the words like a bomb and waited for the explosion. I touched my expanding tummy. 'Surely you must have noticed?'

Ernest stepped away initially. He turned his back on me and held his face in his hands. Then he sprinted back to me and swung me around in his arms, so high that my feet lifted off the ground. He laughed into my ear and told me that he loved me and that everything was going to be fine. He promised that he would speak to his parents. They would be over the moon, he said. 'There's nothing more important than family,' he said.

I hoped he was right, but am I being naive by thinking that a relationship between a working-class housemaid - albeit an educated one - the daughter of a factory worker, would ever be accepted by upper-class people such as the Comptons? Yes, maybe. Probably. But optimism combined with young love is an extremely strong force.

Now, as I try to decipher the look on Mrs Compton's face, my optimism is shrinking. I am struggling to decide whether she is angry, disappointed, and appalled, or whether she is in fact over the moon. She does not have the look of an ecstatic expectant grandmother. The chasm between us could not be greater. My plain black dress is littered with dust after a morning's work, my clogs are scuffed, my fingernails need a scrub, and the skin on my hands is dry and chapped. Mrs Compton in her high-necked blouse, decorated with delicate embroidered lace the colour of whipped cream, and her elegant cloud-grey skirt which skims black leather boots is spotlessly clean.

'Ernest told me and his father that you think the baby might be due in February, is that correct?' she says. I nod. 'It will be here before we know it. And are you well? Or are you sickly?'

'I'm quite well, thank you, ma'am. Although I tire easily.'

'Yes, that's to be expected,' she says. 'Do your parents know of your condition?'

'No, ma'am, although I expect they will do before long.'

'No, no,' says Mrs Compton with a sudden shake of her head and a wag of her index finger. 'They do not need to know.'

'I don't understand, ma'am.'

Mrs Compton puts her cup and saucer onto the table and shuffles forward in her chair. For a moment, I think that she is going to grasp my hand, but she doesn't. I still can't fathom what she's thinking. She smiles at me but her eyes are as cold as flint.

'I would like to discuss something with you, Violet,' she says. 'We have a plan and I think you will agree that it is something that will benefit both of us.'

Chapter Two
September 1908 - Violet

I almost pass Cook on the back stairs as I quickly make my way back down to the servants' floor in the basement of the house. She stands in the middle of the step, about halfway up, her feet firmly stationed, her hands resting on her wide hips. With my head down, it's her feet that I spot first and I stop suddenly before we collide.

'Violet Pearson, where have you been?' she commands. 'I've been searching high and low for you. We have enough to do, don't you think, without your shenanigans holding up the job? It's like looking for Harry Houdini.'

I don't have a chance to explain, which is just as well because Mrs Compton has sworn me to secrecy, before Cook waves her arms at me and forces me to retreat backwards, with a warning that bad luck will befall the whole household if we are to cross on the stairs.

Back on the ground floor, I follow Cook into the dining room to begin laying the table for dinner, a job which is usually done by Barrow, but which he delegates to Cook when he is busy with the master.

'We've got five for dinner tonight,' says Cook. She bends down and peers at the sheen on the mahogany table. Satisfied that her hunt for smears is unsuccessful, she walks around the table, moving the chairs an inch this way, an inch that way. I have often found her eye for detail inspirational - nobody could argue that the dining room ever looked less than perfect after Cook's eye had been cast around - but today I find it irritating beyond measure. What does it matter that the master's chair at the end of the table is not at an exact right angle to the window, or that the three chairs down each side of the table are not equally spaced? Would anyone truly notice? If they did, they wouldn't be so rude as to comment.

'Who's the fifth guest?' I ask, as I pull open the top drawer of the sideboard and begin to count out the cutlery.

'Not those, not those,' says Cook. She abandons her chair-straightening mission and rushes over to me. She snatches the cutlery from my hands and gently places the pieces back in the drawer. 'We need the best silver tonight.' She nods and smiles to herself. 'Well, come on then, what are you waiting for?' She pushes the drawer shut and points to the one underneath it, where the second, and the best, set of cutlery is kept. The one reserved for Christmas and special dinner parties with The Comptons' favourite guests.

As I bend down, I can feel her eyes burning into my back. The hot knowledge of tonight's guest is too much for her and I know that she will tell me eventually, but I humour her and ask again who it is that the master and mistress are expecting for dinner.

'Reverend and Mrs Flynn,' she says, with a sigh of satisfaction that the secret is finally out, like a butterfly escaping from its cocoon. 'It is such an honour. The reverend is a very busy man, you know. Much in demand for dinner, I would imagine.' She makes the sign of the cross and closes her eyes for a second, as though our guest was Jesus Christ Himself and the Comptons were hosting the Last Supper.

Mrs Flynn is Mrs Compton's sister. If I owned my own house, especially one with a dining room this size, with a flurry of servants to wait on my every need, I would expect my sister and her husband to visit often, once a week at least. I want to tell Cook that it isn't an honour at all. They are family. That is what families do. But right now, I'm struggling to think straight. My jumbled thoughts race around my head, leaving no space to consider Mr and Mrs Compton's dining partners. It is only when Cook bustles around the table, taking each knife and fork from me after I have polished them and placing them on either side of a gold embossed white china dinner plate, whilst simultaneously mumbling the name of the dinner guest to herself, that I realise that there should be an extra place setting. We are one short.

'Don't we need six places at the table?' I ask.

'No, just five,' answers Cook.

'Are you sure?'

'Of course, I'm sure,' she says. 'Barrow himself told me before he went out.'

'So, Mr Compton here,' I say, touching the top of his high-backed dining chair at the head of the table. 'Mrs Compton over there at the other end, Mrs Flynn and her husband here.' I point to the chairs on either side of the master's.

'Yes, yes, like I said, Mr Compton, Mrs Compton, Reverend Flynn, Mrs Flynn, and Miss Mary.' Cook points to all of the chairs in turn. 'Now then, where are the napkins?' She claps her hands together loudly. 'Violet, chop chop! The napkins!'

'Isn't Master Ernest dining at home tonight?' I turn my back and busy myself in finding the linen napkins in the sideboard so that Cook is unable to read any expression that might unwittingly cross my face.

'No. He left for Oxford this morning,' she says.

'Oxford?' I turn too quickly and a fleeting dizzy spell forces me to hold onto the edge of the open drawer. A couple of napkins fall from my grasp and I watch as they flutter to the floor.

'Violet!' Cook's admonishment is swift, as I expected it would be and I scoop the napkins up and begin straightening them out. She rushes over to inspect and only allows me to place them across the plates when she is sure that no dust has dared to cling to the delicate fabric. 'Okay, good,' she says. She steps back and admires the job so far. 'We just need some water glasses tonight. Put the wine glasses back, please. You know the Reverend isn't a fan of alcohol.'

I collect the wine glasses and place them back in the dresser. As I begin to pass Cook the larger water glasses, one at a time, I am anxious to ask her what she knows about Ernest's trip to Oxford, but how can I do this without arousing suspicion? I am as sure as I can be that she doesn't know about my love affair with him and I silently thank Philip for that. If she knew, she would have had me dismissed on the spot. A new maid would be hired before anyone noticed that I was gone.

'Will Master Ernest be away long in Oxford?' I ask, eventually, with as much composed indifference as I can muster.

'Until Christmas, as far as I know,' she says.

'Christmas?'

She holds a glass into the air and twirls it around before setting it on the table. I try to steady my voice, even though I am on the verge of tears. The thought that Ernest could have left to go back to university without saying goodbye is punching a hole in my heart. The pain is palpable.

'But, I didn't think the new university term started until next week?' I say.

'That one has a smudge on it,' says Cook. She returns one of the glasses to me and I pass her a fresh one.

My question is lost amongst the crockery and glasses and I have no option but to continue my work until such a time that I can escape to my room. The hope that Ernest has managed to sneak upstairs and has hidden a love letter underneath my pillow is the only thing that keeps me going throughout the day.

'If Mr Barrow finds any fault with this table, Violet dearest, I'll eat my hat.' Cook laughs to herself and I follow her out of the room.

Mr Barrow has been Mr Compton's valet and butler since the age of the dinosaurs and has the fierceness of a tyrannosaurus rex. During my time at Compton House, I have managed to avoid his wrath thus far but I have heard the way that he has spoken to the other members of staff, and on this occasion, I am glad that I did not set the table on my own. If he has anything to say, then at least Cook and I can bear it together. Although, I won't have to put up with him much longer. Not if I accept Mrs Compton's offer, that is. Whether I do or not decides very much on what Ernest wants to do.

If only he wasn't so far away when I need him.

*

After dinner, I finally make it back to my room.

Mr Barrow has been in a particularly bright mood all evening, having had an exciting afternoon out with Mr Compton, and had brought back with him two bottles of wine and a fruit cake, an unexpected treat. Mr Barrow persuaded everyone to stay around the kitchen table for a game of cards. I stayed for one game but then told them that I was tired. It has been a long day.

I dash to my bed and frantically search for Ernest's letter. The bed appears to be untouched; it is as neat and tidy as when I left it this morning, and the books on my bookcase appear to be undisturbed. Nevertheless, I search under my pillow, under the mattress, in the drawers of my unit, and also under the bed. Then I take each of the books from the shelves and shake them open, but find nothing. I sink onto the bed with a racing heart and jumbled thoughts. My mind is so saturated with disappointment and hurt.

I take out my notepad and pencil and begin to write Ernest a letter. Mrs Compton told me earlier that they hadn't discussed their offer with him. She told me that I should keep it to myself, as he was entering his final year of studies at Oxford and they were of the view that he should be left alone to concentrate. I had bitten my tongue, but my expression must have given me away because Mrs Compton's face took on a cold glare. She told me that if I interrupted Ernest's studies in any way, the offer would be immediately rescinded and I would be left to bring up a baby on my own, out of work and penniless.

Well, let's see what Ernest has to say, shall we? He won't abandon me. I know he won't.

Dearest Ernest,

I'm shocked and upset that you have gone away to Oxford without speaking to me, but don't think for one moment that I blame you. I most certainly do not. I know that you had no choice. I know that you would never leave prematurely of your own accord and you certainly wouldn't leave without saying goodbye to me and smothering me with kisses. Your parents, undoubtedly, gave you an ultimatum. They have given me one, too.

Today has been a day that I will never forget.

I desperately wish that you were here so that I could talk to you. We have so much to discuss and so many decisions to make. I know that we are both still young and you are not yet earning your own money, but you will be soon, and I have some savings. Surely we should not be allowing other people to decide our fate? We are both adults.

I know that you don't know what I'm talking about, and you are probably wondering why I am talking in riddles. I can imagine you reading this letter quickly, skimming over my words, hoping to get to the point. So, I will do. But please take your time to read on. Do not rush; do not allow your emotions to govern your next steps. It is important for you to keep a cool head so that we can make the decision that is right for us both.

Your mother called me into the drawing room this morning and told me that she and your father know about the baby. I am sure that I don't have to tell you what their reaction was. You, no doubt, experienced their wrath firsthand when you told them. After sending your father out of the room, your mother poured me some tea and asked me to carefully consider the offer that she was about to make to me.

She told me that, firstly, I have to get any notion of you and me being together out of my head. She said that it would never happen. They will never accept me into the family as your wife. (Did she say that to you? Please tell me you are willing to talk to them and try to change their minds.) Secondly, she said she refuses to let your life be ruined by me and a baby. She actually said "a baby". I wanted to correct her and tell her that I am carrying "our baby" and that the child is her grandchild, but I remained silent.

She told me that she was within her rights to end my employment immediately, without a reference, and I would be forced to go back to live with my parents and I would end up working in a dirty factory. She asked me how many children were still at home and when I said that my two younger sisters and my brother were all at home, she said that I needed to think clearly about whether I could go back to sharing a bedroom, after having my own room at Compton Hall for the past two years. I think she was trying to scare me, but actually going back to live within the bosom of my family would be a blessing for me.

I did not tell her that. I waited for her to tell me what my options were. I was intrigued with what she would come up with. Although, I would never have guessed what she was about to say. Never in a million years would I have thought that she would ask me to give our baby away. But that's what she did! Can you believe it? She said that you don't know anything about her proposal and she swore me to secrecy, but I can't have any secrets from you, my darling. It seems so wrong not to tell you what they are planning.

She wants me to sell our baby to her sister - your aunt and her husband, that nasty and horrible Reverend Flynn.

She wants me to leave Compton Hall early in December (she made it clear that it would be before you return for the Christmas holidays, so we shan't see each other) and go and stay in your summer cottage in Bowness-on-Windermere until the baby is born. Then I am to pass the baby to the horrible Reverend and Mrs Flynn, who will bring it up as their own.

I can't do it, Ernest. I won't give our baby away.

Could we speak on the telephone? I need to hear your voice. I need you to tell me that everything will be all right.

I will busy myself in the kitchen after everyone has gone to bed on Saturday night, so if you ring at eleven in the evening, I will pick up the phone in the servants' hall.

Sending all my love,
Violet xx

I fold the paper in half and slip it into an envelope. I address it with the simple address of 'Ernest Compton, Student, The Law Department, Oxford University'. The Compton family is notorious and I know that the letter will find its way to him. I have allowed a full week for the letter to reach him and for him to telephone me, even though it will kill me to wait that long. I don't know how I am going to bear it.

Cook hums to herself as she climbs the stairs a little while later. My bedroom door is ajar. She mustn't see me still awake, she will want to know what I am doing, so I jump up and quickly close it. Her humming stops for a second. I can imagine her debating whether or not to knock, but thankfully she continues past my door and I can hear her bedroom door creak open, and then close again as she retires to bed.

Chapter Three
September 1908 - Violet

The following morning, I am engrossed in the task of making Mrs Compton's bed when she returns to her room. Eliza, one of the junior maids, is cleaning out the fire. I immediately straighten up and resist the temptation to hold onto the aching pain in my lower back. I will never give Mrs Compton the satisfaction of knowing that the work she asks me to do is arduous.

'Sorry, ma'am,' I say. 'I didn't expect you back from breakfast so soon. We can come back and finish your room later.'

Eliza jumps to her feet. She drops the hearth brush with a clatter. She stares at the mistress like a frightened rabbit who senses a predator.

'No, Violet. Stay here. Eliza, please leave us,' she says. Eliza scuttles from the room. 'We need to talk, don't you think?' she adds when Eliza has left and she has closed the door behind her.

She poses it as a question, but I am aware that I have no choice in the matter. She is the mistress of the house and I do as I am told, although she is the last person I want to speak to, given the circumstances. Given what she said to me last night. However, I nod and she tells me to sit down.

'Sit, sit!' she repeats impatiently when I hesitate as I glance around the room, wondering where she wants me to go.

Lowering myself onto the edge of the unmade bed, I watch Mrs Compton pace over to the window and back again like a nervous caged lioness.

'You are making my life extremely difficult, Violet,' she says. She stops pacing and stands at the end of the bed, gripping onto one of the brass knobs. I twist to look at her and wish that she hadn't asked me to sit. I feel extremely uncomfortable perched on the edge of Mrs Compton's marital bed. 'Mr Compton and I made you an extremely generous offer and you have thrown it back in our faces.'

'But, ma'am…'

'Don't interrupt me, Violet. I specifically bade you not to speak of the offer to anyone. Nobody!'

'I haven't, ma'am.' My heart is racing with indignation and I want to stand up to her and tell her not to speak to me in that tone. I might be working as her housemaid, but I am carrying her grandchild, after all. A future Compton who will demand respect and admiration.

It frustrates me that she knows nothing about me. All she sees is my uniform and the occupation in which I am currently employed. My education, which was excellent thanks to the dedication of the teachers at my school; the bookcase groaning with books of all kinds in my room; my ambition to read more, learn more, and better myself means nothing to her. But, of course, I silence myself, again. Even if I began to speak, she wouldn't listen to me.

'I told you not to discuss the offer with Ernest. I won't have his life ruined. He has worked extremely hard to get where he is and he needs to concentrate on his studies without distraction. I thought I had made myself clear.' I turn my head away so that she cannot see the angry tears that are beginning to fall onto my cheeks. 'But you disobeyed me, didn't you?'

'I haven't spoken to him,' I whisper.

'I beg your pardon?'

I turn to face her. 'I said that I haven't spoken to him.'

'You wrote to him!'

She reaches into the pocket of her skirt and retrieves my letter to Ernest. My private words are clutched in her fist. Like a caged and frightened bird, they have no chance of escaping. She waves the letter in my face, before throwing it angrily onto the bed. It is so close to me. I want to reach down and grasp it. The letter was never posted. How stupid I was to ask Philip to post the letter for me. Because he knew about me and Ernest I thought I could trust him, but ultimately, his betrayal does not surprise me. Just because he knows about me and Ernest does not mean he condones our behaviour. I should have known better.

'Ernest doesn't want anything to do with you, Violet. You know that, don't you?'

'No, that's not true.' I stand and face her and a tiny shot of pleasure zips through my body when she steps back slightly.

'You silly little girl,' she says. 'That's why he left for university early, so he didn't have to speak to you.' She snatches the letter up, turns her back on me, and walks towards the window again and I can hear her breathing heavily. Then she walks over to her dressing table, opens the top drawer, and deposits my letter in amongst her jewellry.

27

She turns the tiny key, which she then pushes into the pocket of her skirt. She will burn the letter in the fire later this evening, I imagine.

Time moves on as I stand and wait, still and silent, for another confrontation. I hold my hands tightly behind me. The temptation to lash out at her is too much. I don't believe what she is telling me about Ernest. It can't be true. She is just being cruel.

'Mr Compton and I don't want you in this house any longer, Violet. I know we said you could stay until December but, well, you've only got yourself to blame.' She speaks to the windowpane as if the person she is addressing is outside, taking a leisurely walk around the garden, taking in the cool autumn air without a care in the world. 'You can pack your bags and leave immediately, and return to your family.' She pauses a moment, waiting for her vicious words to sink in. 'Without a reference.' I remain quiet. 'Or Philip will take you to the train station to begin your journey to Cumberland at the end of the week. Which is it to be?'

She walks back over to me, her equilibrium returned, and stands at the foot of the bed. The only clue as to her inner feelings is the way she wrings her hands, twisting and turning her fingers. When she sees that I have noticed, her fingers still.

'If you had any sense, and I know you're an intelligent girl, Violet, you would take my extremely kind and generous offer. I can't see that you have a favourable alternative. I will not allow you to stay at Compton Hall.'

'I'll go to Cumberland, ma'am,' I say. She is right, of course. If she is determined to keep me and Ernest apart, and he is determined not to fight for me, then what alternative do I have?

Mrs Compton looks shocked and I can see a smile playing about the edges of her mouth as she tries to maintain an expressionless face. It is clear that she expected me to stubbornly cling to my independence and walk away. But she and I both know that independence isn't a gift for the likes of people like me. Even an education can't help me if I have a baby to care for and no husband to help me.

'Very well,' she says. 'The train leaves Skipton at seven forty-five on Friday to go to Settle. You can catch the connecting train from Settle to Oxenholme and then onto Windermere. It is a journey I have done many times myself. There is no need to look so alarmed.'

'Yes, ma'am.'

'I will see you before dinner tonight to give you the address and the front door key to Lakeview Cottage, together with directions from the train station. Come to the library at six-thirty.'

'What about the money, ma'am?' My insubordination floats between us, casting a dark shadow over her face. I know that the upper classes don't like to talk about money, but it is too bad. This is what this transaction is all about, after all. I have to think about myself now, as well as my unborn child. I am not doing this as an act of charity.

'You can take half of it with you and then you can have the other half when the baby is born, as we agreed.'

'But I didn't agree to that, ma'am, with respect.' I ignore her frown and the little circles of red that form on her cheeks. 'I want all the money upfront.'

'Impossible!' she screeches. 'You can't…'

'Yes, I can,' I say. I put a protective hand onto my tiny bump. 'I know you do not agree, ma'am, but you need to see things from my point of view. Right now, I need to make sure that I have enough money to take care of any medical needs…'

'Yes, yes.' She waves her hand up and down, batting away my concerns dismissively. 'The medical costs will be taken care of, you know that you don't need to worry about that. Doctor Bradbury in Windermere is one of the best doctors in the business. You will be extremely fortunate to be in his care.'

'I will need a midwife,' I say.

'Of course. I'm sure that there will be a local midwife. Doctor Bradbury will organise everything you need.'

'And I will need money for food and coal for the fire.'

'There will be plenty of coal in the coal store, but we can always have more delivered, if necessary. You will be given your wages, as usual, in return for keeping the house clean and getting it ready for the summer.' She takes a deep breath and then adds, 'I will arrange for a small box of groceries to be delivered every week, together with meat and eggs. You will want for nothing.'

She honestly thinks that a box of food and a warm fire will cinch the deal. 'If truth be told, ma'am, I don't trust anyone, and it is nothing personal, but I need to put myself first. After all of this, I will be considered damaged goods, unlikely to get a husband, and I will be out of a job. I need to make sure that I will have enough money to keep me going for a while after the baby is born, until I am fit to work again.'

'I am sure we can find you a position somewhere, we have friends…'

'No, thank you, ma'am.'

She stares at me for a moment and I wonder if she ever considers what it is like to be someone like me. Is that what she is thinking now? Has she ever put herself into my shoes? I wonder what it is like to be her most days; when I see her reading the morning newspaper, with not a care in the world; when I plump the soft cushions on the luxurious sofa that she will rest on in the evenings; when I race up and down the stairs a dozen times a day with cups of tea for her and whichever friend happens to be calling on her; when I tidy her bedroom and admire the dozens of dresses and hats, rows of pearls and diamond hair pins that scatter her dressing table, and right now, in this moment, I wonder what it is like to be her, a woman with choices.

'But where will you go?' she asks me. 'What will you do?'

If I thought for one moment that she cared, I would sit down again and discuss with her what my options would be. 'I will find another job, ma'am. Maybe in a department store or a nice dress shop. There is always work for someone like me.' My dreams of one day being a teacher or even a writer of children's stories have nothing to do with her and I'm not going to share them.

She nods, seemingly satisfied. 'Yes, well, like I said, fifty now and fifty when the baby is born…'

'No,' I say, firmly. I lift my chin and meet her gaze. 'All of the money now, or I will go home to my family and you will never see the baby again.'

'Okay, as you wish,' she says quickly glancing at the door, as though listening for eavesdroppers. 'You can have all the money. But if you run home to your family, or you dishonour our agreement in any way, I will send the police to your parents' house. Do you understand? I will tell them that you stole the money. You will be in prison before you can say "not guilty."'

I tell her that I understand and that I have no intention of going to my parents' house. I assure her that I will write to my family and tell them that I have been tasked with looking after the Compton's summer cottage in Cumberland for a few months, and I will promise to write to them often, but I will tell them that I am not able to visit, because I cannot leave the house unattended, due to the fact that it will be being decorated. Mrs Compton seems to like this idea and says that I should make a point of telling them that there is a lot of work to do to get the house ready for the summer season and that I will not have any free time, except for half a day a week. She says that I must strongly discourage my family from visiting, in fact, I should tell them that they are forbidden from doing so, and I tell her that I have no intention of letting them see me for the next few months. This is true. I blink away the tears as I tell her that I don't want them to know that I have agreed to sell my baby. Mrs Compton says that I am not selling my baby, I mustn't see it like that. She takes hold of both of my hands and tells me that I am doing a very gracious and unselfish thing. Giving a baby to a childless couple, especially a couple as deserving as the Flynns, is the best gift that anyone could ever give to another human being.

She has actual tears in her eyes. I tug my hands away and I tell her that I need to go now and pack my things. How dare she become emotional like that! I am the one who is forced to sell my child simply because of who I am and the circumstances that I find myself in. The unfairness of it makes me angry beyond words. I straighten her bed covers as quickly as I can and leave the room.

I run to my tiny bedroom. The place that has been my own personal sanctuary for the past couple of years.

'Things will work out just fine,' I tell my baby bump. I can feel her fluttering around in there. Her miniature arms and legs tickle my insides. I instinctively feel that she is a girl.

Despite my reservations, worries, and woes, I tell myself that I know that we are both going to be okay. I tell myself that I will enjoy spending the next few months in the Compton's cottage. I have never been to Cumberland before. I have heard that it is a very special place and is especially beautiful in the winter when it sparkles with frost and icicles.

I tell myself that I am doing the right thing and that my daughter will be much better off living with Reverend and Mrs Flynn. What a joy it will be for her to grow up with wealth and the privileges it will bring her. Then the thought of her as a little girl, sitting cross-legged on the floor of her nursery, surrounded by piles of toys and books, stops me short. The pain in my heart is unbearable. I am going to Bowness-on-Windermere, close to the home of the famous author, Beatrix Potter, yet I will never be able to read one of her beautiful books to my child.

I lie face down on my bed and sob into my pillow.

Chapter Four
September 1908 - Violet

There isn't much of a fuss when I leave Compton Hall. You would think that after two years of loyal service, I would be given a small gift. A cake to take with me, or a pair of lace handkerchiefs, or a fragrant bar of soap at least. That's what I would have given my housemaid if she was leaving my employment. In return for a baby, it isn't too much to ask, is it? I would have gathered the staff in the hallway and instigated a round of applause when the maid came down the stairs, and then I would have smothered her with gifts, tokens of appreciation for her hard work. But, like my mother says, it wouldn't do for us all to be made the same. How boring would it be then?

Cook is the only person who seems sorry to see me go. She made me a cup of tea and a small bowlful of porridge this morning and, now, as I take the empty bowl to the sink to wash, she takes it from me.

'Now, now, don't bother yourself with that,' she says, as she immerses the bowl into the soapy water and concentrates on scrubbing it more than is warranted. 'You go and get yourself ready. I have made you a nice cheese and pickle sandwich for your journey. Go and collect it from the cold store. Then you had better wait in the hall. You don't want to keep Philip waiting.'

I am already dressed and my suitcase is packed with my meagre belongings and some books that I cannot bear to leave behind, but I don't argue with her. I hate goodbyes as much as the next person. Cook sniffs and I can tell she is about to cry, so I hug her tightly from behind, wrapping my arms around her ample waist, and ask her to promise to write to me and fill me in on all the gossip. She pats my hand, covering it with soap suds, and says that, of course, she will, and she wants me to write back and tell her about Lakeview Cottage and all the interesting people in Bowness.

As I walk over to the cold store to collect my doorstep slices of brown bread and cheese wrapped in paper on which Cook had scrawled *With love from Mrs Meadows* together with a large love heart, I wonder what she would say if she knew the real reason for my departure. She has no clue that I am carrying Ernest's child. She likes to see herself as a woman of the world, but she isn't at all. Her world consists entirely of the kitchen in Compton Hall and the surrounding area between here and St Ann's Church in the village.

Cook told me last night on more than one occasion how lucky I am to be given this chance. Taking on such a prestigious house was an honour indeed, she had said, particularly at my young age. The mistress must think very highly of me. I nodded and forced myself to agree with her. I smiled and then concentrated on dipping my chunk of bread into my vegetable soup so I did not have to meet Philip's scowl across the table. Cook reminded me to work hard to get the cottage spick and span and I assured her that I would.

I give Cook one last hug and make my way to the hallway. Seven o'clock is slow to appear. I keep my eyes on the clock, my suitcase at my feet and the key to Lakeview Cottage safely tucked into the deep pocket of my overcoat.

Eliza rushes down the stairs on her way to the drawing room, fire rake in hand, and wishes me a hasty goodbye, but Mr Barrow is nowhere to be seen, and neither are Mr or Mrs Compton. Not that I am keen to speak to any of them this morning. The last encounter with Mrs Compton was frosty, to say the least. I could tell that she had plenty that she wanted to say, but she was keeping her words tucked away deep inside, no doubt frightened of getting on the wrong side of me in case I changed my mind. Until the money has changed hands, I have the power to decline the offer, leaving her sister and the horrible Reverend Flynn childless.

Unlike our first meeting in the drawing room, which was quite convivial - friendly I might say - Mrs Compton did not ask me to sit down in the library, nor did she offer me any tea. I stood in front of her like a recalcitrant schoolgirl, trying my best to stem the flow of my tears. I brushed them away surreptitiously every time Mrs Compton looked down, which was quite often, as it seemed she had difficulty making eye contact with me. If she noticed my emotion, she did not allow herself to react. Her British stiff upper lip came into its own. She pushed a long metal door key into an envelope, along with a folded sheet of thick cream notepaper on which she informed me were the directions to the cottage from the train station at Windermere. She licked the envelope, closed it, and placed it on the low table in front of her.

'There you are,' she said, keeping her head down, studying the envelope for longer than was necessary. 'There are comprehensive directions in there, but you won't have any problem finding the cottage. Turn left out of the train station, walk down the hill, and then turn left at the bottom of the road when you reach the lake in Bowness.'

'Thank you, ma'am,' I said.

'Regarding the money,' she continued. 'We don't have such a large amount of cash in the house, so I cannot give you any now, but I will bring it to you within the next few weeks when I visit. The full amount, I promise.'

I didn't know what to say. Thoughts and questions clambered about in my head and fought to get out, but I didn't speak. I simply reached for the envelope and left the room. Fortunately, I have not seen her since.

I hear footsteps behind me. It is Philip, marching up the servants' staircase and into the hallway just as the clock strikes seven. Without looking at me or speaking to me, he picks up my suitcase, carries it outside, and places it into the boot of Mr Compton's waiting car. I follow him and close the front door gently behind me. As I approach the car, I am not sure whether to sit in the front seat or climb into the back. Philip doesn't give me any indication, so I opt for the front, guessing that the pompous chauffeur wouldn't hesitate to put me right if I make the wrong choice, the back seats generally being reserved for Mr and Mrs Compton.

The journey to the train station doesn't take long, but it feels like hours. The oppressive silence in the small car sits uncomfortably between us like a fortress. Philip keeps his eyes firmly ahead and I keep mine to my left, looking out of the window. I do not want him to communicate with me. I have no idea how much he knows of my situation, but there is no doubt that he would have read my letter to Ernest before he handed it over. I do not want to hear his views on how my disgraceful actions could have brought shame to the family, had it not been for Mrs Compton offering me a way out of the mess I had made for myself. I am ready for him, poised to fight off his piercing words, and I am glad when he chooses to ignore me, as I am not in the mood for a battle.

Surely he cannot condone the fact that Mrs Compton has offered me money in exchange for a baby? I want to ask him, whilst it is just him and me in the car. I want to tell him that Ernest loves me and that he will make everything right. It doesn't matter that my letter was intercepted. I will write him another one. Nobody can stop me when I'm at Lakeview Cottage. I can do what I want. But I cannot bring myself to begin the conversation.

Instead, I concentrate on watching the view as it whizzes past, and I wonder how the Yorkshire hills differ from the ones in Cumberland, whether they have purple heather or emerald-coloured moss, or a mixture of both? I had heard that the hills are peppered with dark grey granite and sheep. Lots and lots of sheep.

Finally, the car journey comes to an end. Philip drops my suitcase onto the road. As he is getting back into the car, he says, 'You've only yourself to blame for this. Ernest doesn't want you. He never has.'

'That's a lie,' I say.

He shakes his head. ' If you believe that, you're more of a fool than I thought. Why do you think he went off to Oxford without speaking to you?'

'He didn't have chance to speak to me,' I say.

'Rubbish,' he says.

He gets back into the car and drives away without a second look, leaving me with more unanswered questions than ever before. I know Ernest loves me, but it is true that he didn't make an effort to come and find me before he left. Maybe I was just a bit of fun to him. A play thing.

It is now seven-thirty. I am alone at the entrance to the station, with fifteen minutes to spare until my train is due to leave. Suddenly, I am terrified. I have never travelled alone on a train before. What if I miss the connecting stops? What if I get on the wrong train? I am not sure whether I am doing the right thing at all. Spending the next few months alone in a strange town whilst pregnant suddenly feels like the worst idea in the world.

'Everything all right, miss?'

I turn to see a young station guard standing behind me. He looks no older than my brother, Thomas, and has a kind face. His concerned smile and his bright blue eyes that remind me of my brother bring sudden tears to my eyes.

'Now, now, don't cry, miss,' he says. He pushes his hands into his jacket pockets and then his trouser pockets, one after the other. 'I don't have a clean handkerchief, I'm afraid.'

'It's okay, I've got one,' I say, as I dab at my eyes.

'Can I help you with anything? Do you need a sit down for a moment?' I shake my head. 'Which platform are you looking for?'

'I'm not sure,' I manage to say. I pull the various tickets from my pocket, turn them over in my hands, and stare at them. 'Is there a train to Manchester from here?'

'Yes, miss,' says the guard. 'You will need to change at Clitheroe and then at Bury. The next train leaves at eight-fifteen.' He reaches out for the bundle of tickets and I give them to him without thinking. 'There are no tickets here for those trains though, miss.'

'Yes, I know, I just wondered if it was possible that I could get to Manchester from here,' I say. 'I think I might have changed my mind about my journey.'

The young guard returns my tickets. 'See the man in there.' He nods towards a small booth. 'He'll sort you out with the tickets that you need.'

'How much will it be?' I asked him.

'I'm not too sure exactly, miss, about thr'pence, maybe four pence. He will be able to tell you.'

With that, the young guard walks away to help another customer, leaving me and my dilemma alone for a moment. My tickets are all for the third-class carriages. Of course, they are. I would not have expected to be sitting anywhere else, but as I stare at the tickets and the printed words blur behind my tears, I am suddenly enraged. I want to rip them up and throw them onto the floor and stamp on them furiously. The least Mrs Compton could have done would have been to buy me a first-class ticket, at least for part of the journey. It isn't as though she can't afford it. Would she expect her grandchild, the child of her son, to travel third class? I think not. As the doors to the station open behind me and two ladies enter, chattering and laughing, I am brought to my senses, and I move to the side out of the way, kicking my small suitcase along the floor. I sit down on a wooden bench while I gather my thoughts.

My mother would love to see me. I know how much she misses me. I haven't been home for weeks. I can picture her face when I tell her about the baby. She might be worried about me initially; my mother worries about anything and everything, so that is to be expected, but I know that she would wrap me in her arms and whisper into my hair that everything was going to be fine. With so many mouths to feed already, what is one more? she would say. My mother would clap her hands together in excitement and would send Rose to the grocer's shop for another loaf of bread and some sliced ham and we would feast like kings when Father and Thomas got home from the factory. Father is a kind and gentle man who loves his family more than life itself, so he would be more than happy to see me ensconced back in the family home.

But I know it isn't the right thing to do. How would I go to work? It would not be fair to ask my mother to look after a baby while I was out of the house all day. My life would be immeasurably difficult and I tell myself that I need to forget seeing Manchester and my family for a while.

Ernest and I should be together. He is a gentleman and, despite his parents' objections, I know that he will fight for me. When he gets a minute. He will be busy with his studies, but when he has settled in, he can write home and tell his parents that I wish to study to become a teacher. I am not just a housemaid. There is a real chance that we could be married one day when he has finished at Oxford. Then we can have more children, and our lives will be perfect.

I pick up my suitcase and make my way into the body of the station to wait for the train to Settle, which is to be my first stop. I can see the two ladies who came in behind me now standing on the opposite platform and I wonder where they are going and what is the purpose of their journey. The wide brims of their hats, adorned with feathers and ribbons of various shades of gold and green, bob up and down as they giggle. They grasp each other's forearms, as though needing to steady themselves against the hilarity of the stories they share. One of them catches me looking and pauses briefly to give me the once-over. She quickly looks away when she sees that my ordinary black bonnet, grey overcoat, and scuffed boots are not worth looking at.

Their train arrives before mine. The small station is filled with smoke, the screeching of brakes, the blowing of whistles. Doors are opened and a guard shouts for everyone to board. I watch the train as it pulls away, imagining the two ladies settling themselves into the comfort of one of the first-class carriages, on their way to Leeds for a day of shopping, lunching, and gossiping. Thankfully, my train arrives a few minutes later and I cannot afford to waste any more of my thoughts on them. I have positioned myself at the far end of the platform, towards the back of the train, which means that I do not have to walk past any more privileged travellers in the front carriages.

As the train stops at the platform, I spot an elderly man and woman alight from the carriage at the back. I make my way towards it. They seem to have been the only passengers in that carriage, a fact that I am thankful for. I climb inside, heave my suitcase into the overhead hammock, and sit in the seat nearest to the window, facing the direction of travel.

I force my eyes closed and grip the seat with both hands, to stop myself from jumping off the train. As the guard's whistle blows and plumes of smoke filter towards the carriage from the engine, the train pulls slowly away. A flock of pigeons is disturbed from their resting place on top of the platform canopy; their noisy wing-flapping drowned out by the cacophony of the train's movement. They disappear over the top of the train, seemingly unperturbed by the sudden downfall of rain.

Finally, I let go of the seat.

My choice is made.

My future is decided.

My journey to Cumberland has begun.

My fight for Ernest has begun.

Chapter Five
September 1908 - Mary

This morning Violet left us. I woke early, pushed back the sheets, and settled myself in my chair by my bedroom window with one eye on the driveway outside and one eye on the clock, waiting for a reasonable time when I could ring down to the kitchen for some tea. I watched Violet climb into Father's waiting car just after seven. Philip almost threw her small suitcase into the boot and I wanted to rap on the glass and tell him to take more care with her things. The poor girl doesn't have much.

I called her to my room last night and asked her if she had a decent winter coat. Cumberland can be so cold, I told her, much colder than in Skipton. The wind whips down the hills and wraps itself around unsuspecting legs. It can be quite a shock to the system. She shook her head and stared at the carpet, her pretty cheeks suddenly pink. I told her that she would be doing me a huge favour if she took mine. I threw open one of my wardrobes and took out the grey overcoat I had bought last winter in Skipton. I told her I had had it for years and that it no longer fit me. Whether she believed me or not, I couldn't tell, but she tried it on and a huge smile brightened her face. She stroked the buttons and thanked me profusely.

I wanted to tell her that I knew what she had agreed to do. I overheard the conversation between her and my mother a few days ago. I was secretly impressed at the way Violet stood her ground and asked for the money upfront, although I am sure that her small victory won't mean anything to her when her newborn baby is taken out of her arms.

As soon as I heard Violet's footsteps down the stairs and I knew that Mother was alone, I went into her bedroom and begged and pleaded with her to allow Violet to stay. She could marry Ernest and they could be happy if only they had the chance, I told her.

'Don't be preposterous,' Mother had said. She was sitting at her dressing table, a pot of face powder in her hand.

'I think you're being too harsh with Ernest, really I do,' I had persisted. 'Violet seems like a nice girl, she's intelligent and she's carrying your grandchild.'

I thought that would have done the trick, and for a fleeting moment Mother seemed to be about to relent, but then she told me that Father would never let him marry a housemaid. 'They're simply not a suitable match at all,' she said. 'It would never last. They come from completely different worlds. He will get over her and meet someone else. Oh goodness.' She laughed suddenly. 'Can you imagine if Ernest and Violet are married? We would have dozens of people at the wedding breakfast who wouldn't know which fork to choose. We would have napkins tucked into collars, glasses of beer at the table. It would be chaos.' She continued to chuckle to herself.

I needed to get away from her before I said something that I would regret. I told her that I was in the middle of writing a letter and I had to get back to it.

'Darling, before you go, can you do something for me?' She seemed unaware of my urgency to leave her.

I stopped at the door. 'Yes, Mother, what is it?'

'I need to write to the greengrocers and the butchers in Bowness to arrange for a weekly delivery to Lakeview Cottage. I simply don't have time this morning before the post. Please could you send them a quick note? It won't take you long, as you have your paper out already. There are plenty of stamps in your father's study.'

I agreed and went straight to the kitchen where I asked Cook to give me a list of Violet's favourite foods, so that I could make sure they were delivered to her. The poor girl has no idea what she has agreed to and what heartbreak it will inevitably bring her, so the least I could do would be to make sure she is stocked up with decent food. Cook told me that I was spoiling the girl and that there wasn't any need to order anything special, but at that moment Violet appeared in the kitchen and Cook sent her a wink and a sly smile. I told them both that it was a pleasure and I would make sure that the shopping lists made their way to the greengrocers and the butchers in the afternoon's post.

After I had signed off the note to the greengrocers, I added a P.S. to the end, asking the family to keep an eye on Violet, to make sure she was okay and that she wasn't too lonely. I wanted to ask them to invite her to church, invite her over for lunch every now, and treat her like one of the family. But I knew that was a step too far.

*

There's a knock on the library door shortly after twelve. It's Eliza.

'Doctor and Mrs Bradbury have arrived, miss. Barrow has shown them into the drawing room. The master and mistress are already there.'

'Is James with them?'

'Yes, miss.'

'Thank you, Eliza. I'll be straight down.'

She gives a little curtsy and closes the door behind her. I dash to my bedroom along the corridor to check my hair and straighten my skirt for the hundredth time. I haven't seen James for weeks, not since we left Lakeview Cottage after our summer holiday. He promised that he would visit before long and I silently thank Violet that his visit has come sooner than expected. Mother told me that she would be asking Doctor Bradbury to come over to Compton Hall for lunch so that she could update him about Violet's situation.

Doctor Bradbury and his wife have been friends with my parents for many years, a long time before James and I became a couple. Both sets of parents, I am sure, always hoped that their children would eventually fall in love. Towards the end of last month, when the two families shared lunch on the lawn at Lakeview Cottage and the men chatted about business and politics and the women chatted about love and fashionable evening gowns, Mrs Bradbury whispered that she hoped her son might soon 'pop the question.' I laughed and told her to take it easy; we were courting, but there had been no talk of marriage, not yet anyway. Secretly, however, I was delighted that James had

47

finally noticed me after years of me being in love with him. When his family had left, I had giggled with Mother as I got ready for bed and told her how much I loved James and what a perfect husband he would make. Mother said that I was lucky to have fallen in love with someone whose parents were so delightful. We both agreed that they were charming, amiable, and respectable people and it was even better that James wanted to become a doctor, too, just like his father.

As I make my way down to meet them now, I can't help but feel sorry that Ernest's love match hasn't been so straightforward for him.

At the bottom of the stairs, a wicker picnic basket packed with cheese sandwiches, slices of pork pie, a jar of homemade chutney, and sultana scones, all covered in a red and white checked gingham cloth is sitting at the foot of the chaise-longue, waiting to be collected. I lift the edge of the cloth and add a bottle of wine, a corkscrew, and two glasses. As I am tucking the cloth around them, James appears at my side. He wraps his arms around my waist and kisses my neck.

I turn quickly and throw my arms around his neck and we kiss for a few moments until I reluctantly push him away.

'Come on, let's get outside where we can be on our own,' he says.

'What about your parents?' I ask.

'You can say hello to them later, stop worrying.' He grabs the picnic basket and we make our way outside to the table and chairs at the side of the house, overlooking the garden, the lake, and the fields beyond.

Eliza has left woollen blankets draped over the back of two of the chairs. I pull mine onto my lap and tuck it under my knees. I finger the tiny fringe on the edge of the blanket and the expertly patched hole caused by an errant spark that escaped from a long-forgotten fire. James is carefully unpacking the picnic. His blanket, still neatly folded over the back of his chair because he is always warm, has a stubborn coffee stain from a cherished morning spent watching the sunrise, after Ernest and I had been out to a birthday party and were too drunk to be able to sleep. Each imperfection is a memory, a story woven into the very fabric of each blanket. Wrapped in their soft folds are warmth and nostalgia. Silent witnesses to the passage of time.

James pours the wine. We clink our glasses together and sit in companionable silence for a few minutes, as we listen to the birds singing. When I look at him, I can feel the negative emotions from the past week and this morning gently dissipate, like dandelion seeds in the summer breeze. His infectious smile instantly warms me.

'This is a lovely place,' says James. 'You're incredibly lucky to live here.'

'It has been in the family for a long time,' I say. 'My great-grandfather bought it for himself and his wife when they were first married.' I take a sandwich out of the basket and bite into it. I stroke the top of the table with my fingertips. 'We have had so many wonderful meals around this table,' I say. 'I always preferred eating here as a child, rather than inside in the formal dining room, especially on a warm day. Although, I have to say that I would much rather be in Cumberland. Lakeview Cottage is my favourite place in all the world.'

Flashes of long-ago summers, reading books in the garden, glasses of homemade lemonade, lazy afternoons lying on the grassy mound by the lake and staring up at the moving clouds, swimming in Lake Windermere, and walking home soaking wet wrapped in a huge towel make me smile. Those were special days. Ernest and I had so much fun when we were young. By the end of each summer, when we had to return to Compton Hall and resume our studies within the confinements of the four walls of the school room, we were tanned, happy, and full of life.

I wonder where Violet is on her journey and whether she has yet arrived safely. It's a shame that she won't experience Lakeview Cottage in the summer when it is at its best. Nevertheless, I hope she will fall in love with the place and treat it as home, for the short time she is there.

'I know about your housemaid, Violet,' says James. 'I know she's on her way there.'

'You do?'

'Yes, Father told me that was why he had been asked to visit today. Your mother put all the details in the letter, so we really didn't need to come, but of course we all wanted to.'

'Do you think she'll be all right?' I ask. 'She doesn't know anyone over there, and she's young, and pregnant...'

'She'll make friends,' says James. 'You shouldn't worry. People like her are robust.'

'People like her?'

'You know, working-class people. They seem to cope with things, take things in their stride.'

'James, how can you say that? That's a terrible thing to say.'

'What? I mean...'

'That their feelings are not as valid as ours, that they don't feel as intensely?'

'I didn't mean it like that.'

I shouldn't take out my frustrations on James and I decide that if I continue this line of conversation, it will almost definitely result in a spat. So I sip my wine and hold onto his hand to let him know that I would rather not disagree with him.

I picture Violet sitting on one of the small armchairs in the bay window in the drawing room of Lakeview Cottage. It is one of my favourite spots in the whole house. The chairs are comfortable and I have always liked the blue and grey tartan fabric. I don't know if it is a real Scottish tartan, but I love it all the same. It is elegant, but simultaneously warm and comforting. I have spent many hours over the years sitting there and watching the activity on and around the lake: rowing boats being manoeuvred by young men who have over-estimated their prowess and tried, but failed, to impress their young ladies and have ended up rowing around and around in a circle; nannies with small children, throwing handfuls of breadcrumbs to the ducks and geese at the water's edge; courting couples walking hand in hand along the promenade. My favourite time to watch the lake is always first thing in the morning, when it is still peaceful, before the village properly wakes, when the early morning sun shimmers onto the ripple-less surface before it gets disturbed by the steam ferry and the dozens of legs that paddle at its shore. I hope that Violet will enjoy sitting there as much as I do.

'I was sixteen by the time Mother allowed me and Ernest to travel on the ferry by ourselves,' I tell James. 'Can you believe that? Ernest, despite being two years younger, was given strict instructions to take good care of me. He promised Mother that he would sit on the side closest to the water, to stop me from falling into the lake and that if I did fall in, he would immediately dive in and save me. Hopefully, I'll get to her before she drowns, he told her.'

James laughs and tops up my wine glass. 'I can imagine your mother being a worrier,' he says.

'Yes, she was. She went into a total panic at the thought of such a tragedy, that she instantly rescinded her agreement to the ferry ride. She said we were both far too young and that it wasn't safe. Father had to step in and assure her that Ernest was teasing her. Reluctantly, she had laughed and we ran out of the door before she could change her mind. I miss being young, do you?'

'No, I don't think so. How can I? I didn't have you then.'

He leans across and kisses me, and I kiss him back and tell him that I love him. But I long for carefree days, before I became an adult, when life was simple.

I will never forget the gentle cool wind on my face that day, my first ferry ride without my mother, as we set off from Bowness on the slow journey to Ambleside. I closed my eyes, held tightly onto my bonnet to stop it from blowing away, and pretended that I was travelling up the River Nile, or somewhere equally exotic. In Ambleside, Ernest and I had strolled around the village, which was teaming with summer visitors. I felt so lucky that we could spend the summer months there and felt sorry for those people whose visit was any shorter.

After we returned home safe and sound, Mother allowed us to ride on the ferry regularly. We always bought a return ticket, but sometimes didn't alight at Ambleside. We stayed in our seats and rode on the lake for the pure pleasure of it.

'Ambleside is a special place, isn't it? It will always be our special place,' says James, as though reading my mind. 'This summer has been the best of my life. Those long days in Ambleside, well…'

He takes hold of my hand and kisses each of my knuckles in turn. I can tell by the look in his eyes that a marriage proposal is at the forefront of his mind. I wonder whether he intends to do it here, right now. Each slightest movement makes me think he is going to position himself on one knee and produce a diamond ring from his jacket pocket. I am surprised that he can still love me after discovering Mother's despicable plan to snatch a young baby from the arms of its traumatised mother.

Chapter Six
September 1908 - Violet

Mrs Compton hasn't given comprehensive directions at all. In fact, the directions are extremely sparse and I wonder whether the cottage really is as easy to find as she said, or does she not care whether or not I get lost? I suspect the latter, but I swallow down the bitterness that rises into my throat.

As I stand on the road outside the station at Windermere, trying to get my bearings, I notice a small horse-drawn carriage. A beautiful chestnut mare stands patiently waiting for its owner and I wonder who they are and where they are going. If it were a Hackney Carriage, I would treat myself to a ride. I would stand on the pavement and wait for the driver to hold out his arm to assist me as I climbed into my seat. Then I would settle back, make myself comfortable, and pull the red and gold tartan rug over my knees while I waited for him to tie my suitcase to the back of the carriage. I would pretend that I was the owner of Lakeview Cottage, the lady of the house, and I would enjoy the journey with composed nonchalance, as though I had been driven in such luxury a thousand times and had spent dozens of summers in my second home.

But no. That life is not mine. I cannot allow my thoughts to gallop away from me like this. Happiness doesn't come from wanting what you can't have. I know that; my mother told me enough times.

So, I begin the walk down the hill from the train station, following Mrs Compton's direction to turn left and walk towards the lake. It is still raining. Not a torrential downpour that chases everyone indoors to shelter temporarily in warm cafes, giggling and shaking sodden umbrellas whilst they search out vacant tables. But a light shower, icy blue, a mist which lingers long enough to dampen spirits and spoil plans. A confirmation of the end of the summer. I put my head down and face it.

It is past lunchtime, and my stomach rubbles as I pass a small baker's. The door is open and the smell of freshly baked bread floats out of the door and wraps itself around me, like one of my father's warm hugs. I am suddenly homesick and tearful and, even if I wanted to buy some bread, I know that I can't possibly go inside the shop now, not now that my tears are flowing so freely. I don't want to make a spectacle of myself and have people asking questions. What is wrong, miss? Where are you going? Who are you? So, I walk on, past the baker's, past a butcher's and an ironmonger's, and past a small public house on the corner, where a young boy is washing the windows with a dirty rag, splashing more water on himself and the pavement than on the glass.

The pavement through the town is narrow and I am conscious of bumping into someone's legs with my suitcase, but a couple of passing gentlemen tip their hats and step into the road to allow me to pass. I wonder whether they assume

I am a lady, or do they give this courtesy to all women? I conclude that my overcoat - a hand-me-down from Miss Mary - is elevating my status somewhat. I would like to smile and say thank you, but my tears prevent me from making eye contact and I keep my eyes focused on the ground.

After what feels like an hour, but is probably only ten or fifteen minutes, I begin to wonder whether I have taken the wrong turn. The rows of shops have given way to houses. Not narrow terraced ones like the ones in Manchester where my family live, with peeling paint around the window sills, but smart, well-cared-for houses, each standing in their own garden.

I put the suitcase, which is feeling heavier and heavier with each step, onto the ground and, again, take out the sheet of paper with Mrs Compton's handwritten directions. I have read the note so many times already that I know exactly what it says, word for word. But somehow I need the reassurance that I am going in the right direction.

'Turn left out of Windermere Station. Walk down the hill, past all the shops, until you reach the lake. The cottage is on the left.'

I cannot believe that is all that she has written, although I know it's true. There is no mention of what happens when the shops end. I cannot see a lake and I begin to wonder whether I have missed it. I turn the paper over in my hands, knowing that the underside is blank. I screw it up, throw it onto the pavement, and stamp on it. I twist my leg this way and that way until the paper begins to disintegrate into the puddles. My heart is beating hot, furious blood around my body and I suddenly feel the intense claustrophobic pressure of too many clothes. Despite the persistent rain, I pull off my hat and unbutton my overcoat. I want to sit down, but I can't see anywhere to sit. I turn around, looking frantically up the road and down. There are no benches, no public parks that I can see, no open spaces at all, just a narrow road with tall, dark trees protecting the houses on either side of me. A wobble forces me to hold onto a low brick wall of one of the houses.

'Hey, steady the buffs. You all right, love?' I can hear a voice whispering at my side, although it seems like miles away. A strong arm holds onto my elbow as a wave of dizziness washes over me. I clench my eyes closed for a second and when I open them, I see a young lady about my own age standing at my side. She is wearing the ubiquitous long black dress and white pinafore of someone in service and her hand, red raw, is the hand of someone who spends her life cleaning, scrubbing, and mopping. 'Here, come and have a sit down,' she says.

I am about to tell her that I cannot see where I can sit, but she leads me up the garden path of the house whose wall has been supporting me. The gleaming black front door is partially open and the stained glass in the middle of the door catches the sun and throws speckles of colour on the tiled hallway beyond. For a moment, I think she is going to take me inside and I am ready with my objections, but she ushers me to a low wooden bench in the front garden, underneath one of the windows, and I gratefully fall onto it, despite the fact that it is damp.

'There you go,' she says. 'You will feel better in a minute. You are ever so pale.' The young maid scuttles off and retrieves my suitcase and the discarded notepaper from the pavement. Mrs Compton's words are now smudged and covered in mud.

'I don't suppose you need this now, do you?' she asks, as she buries the paper in her apron pocket. There's a twinkle in her eyes and I wonder what she thinks of me. I am ashamed of my public outburst of emotion and wonder who else has watched me from behind their lace curtains. 'Is it a love letter?' She smiles at me and winks. She is probably around my age, and her smile lights up her whole face, causing a single dimple to appear in her left cheek and the skin around her mischievous eyes to crinkle. She has eyes like a forest; deep, welcoming, green with dapples of brown. She's a pretty little thing. I wonder how much she knows about love letters and whether she has ever had one of her own. 'No matter,' she says. 'You don't need to read it ever again. It's gone. Forget about him. If he gives you tears, then you should not be giving him your heart, that's what my mum always says.'

I wipe my face with the back of my hand. 'Thank you, I'm okay now. I really should…'

'What was that?' she asks, cupping a hand around her ear.

'I said thank you,' I reply, a little louder.

'Don't worry about it,' she says, brushing away my objections with a wave of one hand while resting her other on my shoulder to stop me from getting up. She perches on the bench next to me. 'I'm Clara.' She holds out her right hand and I take it in mine and give it a shake.

'Violet,' I say, slowly and loudly. I can see her watching my lips as I say my name slowly.

She laughs and tells me that she is a little hard of hearing sometimes, but not completely stone deaf.

'Do you want a glass of water?' she asks, and before I have time to object, she rushes off into the house. A minute later, she reappears and pushes a glass into my hand. 'Here, have a drink. It will make you feel better. You still look a bit peeky.'

'Do I?'

She nods as she studies me, a little too closely. 'Have you eaten yet today?'

I smile as I realise that, despite the expensive, albeit second-hand coat that I'm wearing, Clara spots that I am a working-class girl, like her. Surely she would not be so forward with a lady, asking personal questions and staring into her eyes, searching for answers. I decide that, even though I have known her for less than ten minutes, she makes me feel comfortable and I find myself happy to talk. I tap my suitcase and tell Clara that the sandwich Mrs Meadows made for me this morning is still in there. I tell her about the various train journeys I have had and that I did not feel comfortable eating on the train, so I was waiting until I got to the cottage. As if on cue, my stomach grumbles loudly and we both laugh. I explain that I will be looking after my mistress' cottage for a few months, cleaning it and getting it ready for them to use in the summer.

'I'll be fine, honestly,' I say. 'I'm sure I'll be there soon, although I've got to say that the cottage seems to be getting further and further away from me and I wonder if someone is moving it, just to play a trick on me.'

Clara laughs and says that it feels like that sometimes when you feel exhausted. 'Just take it one step at a time,' she says. 'Everything in life can be overcome by taking one step at a time. I think that when I've got to clean the fireplaces in this big monstrosity of a house every morning. There's six of the bloody things. Six of them! I mean, who needs that many rooms? I don't know why they can't just stay in one. I swear they walk about from one room to the next just because they want to make my life as difficult as possible.' She laughs.

I think about Compton Hall and the dozens of fireplaces in there. It takes three maids to keep the place clean. Clearly, Clara hasn't worked in a house as large as that before. Then, I think about my parents and my sisters and brother at home and their small kitchen where everybody stays hunched over the fire to keep warm in the winter. The three small bedrooms upstairs are freezing cold and the front room is only used during the spring and summer when it's bearable to sit without a fire, or on special occasions like Christmas, when the fire is lit with precious coal.

'Yes, people who live in houses like these don't know how lucky they are, being surrounded by such beautiful things,' I say. I turn around and peer into the bay window behind me. A long dining table surrounded by eight spindle-backed chairs dominates the room. A silver candelabra holds five tall slim candles, waiting patiently to be brought to life, to be the centre of attention during an extravagant meal. 'Who lives here?' I ask, taking a sip of my water.

'Mr and Mrs Douglas they're called. Not married long, no children yet,' says Clara. She tuts and rolls her eyes and I smile, encouraging her to tell me more. I suspect that she has a story or two to tell. She lowers her voice to a whisper and cups her hand around her mouth, screening her words from any passers-by who may inadvertently hear what she is about to say. 'I can't wait for her to have children, if truth be told,' she says. 'If only to put a stop to the incessant parties. The music, the wine, the lecherous men. I can't stand it. It's virtually every weekend, unless they are away visiting friends. A child will settle them down.' She nods sagely.

I unconsciously put a hand to my stomach at the talk of children, but then quickly remove it. This child is not mine. I have to stop believing that it is. I don't want anybody to know that I am carrying a child. That's what Mrs Compton said. Keep myself to myself, do not get too friendly with the locals, it will only lead to questions that nobody wants to answer.

'It's for your own good, Violet,' Mrs Compton had said last night. 'It will all work out in the end and when this unfortunate business is over, you can get on with your life and no damage will be done to your reputation.'

Mrs Compton threw her words at me and they landed painfully. I steadied myself, holding onto the back of the chair, to prevent them from knocking me over. I was relieved that she then pushed the envelope containing the directions towards me, together with the house key, and that the meeting had soon after come to an end. I had run upstairs to my room and beat my pillow with my fists until all my energy was spent. I then perched on the end of my bed and waited for my breathing to return to normal before I went back into the kitchen, where I kept myself busy making tea and cutting slices of cake for Cook, Mr Barrow, Philip and the junior maids before the family's evening meal forced us back onto our feet and back to work.

I can feel Clara's eyes burning into the side of my face. She must have noticed when my hands shot to my stomach in the tell-tale way that expectant mothers often cradle their unborn child. She waits for me to explain, to fill the silence, but instead, I take another sip of the water and then stand up, holding the glass out towards her.

'Thank you, Clara. I feel better now, I must go.'

'Well, if you're sure,' she says.

'Yes, I have a lot to do when I get to the cottage, and you're getting soaked sitting out here with me.'

'Oh don't worry about that. It's only a bit of rain. You can sit for a moment longer, the master and mistress aren't here. They won't be back until later tonight,' she says.

'Where is it you are going?' she asks.

'Lakeview Cottage,' I tell her. 'I don't suppose you know where it is?'

'Just at the bottom of the road. When you get to the lake, look to your left and you will see the house on top of the hill. You can't miss it. My family deliver groceries to that house every summer when the Comptons are there.'

'Oh really. Mrs Compton said that she would arrange for a box to be delivered for me.'

'Yes, there will be one on its way to you,' she says. 'Mum mentioned this morning that someone was moving in.'

'Well, I must be going,' I say. 'I will see you again, no doubt.'

'Yes, see you again,' she says.

As I walk away, I kick myself for feeling dizzy right there, right where someone was watching. I am already breaking Mrs Compton's rule of not getting friendly with the locals.

Chapter Seven
September 1908 - Violet

I am here now.

I had almost given up my search when, finally, the lake came into view. Lake Windermere. I have never seen anything as magnificent. The silver water lies as still as bath water. Mrs Meadows told me about the island in the middle of the lake, which people row their boats to in the summer, although I can't imagine that there is anywhere to land; the island seems to be completely covered in fir trees, like a dense luxurious carpet.

Then I come upon the house. It is just as Mrs Compton and Clara said - when I reach the lake, I can't miss it. The sign on the grey stone gatepost tells me I have arrived at the correct place. The giant wrought-iron gates at the bottom of the drive are open and I am sure whether this is normally the case, or whether Mrs Compton has arranged for someone to open them in readiness for my arrival, but I am grateful.

I look up and see Lakeview Cottage perched on the top of a small hill, the imposing facade looking down to the lake with the supercilious air of the upper classes oozing from its mullioned windows. Its slate roof, the colour of charcoal, support four tall chimneys, causing the house to seem even more impressive. Nobody had told me how huge this place is. It's not a cottage at all, it's a mansion house.

I have to stop twice on the steep climb to the house to catch my breath, putting my suitcase onto the gravel drive and resting my hands on my knees as I take in mouthfuls of air.

Now, as the front door slams closed behind me, I release the burden of my suitcase and burst into tears again. Is it the travelling that is making me emotional, or the intense tiredness? I seem to have been crying such a lot today.

I stand with my back to the front door, my heart beating. I take a deep breath and wipe my tears away with the sleeve of my coat. There is nobody here to comfort me, so there doesn't seem much point in giving in to the feeling of overwhelming panic right now. I can hear Cook's voice telling me last night how wonderful my adventure is going to be; how having the responsibility of caring for such a magnificent house is a true honour. She prattled on about the summers she has spent at Lakeview Cottage in the past, and what a joy it was to be able to walk to Lake Windermere on her day off and enjoy the beautiful scenery. It was then that I wanted to tell her the truth. I wanted to take hold of her constantly-cleaning hand, sit her down at the freshly scrubbed kitchen table, and tell her about the baby. I wanted to tell her that my job is to provide Mrs Compton's sister with a child, not simply to prepare their holiday cottage for summer parties and gaiety. But the words stuck in my throat, forced down by tears and complicated emotions that I did not have the energy to decipher, so I agreed with her that yes, I was extremely blessed, and that yes, I would take care of the place and yes, I would make sure that I polished the brass on the front door so that it glistened in the sun.

I run my fingers across a large, square mirror hanging on the wall. It is speckled with dust and I notice an abandoned and partially broken spider's web clinging to one corner. There is no sign of the spider, although it isn't easy to see, as the dark wood panelling and the olive green wallpaper have sapped the delicate autumn light.

I wander into the first room on the right, which I discover to be a dining room, at the centre of which is an oval-shaped table. I am thankful that there are only ten chairs around it, rather than the fourteen that I am used to cleaning. Each one is made from intricately carved mahogany with a tapestry seat cover, and each one, like the hallway mirror, is layered with dust. A silver candelabra stands in the middle of the table, holding three half-burned candles. The remnants of a long-ago dinner.

Cook had told me last night that half a dozen locals from Bowness and Windermere are usually employed by the Comptons during the summer, as cleaners and gardeners. No doubt they work hard as the Comptons' every whim is catered for, along with the needs and wants of their demanding visitors every summer. As I walk back into the hallway and stare at my reflection in the mirror, I wonder who is usually responsible for cleaning it before their arrival and I wonder whether they love working for the Comptons as much as Cook does. Will the staff still come next spring? Nobody has told me. It is of no matter to me; I will have long gone by the time the regular staff begin work. I have calculated that the baby is due in February.

I wander over to the window and look out onto the driveway and the gates beyond. The windowsill is covered with tiny specks of black soot. Still, it could be worse, I tell myself. The house does not have to be cleaned all at once. I can take my time, one room at a time. I don't have anyone cracking any whip behind me. A very pleasant change indeed. I can rise tomorrow morning at whatever time I wish, and begin work at whatever time I wish.

On the other side of the hallway, I discover a sitting room. A stone fireplace dominates one wall and is surrounded by three elegant brown leather Chesterfield sofas. Countryside paintings fill the walls - scenes of sheep grazing in green fields, horses and hounds cantering over hedges on the hunt for the elusive fox, and snow-topped hills dotted with dancing daffodils. A tall slim bookcase rests in the corner against the back wall. Three of the shelves are packed with books, but the top shelf is empty, except for a tiny white ceramic vase. I pick it up and rub the dust away with my fingers. It is pretty. Tomorrow I shall have a look around the garden for some late flowers to go in it, but for now, I leave it where it is.

The room has a slightly more welcoming feel than the dining room. Two matching armchairs, with wooden arms and blue and grey tartan upholstery, face each other under the bay window. A small round coffee table on three elegant wooden legs sits between them. I sit down at one of the chairs and take in the view. The relentless drizzle drips down the glass in the window and I watch as the oak trees on either side of the driveway grow heavy with rainwater, until their depressed leaves bow in submission.

My eye is directed to the huge lake beyond and I lose myself for a few moments watching a ferry boat arriving and docking at the pier. I am surprised to see the passengers alighting without luggage. Courting couples linking arms, nannies holding tightly to their charges, and ladies and gentlemen of various ages walk along the pier to the promenade. It occurs to me that they have taken the boat purely for pleasure and I wonder where it goes to and how much it is.

I continue watching as one of the nannies buys what looks like a bag of sweets from a cart for two small children. Their excitement makes me smile and I am disappointed when they walk out of view. I blink away more unwanted tears. I don't know why the children - children I have never met and will never see again, in all likelihood - grabbed at my emotions, suddenly and unexpectedly, like the branches of a tree snagging on your clothes as you walk past.

I leap to my feet. I need to move myself. There are things to do. I don't have the luxury of sitting down all day. This is a time-wasting window; one that draws you in with the promise of adventure, of better times, on the other side.

I find the kitchen at the back of the house next to what appears to be a study. It isn't in the basement, like at Compton Hall. Here, the kitchen overlooks the garden which is protected by immaculate beech hedges, whose golden leaves shake in the breeze as they bravely cling to their branches. The wind is getting up and I pull my coat tightly around me with a shiver, as a gust of wind howls into the kitchen under the loose-fitting back door. Two blackbirds shoot out from underneath the hedge and settle together in the flowerbed underneath a couple of bare rose bushes, where they proceed to peck at the ground, flirting and skirting around one another, until suddenly they fly off again, disturbed by some unknown noise or movement.

I wonder what colour the roses will be in the summer. I will be gone before they bloom.

I test the tap over a white stone sink and am surprised to find running water. I was expecting to have to use an outside tap and a steel bucket as penance for my sins, but I should have realised that the Comptons would only have the best, most modern kitchen, even in a house that they only use for a couple of months each year. I find a glass on a nearby pine dresser and pour myself a drink, and then another. It has been a long time since I had a proper drink, apart from the couple of sips at the house where Clara works. I stare out into the garden, wondering for the hundredth time that day whether I am doing the right thing. Before I unpack my case, I could walk right out, back to the railway station, and could be in Manchester before I change my mind again. But I am tired. Oh so tired.

I wish I could talk to Ernest. He has no idea where I am or where my future lies. I am sure his mother will tell him, if she hasn't done so already, that I have left Compton Hall. But will she tell him that I am here? Will he know that I still love him, or will he presume I will make other plans and perhaps marry someone else? Would he get jealous if I told him I plan to marry Arthur, the greengrocer's son from Skipton? Arthur would marry me, I know he would. For a moment, the possibility seems real. I could write to Arthur and ask him to come and see me and I could tell him what a predicament I am in. Arthur is a nice boy but… another sob rises to my throat as I push thoughts of Arthur away. He is not the one for me. Ernest is. Ernest is the only man I want. I can't wait to write to him. My letters won't be intercepted like they were before. I can write to him as often as I wish and I can take the letters to the post box myself. I am sure there will be paper somewhere in the study but if not, I can buy some. He needs to know that his mother intends to take the baby from me.

The thought boosts me a little. I know, deep down, that Ernest could not marry me, not right now at any rate. He does not have a job and his parents wouldn't support him, not unless he was planning to marry a lady of their choice. We will have to wait until he has finished at university and then we can be together, when he is earning his own money as a lawyer and I can begin my studies to be a teacher. Perhaps I need to harden my heart against the little one growing inside me. This one isn't meant for me. It isn't the right time. It is God's will. But I will have another child with Ernest when we are married. I know I will.

I take a deep breath and I tell myself to accept my current situation, as nothing is going to change it. There is time for change in the future, but not right now.

I dry my face again and decide to explore the rest of the house.

As I look around the dismal hallway and peer up the dark stairs, I have decided that I already don't like it here. I am sure the house looks more impressive in the summer, but now, I immediately want to go home. Not to Compton Hall, but home to Manchester, to the tall mills and choking fog and the over-crowded streets. I do not want to stay in this empty, soulless house. I want life and light. At Compton Hall the light floods into the hallway from bright windows on either side of the south-facing door. Colourful ceramic plant pots of various sizes house elegant parlour palms, which stand on sentry along the wall leading to the drawing room. The door to the servants' stairs on the left is forever opening and closing as we go about our daily tasks. Laughter and chatter float up the stairs behind us. On the other side of the staircase, a bright fuchsia pink chaise-longue invites you to take a seat on the way to the dining room, not that anyone does.

Here it is dark.

Chapter Eight
September 1908 - Violet

A sharp knock on the kitchen door wakes me. I wonder whether the noise comes from my dream. It sounded like the frantic wheels of a train, not bringing me here, but whisking me away from all my troubles, from this location and far far away from Mrs Compton and her childless sister and the horrible Reverend Flynn. But a second knock confirms that I am not dreaming. I jump up and run over to the back door, only to find it locked.

'Just a moment,' I shout through the solid wood door, hoping that whoever is on the other side won't disappear before I can find the key.

'Delivery for you,' says a boy's voice.

'I am not sure where the key is,' I tell him. 'Could you please take it to the front door? Oh, it's okay, I found it.' I grab the key from the windowsill and open the door.

The boy, no older than twelve or thirteen, holds out a wooden box overflowing with groceries. I look over his shoulder and spot a rusty old bicycle propped up against the dustbin. The boy grins with pride, as though sensing my question about how on earth he managed to ride the bicycle and hold onto the box at the same time. 'I balanced it on the handlebars,' he says before I can ask, his infectious grin growing wider. His eyes shine and I feel myself smiling back at him.

'That's very impressive,' I say.

'He is fibbing again!' Clara jumps out from where she was hiding behind the wall. 'Don't believe a word!' She laughs as she holds a long piece of rope in the air. 'Don't worry, Vi, your grocery box was perfectly safe, tied securely onto the back by yours truly.' She bows low and I curtsy back at her and thank them both. 'This is my brother, Billy,' says Clara. 'When he said there was a delivery for Lakeview Cottage, I thought I would come over on the off-chance that you were here and see how you are.' She takes the box from Billy's outstretched arms and pushes her way into the kitchen. 'Where do you want it? On here will do, don't you think?' She indicates the pine dresser in the far corner of the kitchen where I had found the glass earlier. Clara puts the box down and turns towards me. 'That's all right, isn't it? It's out of the sun there. Not that you need to worry about the stuff getting too warm - bloody hell, Vi, it's freezing in here.' She rubs her hands together and blows on her fingertips, which makes me laugh.

'I couldn't find any matches to get the stove working,' I say.

'The stove, did you say?'

I nod, I had forgotten that Clara was hard of hearing.

'That's easy,' she says, dashing out of the room. Within a minute, she is back, waving a box of matches triumphantly in the air. 'Just like I thought. Found them in the dining room. I thought there might be some in there, for the candles.' She puts the box on the table, then rushes over to me and rubs her hands up and down my arms quickly. I can feel the heat immediately, which travels into my neck and cheeks. I am not used to this level of familiarity from someone I have only just met, although it is not unpleasant.

'Billy, off you go now, and close the door quickly before we both freeze to death.' Clara waits until her reluctant brother closes the door behind him and cycles away. 'Truth is,' she says in a whisper, as though Billy might still be listening at the door, 'I thought you might need a friend. Here, sit yourself down, you still don't look a hundred percent.' She holds onto the back of the rocking chair next to the oven, waiting for me to take my place in it, which I do.

'I have already been sat here for goodness knows how long,' I say, with little protest. 'I fell asleep and it was only your Billy's knocking that woke me up just now.'

'Well, you need your rest,' says Clara, with the conviction and authority of a matron in charge of a maternity ward. 'How far gone are you?'

'What? How…?'

'It's obvious,' she laughs. 'A young woman, crying and fainting in the street, looking pale and pasty and tired. The clues are all there if you know what you're looking for. Plus, I don't know if you've noticed, but you have a little bump right there.'

'You're a proper detective, aren't you?' I can't help but laugh, as I relax into the chair and rest my head against the high back. I close my eyes. 'Around four months,' I say, after taking a deep breath. 'I can't hide the bump much longer.' I slowly open my eyes and allow the tears to escape.

'I can't seem to stop crying today, and I am so tired. I have never felt tiredness like it.'

Clara nods and hands me a linen tea towel from the hook on the back of the door. Like earlier, I know that she is waiting for me to tell her more.

'Nobody is meant to know,' I say eventually. 'Except for the doctor, of course. Mrs Compton has arranged for a local doctor to come and see me regularly. She said I should keep myself to myself and not go *flaunting* myself outside of the cottage. She's letting me stay here until the baby's born. As you know, she's arranged for groceries to be delivered, so I shouldn't have the need to go out shopping. And, well, that's it.'

I shrug my shoulders.

I have said too much. I cannot possibly spill everything out to this person that I have only just met, as kind as she may appear. She may have spotted my pregnancy, but how can I possibly explain the plan to sell my baby? The whole thing is so absurd and I struggle to get my own head around it sometimes, so I am sure that Clara won't understand. It is a conversation for another time, on another day. If that day ever comes.

'She has been very kind really, all considered,' I say.

'Mmm, very kind you say?' says Clara. 'Are you permitted to go for a walk, or are you expected to coup yourself indoors all day, so you don't *flaunt* yourself?'

'No, no, I can go for a walk,' I say, feeling instantly brighter at the thought of getting out and about in what I had been told was a beautiful place. 'Mrs Compton said that I should wrap myself up in my coat and maybe wear a long scarf to cover my growing bump, so that people don't talk, but yes, I can go out, for some daily exercise.'

Clara nods, but I can see that her forehead is wrinkled in a frown. 'He's the daddy, is he? Is that why she has sent you into hiding so that he can keep their dirty little secret?'

'Who? No.'

'He wouldn't want to spoil his impeccable reputation, would he? They're all the bloody same.' She crosses her arms and stands with her back resting on the oven. 'You're not a prisoner, Vi, you know that, don't you? You can go outside as often as you bloody well please.'

'Oh, I know, but...'

'To hell with him, to hell with them both for putting you in this situation. If I were you...'

'No, no, Clara,' I interrupt her when I realise what she is thinking. 'The baby isn't Mr Compton's. He is not the father.' An image of old Mr Compton with his greying moustache and his waistline as large as any woman about to give birth flashes into my mind. 'I would never...'

'Well, we women don't always get a say, do we?'

'But I did,' I say. I move forwards so that I'm perched on the edge of the rocking chair, my feet firmly planted on the floor to prevent the chair from moving backwards and forwards. I need her full attention. I don't want to have to explain twice if she doesn't hear me the first time. 'The baby's father is called Ernest. We love each other.'

Clara's face softens and I find myself opening up to her and telling her about my affair with Ernest, about how he had pursued me, although I hadn't offered much resistance. I tell her how I have admired him for such a long time, not just because his dark hair and deep brown eyes are intoxicating and it was impossible to succumb to his spell, but because he also has a beautiful soul. I remember the first time that he had held me and whispered into my ear that I was the most beautiful woman he had ever seen, and my heart had beat so fast and my cheeks had burned so brightly that I thought I would need to sit down. I had clung to his waist and tipped my head to the side, allowing him to smother my neck with kisses. I don't tell Clara such personal details, of course, but I find myself telling her about the day in Skipton when I had told Ernest that I was pregnant, and how his face had lit up and how he had assured me that everything would be fine.

'But nothing works out like that for people like us, does it?' I say, with a sigh. 'He was sent away to university without being given the chance to speak to me, and here I am, sent away to have my baby on my own. He doesn't know where I am.' I stop myself from expanding the story any further.

Clara busies herself stacking kindling and coal into the stove and lighting tightly screwed up balls of newspaper with one match after another as I talk. I can see her clenched mouth and thin lips and instantly regret opening up to her so soon. I know nothing about this woman. Clara discombobulated me with her friendliness, but now she is judging me for having a love affair with the son of the family who employ me. I have ruined my chances of making a new friend. I can't blame Clara for thinking of me as a trollop. I only have myself to blame for throwing myself at someone who was so far out of my reach that it would never have worked out between us. I should have known. What a fool I have been. I should have been content to go courting with

Arthur. There is nothing wrong with being married to a greengrocer's son from Skipton.

Now, if Mrs Compton finds out that what should have been a secret pregnancy is no longer secret, I will be out on my ear in no time. I will have no option but to go back to Manchester to my parents' overcrowded house and to bring the baby up without a father. She will never let me see Ernest again.

'Right, well that's done then,' says Clara. She stands up suddenly and wipes her sooted hands on the front of her dress.

Yes, that's done. A friendship that hasn't even started is over already. I clench the tea towel that I am still twisting in my hands. There is no point in any more regrets, I tell myself. They are already stacking up around me like hastily built prison walls. What is done is done.

'Don't think badly of me, please,' I say, as Clara walks towards the door. 'I'm not a tart, honest I'm not. I didn't throw myself at him. We were in love.'

'What?' Clara stops and, leaning with one hand on the sink to steady herself, she begins to untie her boots with her other hand.

'I loved him. I'm not sure whether he genuinely loved me, but I know that I loved him.' I say. 'What are you doing?'

'I'm taking these boots off,' says Clara. 'Then I'm going to make us a cup of tea when that fire gets going. Have you got any milk?'

'Yes,' I say. 'I thought you were leaving. I thought you were angry and that…'

'Oh, I'm angry all right,' says Clara. 'I'm bloody angry at what they have done to you, making you come here and hide away like some prisoner when the only crime you are guilty of is falling in love with the wrong man.'

Ernest is not the wrong man at all, I want to say. He is the perfect man, and I will be the perfect woman for him. One day, I will walk back into Compton Hall with my arm linked through his and tell his mother about my accomplishments and my new job as a teacher.

'I don't think badly of you at all,' continues Clara. 'I think you're very brave coming to live here in a big old house like this for months and months on your own, not knowing a soul. I don't know whether I would be able to do it. You shouldn't be expected to do it. Life isn't fair on women like us.'

'Well, I can agree with you about that,' I say.

Clara tugs off her boots and places them side by side on the mat behind the back door. Then she fills the kettle with water and places it on the hob.

'That will take a while to boil,' she says. 'But no matter. Now, I know for certain that there are some biscuits in this box somewhere. You look like you need feeding up.'

She begins to systematically empty the grocery box, laying the produce out on the kitchen table for me to see. She pulls out a small cauliflower, half a dozen carrots, two small hessian bags of potatoes, and a green cabbage before she gets to the biscuits, which are nestled next to a bag of eggs.

'Here they are!' she shouts, triumphantly. 'What biscuits can't cure aren't worth worrying about.'

*

As Clara is leaving an hour later, Tom, the butcher's apprentice, arrives with four rashers of bacon, a string of sausages, and a small chicken, all wrapped tightly in grease-proof paper.

Clara opens the door to him, flooding the kitchen with weak autumn sun. 'This is Violet,' she says, once again in charge of the situation. 'Violet, this is Tom. We went to school together, didn't we, Tom?'

Tom nods shyly. 'Pleased to meet you, miss,' he says, taking off his flat cap and clutching it between his fingers.

'Violet will be looking after the house for a while, cleaning and such like,' explains Clara. She winks at me and, although I am thankful for her explanation, Tom does not seem interested in who I am or why I am here. People have their own lives to live, filled to the rafters with their own worries and tribulations. Tom walks over to the cold room directly opposite the oven, and places the meat on one of the shelves, as though he has been here hundreds of times and knows the kitchen as well as he knows his own.

'He's a nice lad,' says Clara when Tom has gone. 'He won't gossip, but if he's asked any questions then…'

'Yes, thank you,' I say. 'But you know I'm meant to be keeping the pregnancy a secret, so please don't tell him anything. Mrs Compton…'

'Never mind her,' says Clara. 'She's not here. What Mrs High and Mighty Compton says or wants is not your concern anymore. There's no need to keep it a secret.'

Clara begins to squeeze her feet back into her boots, laces them up quickly, and is gone. I watch her as she walks down the driveway, holding onto her hat tightly. The earlier rain has gone, but there's a strong wind blasting through the trees, shaking the last of their leaves onto the lawn.

I push the kitchen door closed, and I am alone.

Chapter Nine
October 1908 - Violet

The first day of my second week at Lakeview Cottage has brought me a letter from home. The postman had made his delivery before it was daylight and the surprise was waiting for me on the floor in the hallway as I made my way down the stairs this morning. I grasp it to my chest as I wait for the water to boil for my first cup of tea of the day. The kettle takes an age and I am tempted to open the letter now and devour it hungrily, but I am forcing myself to wait until I am comfortably settled and seated.

Finally, the kettle boils and after filling the teapot to the top, I add it to the tray containing a cup and saucer, a small jug of milk, and a thick slice of bread and butter, and take it back to bed, holding the letter carefully between my teeth, so there is no chance of spilling any tea on it. Then I settle myself back into bed and pour a cup of tea before opening it. It is from my mother.

Dearest Violet,

It is lovely to hear that you have been chosen to care for the Comptons' holiday cottage. A holiday cottage, eh? How fancy! It is a shame that your mistress has forbidden you to have any visitors. I can understand that she is precious about her house and she doesn't want all and sundry traipsing around the freshly beaten carpets. But we could still visit, couldn't we?

There's a train direct from London Road Station. We wouldn't come into the house if you didn't feel right about it. But we could take a walk around the lake. I could bring butties and some cake. The kids (she always refers to my brother and sisters as 'the kids') *are dying to see you. It seems like it's been ages since you've been home. Not that I am putting pressure on you. Oh dear, now I've come across as one of those mothers. Ignore me, my sweetheart.*

So, the news from home - well, our Thomas is courting with Victoria Grainger. She's lovely and has been for tea a couple of times. Thomas seems smitten with her. Your dad says Thomas is working hard at the mill and he is very proud of him. We both are.

Rose and Bridgett are studying hard. I have been putting away every spare penny to buy their books. Rose has decided that she wants to be a nurse, so I told her that she has to work hard at that and learn all about wounds and how to clean them. She is a clever girl, just like you. Oh hang on, it's starting to spit and I've got washing out.

There we go, I'm back now. (This makes me smile as I imagine my mother as she dashes outside at the first sign of rain, un-pegs the washing, and then hangs it neatly over the wooden clothes horse in front of the fire before she sits back down to continue the letter. I never would have known that she had taken a break from the writing, and the thought of her chatting away to me as though I am right there in the kitchen with her warms my heart.)

It isn't our washing, it belongs to Mrs Wilkinson next door. She hasn't been so well this week, so I am helping her out. She has offered to pay me, but I won't hear of it, of course. I said that if she lets our girls borrow a couple of her books every now and then, that would do. She was chuffed to bits with that and said the girls are welcome to go over any time. The stuff she has on her bookcase! Novels, history books, the lot!

Write back to me soon, Violet, and let me know when we can come and visit. I'm sure you have made some friends up there, so I don't want to intrude on your days off, but, anyway, sending all my love,

Mum xx

I sip my tea as I wonder how to navigate this. Telling my mother that I am too busy looking after an empty house which I am responsible for cleaning isn't enough of an excuse. She knows that at the very least I will have Sundays off. She will also be expecting us to spend Christmas together. What possible reason could I give that would keep me away from my family at Christmas? By then I will be seven months pregnant and my bump will be impossible to hide unless I keep my coat on for the whole visit.

If I allow myself to think about it too much, I will be living in a constant state of panic. I don't know what to do. I remember what Clara said when I first met her, something about everything in life being overcome by taking one step at a time. I need to concentrate on just one day at a time. Thinking too far into the future is overwhelming.

I take a bite of my bread and butter, when an idea flashes into my head. I could go home now, before my bump gets any bigger. At the moment, I can just about get away with hiding it, especially if I keep a shawl wrapped around me, which I could do without arousing suspicion as the days are getting colder. I could spend a few days with my family, then, when Christmas comes, I will have to tell them a lie; I will have no other choice. I could say that I have been called back to Compton Hall to help with Christmas parties and I won't be able to go back home after all.

Pleased with my plan of action, I take another bite of bread and relax back onto the pillow. When I hear the loud knock on the front door, I assume that it is Billy, calling early with another box of groceries. Friday is the usual delivery day. I dash over to the window, lift up the sash and I am about to call out that he can leave it by the back door when I notice the car. The black, immaculately clean paintwork glints ominously in the early morning sunlight. It is Mr Compton's car. Philip, together with a scowl deep enough to cause his eyebrows to meet in the middle, is staring up at the bedroom window. His chauffeur's hat hangs dejectedly from his right hand.

I slam the window shut and drop to the floor, praying that he hasn't seen me, although I know that he has. My house coat is hanging from the back of the bedroom door, and I contemplate throwing it over my nightdress and telling Philip that I feel under the weather, but I couldn't possibly face a man in my nightwear. He will have to wait for me to get dressed. I crawl over to the wardrobe on my hands and knees and tug at my maid's uniform dress until it falls from the hanger. I haven't worn it since I arrived, and it smells slightly musty, but it is clean and the buttons down the front are quick and easy to manage. I continue my crawl until I am safely out of the bedroom and out of sight. I close the door behind me and in the dark landing, I dress quickly. I don't have time for stockings, but the dress is long, so Philip won't notice.

As I trot down the stairs, I remember that my clogs are in the hallway, near the front door, so I slip my feet into them before I open the door.

Philip pushes in before the door is fully open. He glares at me, peers into the drawing room at the clock on the mantelpiece, and then checks his pocket watch. 'Are you ill?' he asks, without any sign of solicitude.

'It is only seven forty-five, Philip,' I say, closing the door behind him. 'I know what you are intimating, but I can assure you that I am quite well, thank you.' I wonder whether he noticed that I was in my nightdress when I opened the window. He must have. He has an uncanny knack for noticing everything that he shouldn't. Secrets struggle to remain hidden when Phillip is around. I gather my loose hair into my hand and hold onto it tightly. His disapproval sweeps over me, choking me like a fog until I feel the need to re-open the door and allow the fresh air in.

'Would you like a drink?' I try and keep my voice calm, as I would hate him to know how much he rattles me. 'The kettle will still be warm.'

He nods curtly and I walk past him into the kitchen. I place the kettle back onto the range and then remember that the tray with the teapot and milk jug is still upstairs on the bed. I will have to get it, as I have only managed to find one teapot. I will have to ask Philip to take a seat in the drawing room, so that I can sneak upstairs, even though I know he wouldn't be comfortable with that. In the absence of Mr and

Mrs Compton, he would see it as taking a liberty and I know that he would rather stay in the kitchen. But as I turn around to tell him, he isn't behind me. I can hear his footsteps pounding up the stairs. I assume he needs the lavatory after his long journey and has chosen to use the one inside.

'I don't believe it!' he suddenly shouts. 'Violet! Come up here this minute!'

As I reach the bottom of the stairs, he appears at the top, his face scarlet with temper.

'Don't tell me that you've been sleeping in the master bedroom,' he says. 'You impudent little madam. Just because you shared a bed with Master Ernest does not make you mistress of this house. If Mrs Compton knew…'

'I am sure she would have no objection.' I surprise myself by answering him back - I have never in my life spoken back to a man and wouldn't dream of getting into an argument with Philip and his vicious tongue – but thankfully he doesn't appear to have heard me.

'Come upstairs and move your things this minute. One of the small bedrooms at the back is plenty good enough for someone like you.' He turns on his heel and walks away, presumably expecting me to follow him. I do, of course, and when I reach the bedroom, he is standing with his back to the window, facing the door, his hands on his hips like a schoolmaster about to address an assembly of children.

'I saw your face at the window but it didn't occur to me that you would have the nerve to actually sleep there.' He points at the bed. 'And you've had your breakfast here, I can see. Just wait until the master finds out about this. Treating Lakeview Cottage like a hotel. It's despicable.' His face is puce. 'I don't know who you think you are.'

My cold tea and the crust from my bread and butter are laid out on the tray, the evidence of my audacity apparent for all to see. I disconsolately pick up the tray and take it downstairs, without saying a word.

Chapter Ten
October 1908 - Violet

'Hello Vi, are you in?' Clara's voice carries from the kitchen and I have never been so pleased to see anyone in my life. 'What on earth's the matter?' she says, rushing over to me and taking the tray from my hands. She places it on the unit next to the sink and then takes me in her arms and strokes my back as she holds me tight. 'You look white as a ghost. Tell me all about it.'

'Philip is here,' I say. 'He's upstairs. In Mr and Mrs Compton's bedroom.'

'Who is Philip?'

'The chauffeur from Compton Hall.' Confusion clouds her face for a moment. She steps back. I am unable to read her expression. Before I can explain that he isn't a gentleman friend, if that's what she's thinking, and I certainly didn't invite him upstairs, he appears at the threshold.

'Who are you?' he demands. His scowl remains.

'I can ask you the same thing,' says Clara.

She crosses her arms and glares at him. I can sense a battle about to erupt.

'This is my friend, Clara,' I tell Philip. 'She has just called to see me.'

'Oh, isn't that just wonderful,' says Philip, his voice full of sarcasm and derision. 'So you are using Lakeview Cottage as your own property, are you? Sleeping in the master's bedroom; inviting friends over; pretending you're something special. Does she know the truth?' He nods at Clara, who is frantically looking between Philip and me, her mouth hanging open. 'Does she know why you're here? Have you told people you're nothing but a dirty little slut, a housemaid who…'

'Eh! That's enough!' Clara's authoritative manner silences Philip. 'Violet has every right to be here. She's got permission from her mistress, she's working hard, and she isn't doing anything untoward. That's right, isn't it, Vi?'

'Yes, of course,' I say.

'Don't you dare raise your voice at me, madam!' says Philip. 'She is over-stepping the mark and it is my job to make sure everything is done properly, so I can report back to Mr and Mrs Compton that all is well.'

'All *is* well,' says Clara. 'And I am making sure that Violet is well, thank you very much. So you can go back to your mistress and tell her that we are looking after her.'

Philip, who is now breathing heavily and whose cheeks have turned the colour of house bricks, shrieks, 'Did Mrs Compton ask you to make sure she was comfortable in the master bedroom? Was that part of the deal, that she acts like the lady of the house? Breakfast in bed and lazing around until this time.' He shoves his fingers into his jacket pocket, presumably searching for his pocket watch again. 'Damn thing!'

The watch's reluctance to show its face doesn't help to appease his anger, not one little bit. I watch him struggle with the tiny pocket, willing him to succeed.

'Oh, give it up, man,' says Clara. 'I know exactly what time it is.'

Philip's head shoots up. There is a smattering of spittle at the corner of his mouth and I look away, repulsed. 'How dare you!' he says. The words sneak out as a whisper, as though they can't quite believe that a young woman would be so brash and audacious, as though they are not sure whether to make themselves heard and challenge her.

'It isn't easy for her, you know,' continues Clara. 'And she doesn't need any added stress. It isn't good for the bairn.'

'You're right about that. It's peace and quiet that she needs, so I suggest you leave right now.' Philip grabs Clara's arm and manhandles her towards the back door.

'Don't touch me!' shouts Clara, pulling her arm free. 'Who do you think you are?'

As she steps back and lifts her arm out of Philip's reach, her hand smacks him in the nose. It isn't a forceful blow by any means, but Philip reacts as though he has been shot. He covers his nose with his hand and mumbles something about her regretting what she has done, as he leans over the sink. When he finally releases his hand we can all see that there isn't a speck of blood, either on his hand or on his nose. This seems to aggravate his temper, as though he wanted to be wounded, to give credence to his unnecessary temper.

'Just wait until Mr Compton hears about this. He never wanted this,' he sneers, pointing at my stomach. 'He won't stand for it.' He storms out, into the hallway and out through the front door, leaving it wide open. I follow him and, standing at the front door, watch as he takes a small wooden box, covered with layers of newspaper out of the boot of the car. He brings the box back to the house and deposits it on the front step. 'You'll be out on your ear in no time, mark my words.'

Before I say anything, he jumps into the car and drives off in a cloud of exhaust fumes.

'He's a character and a half, isn't he?' says Clara, appearing behind me. She puts her hand on my shoulder and moves my hair back behind my ear. 'Are you all right?'

'Yes, I'm fine, thanks, Clara. I'm sorry about that.'

'What have you got to be sorry about?'

I shrug my shoulders. 'You shouldn't be spoken to in that way. No man should speak to a woman like that.'

Clara laughs and gives me a sudden hug. 'I've heard plenty worse than that,' she says. 'Don't you ever worry about me. I can stand my ground with the best of them.'

'As I now know,' I say. I smile back at her, now that I know she isn't troubled by her encounter with Philip. 'He used to be alright, you know, when I first started at Compton Hall. I wouldn't say he's ever been friendly, but he didn't used to be so angry.'

'I can't see what he's got to be so angry about now.'

'He is the one who spotted me and Ernest kissing in the kitchen a few months back, and he hasn't had the time of day for me since.'

'You don't need the time of day from the likes of him,' says Clara.

'To make matters worse, he has just discovered that I have been sleeping in the master bedroom.'

'You've what?'

I'm not sure whether Clara hasn't heard me, or she disapproves and is finding it hard to believe what I have just said. 'I have been sleeping in the master bedroom,' I say, turning to face her. 'The bed in the maid's room is so small and uncomfortable, I didn't think it would matter to anyone.'

'Did Mrs Compton tell you not to?' asks Clara.

'No, but...'

'Well, then it's none of his business where you sleep. You take your orders from her, not from him. Anyway, I've got to go. I only popped in for a moment. I'm on my way to work.'

'Clara, this isn't on your way to work, this is miles out. But I'm so glad you came to see me,' I say.

'Yes, it seems I arrived at just the right time, didn't I?' She grins, clearly proud of herself for saving me from Philip's wrath. 'Anyway, I've got an afternoon off tomorrow, so my mum says you're welcome to come and have your lunch with us if you like. Just some bread and soup. My mum makes the best pea and ham soup in England. I will come and get you. I don't want you getting lost.'

'Thank you, Clara, that would be lovely. You might as well go this way, now that the door is open.'

'Great, see you tomorrow,' she says. 'And don't let the likes of him upset you. You know he is one of us, don't you? Just because he thinks he's an upper-class lord, doesn't make him one.' She strokes my upper arm and I tell her that she's right.

I pick up the box, cheered by Clara's uncomplicated view of the world, and wave her goodbye.

I close the door behind me and take the box into the kitchen, where I unpack it on the table. Underneath the layers of newspaper is a small round lemon cake wrapped in greaseproof paper, tied together with string. I lift the cake to my nose and take in its smell of citrus, sugar, and Cook's special ingredient, which she used to delight in telling me she added to all her cakes - love. She used to tell me that love was what made the sponges deliciously light. The fact that she has made this one especially for me brings more tears to my eyes. I wonder whether she asked Mrs Compton if she could make it, or was it Mrs Compton's idea? I don't know which one I would prefer.

The letter is less welcome. I don't recognise the handwriting, but whoever has written it has used my full name on the envelope, *Violet Pearson,* which adds to the air of formality. Reluctantly, I rip open the envelope and straighten out the folded paper.

Dear Violet,

I had a trip to Rackhams, and I thought that this blanket would come in useful during the long, cold evenings in the cottage. The drawing room can be draughty and chilly, even when the fire is lit. I do hope you like it.

Mrs Meadows sends her love, together with one of her lemon cakes, which I asked her to bake for you.

The money, as agreed, is all there. You will find it tucked away underneath the wood shavings. For discretion, you understand.

Mother sends her apologies that she is unable to deliver this parcel to you herself, but I can assure you that Philip hasn't been told anything about your arrangement. Mother has been in touch with Doctor Bradbury who will take care of you during the birth. I hope you will be comforted by the

fact. There is nothing to fear. Our families have known each
other for many years and are great friends, and he can be
trusted implicitly.

Please let me know if you need anything else.
Regards
Mary

I read the letter again, unable to believe the words printed
in front of me. So Miss Mary knows that I am here. Does
that mean that Ernest knows? Probably not. Mrs Compton
was quite adamant that she wanted to protect him whilst he
was studying. If he did know, I am sure he would have
written to me, too.

I take out the blanket and hold it to my face. It is white
and soft as a cloud, and the most beautiful thing I have ever
owned. I can't quite believe that Miss Mary bought me the
blanket herself. She was thinking of me whilst out shopping,
and she considered that I might be cold. In the drawing room
of her family's house. Then she considered that I might like
some lemon cake, and asked Cook if she could bake one for
me. How lovely. I imagine Philip sitting at the table in the
kitchen at break-time, eating his sandwich, and reading the
newspaper, and commenting on how delicious the kitchen
smells. A freshly baked cake with lemons is such a
comforting smell that everyone loves. He would have been
furious if he'd known the cake was being baked for me and
even more furious if he'd known that it was at Miss Mary's
behest. I have always liked her and her unexpected kindness
cheers me.

As I make my way upstairs for my wash, I quiet the little
voice in my head that tells me that it was easier for Mrs

Compton to send Philip, rather than make the long journey herself, like she said she would, and that she and Mr Compton, her sister, and the horrible Reverend Flynn are only interested in the care and comfort of the baby, not me.

Chapter Eleven
October 1908 - Mary

It is almost dark by the time I see the headlights of Father's car coming up the drive towards the house. Philip is back. I ring the servants' bell for the kitchen and wait for Barrow to arrive.

'Yes, miss, what can I do for you?' he says, standing in the doorway, as still as one of the men in Father's paintings.

'Philip is on his way,' I say. 'Please ask him to come to the dining room as soon as he has parked the car.'

'Yes, miss,' says Barrow. 'Anything else, miss?'

'No, thank you, Barrow, that will be all.'

'Yes, miss.'

I stand again at the lattice window, half hiding behind the thick velvet curtain, and as the car reaches the house. Then it disappears to the left, towards the garage.

'Hello, dear, I didn't know you were here.' It is Mother. 'We have another half hour until dinner.'

'Yes, hello Mother. I'm just watching the sunset, that's all.'

Thankfully the dining room windows face west, so my explanation is plausible. If I told her my real reason for being here before dinner, which is that I want to speak to Philip in private, to check that the cake and the blanket (and the money, of course) were safely delivered to Violet, and to ask about her condition, whether she is keeping well, whether she has yet made any friends, Mother would be furious, so I keep it to myself.

On the day after Violet left, I suffered a long afternoon tea with Mother in the library listening to her rants about the poor girl, how Violet had set a trap for Ernest, hoping to snare him into an unsuspecting marriage.

'Luckily, I have met girls like her before,' Mother said. 'She is trying to climb the social ladder, and she thinks that becoming pregnant is the way to do it. But let me tell you this, she is not achieving her goals through my son. Not while I have air in my lungs.'

I made the mistake of saying that I didn't think Violet had become pregnant on purpose, that it was such a risky strategy, and didn't seem to work for the housemaids I had heard about, the ones who had lost their jobs in an instant and had been sent away. Their only future prospects were to suffer the stigma of being an unmarried mother, if they were lucky to have their family's support, or to knock on the door of the workhouse and appeal for shelter. I shivered when I thought of it. I had heard that the conditions in those places were worse than anything we could imagine.

'Ah, but she is one of the smart ones,' said Mother, waving a cucumber sandwich in my direction. 'She has her head screwed on, as Nanny used to say.'

'Ernest loves her, though, Mother,' I said. I knew I was playing a dangerous game. My mother was the most stubborn woman in Yorkshire and if she believed there was the slightest chance that her son, the one she had raised to be a gentleman, the heir to Father's fortune, the one who carried the family's reputation into every room he entered, wasn't going to marry a suitable lady, she would move Heaven and earth to steer him back in the right direction. Arranging garden parties and elaborate dinners filled with young, beautiful, and eligible people had been Mother's favourite occupation for years - since I have been coupled up with James, and Ernest has been studying at Oxford, her efforts have waned somewhat - and if she believes there is a risk that her son is going to elope with a housemaid and raise her child, she would immediately get to work arranging more.

'It is lust, Mary. Nothing more, nothing less.' She mistook my disapproving frown for embarrassment. 'I am sorry to be so crude, but you know what men can be like. They're animals.'

'Ernest isn't like that,' I said.

'He might be better than most, he is my son after all and I hate to speak badly of him, but I am certain that lust has been his driver. Now that he is back at Oxford, he will forget about her.'

I quickly changed the subject and avoided further mention of Ernest.

'Where is this sunset you are so keen to watch?' she says now.

'It hasn't materialised, I'm afraid,' I say. 'Too much cloud.'

She isn't listening. She has wandered off to examine the table which, as usual, is immaculately set.

There is a rap on the open dining room door.

'Did you wish to speak to me, miss?' says Philip.

'Ah, Philip, you are safely returned to us,' says Mother.

Philip gives a bow with his head. 'Yes, ma'am.'

'Your journey was uneventful, I trust?' she says.

Philip glances over to me and I shake my head imperceptibly, silently willing him not to speak of the lemon cake or the blanket that I sent for Violet. As I gave him the carefully packed box this morning, I told him not to mention it to Mother, so I hope that he has remembered.

'Yes, thank you, ma'am. Nothing to report. The car coped very well with the steep hills.'

'Excellent. Well, thank you, Philip, I'm sure you want to get some food and rest so we won't require your services any further tonight.'

Philip says thank you and closes the door behind him. Mother continues her walk around the dining table, oblivious to the fact that it was me who wanted to speak to Philip.

Chapter Twelve
December 1908 - Violet

The last two months have flown by. After a two-night stay in Manchester with my family at the end of October, I returned to Lakeview Cottage and gradually settled into a routine. I now find myself lighting my Advent candle for the twelfth time this month. Since the beginning of December, I have begun the practice of lighting it every morning, and sitting in the warm kitchen with a cup of tea and my breakfast, and watching it burn for an hour before I start my work for the day. It is not quite the hard labour of Compton Hall. The endless dusting and cleaning, changing bed linen, and running errands for Mrs Compton that I used to do now seems so long ago. But somehow I am still falling into bed exhausted each night, having been on my feet for the majority of the day.

I am determined to keep myself busy, not because the devil makes work for idle hands - in truth, the devil's work has already been done - but because when I am busy, my mind is quiet. I try not to allow myself to think too much. I try to dismiss any thoughts of Ernest whenever they appear. Thinking about him is too painful. When my fingers are working, I concentrate only on the task at hand. So, I brush and clean the floors, scrub the fire surrounds, polish the door brass and the front doorstep, and then, after my evening meal, I read a book or sew. I found some tapestry cotton in the bureau in the study and Clara has added to my collection with bits and bobs that she said were 'lying about the house.'

But today, I am changing my routine. Sunday, being a day of rest, I am allowing myself to slow down for an hour or so and rest my soul. I am sitting in St. Martin's Church, after Clara persuaded me to join her and her family, waiting for the morning service to begin. Afterwards, I intend to spend a lazy afternoon with my new book. Last week, I treated myself to a small collection of novels and a recipe book when my November wage arrived in the post. A treat indeed. Usually, books are something that I receive as birthday or Christmas gifts, and I am trying to assuage the guilt by telling myself that I deserve them. I need them. I am not living a life of penury, by any means, but such spending on luxury items for myself isn't something that I am used to.

The hundred pounds that Philip, unknowingly I am sure, delivered to me from Mrs Compton has remained untouched. It is safely packed away in my suitcase, which I have stored underneath my bed. I will need every penny of that after the baby is born. Goodness knows what I will do or where I will go. I have tried not to give it too much thought.

'Excuse me, Miss Pearson? Are you Violet Pearson?' I look to my left to see a woman standing at the end of the pew, waiting for me to respond.

'Yes, that's me,' I tell her.

'My name is Mrs Taylor. Me and my husband run a small hotel up in Windermere and I do some odd jobs for Mr and Mrs Compton, now and then, like, when they need me.'

'I'm pleased to meet you.' I offer my right hand for the lady to shake and she takes it gently.

'Hello Mrs Taylor,' says Clara over my shoulder. 'Nice to see you again. Are you well?'

'Yes, thank you, Clara.' Mrs Taylor offers her salutations to Clara's parents, and her brother, Billy, before she turns back to me. 'The thing is, I have had a letter from Mr Compton asking me to go into the house and make up the beds in all of the three front bedrooms. He said he is coming up next weekend with some friends.' She takes a crumpled letter from her pocket and grasps it tightly. 'I have my own key, but I didn't want to be presumptuous and let myself in without speaking to you. I believe you're looking after the place?'

'Yes, that's right,' I say.

Clara digs me in the ribs and a quick glance her way shows me that she is smiling. I am not sure why, but it seems that Clara and her family know Mrs Taylor and my instinct tells me that she is the village gossip. I wrap my coat around my middle and fold my arms across my expanding waistline.

'Oh, well, thank you so much, but I'm sure I can see to that, Mrs Taylor,' I say. 'Thank you for letting me know.'

'He hasn't told you then?' she asks.

Her self-satisfaction at this perceived advantage over me causes her to grin widely. I try not to stare at the large gap where she is missing her two front teeth. I can feel heat rising to my cheeks. I am not sure how to deal with this woman, and I wonder who told her my name, how much she knows about me and the reason that I am staying at Lakeview Cottage.

'No, I haven't received my letter yet,' I say. 'But I'm sure it will arrive with tomorrow's post. Like I said, I…'

'I am under strict orders to make up three of the bedrooms with fresh bedlinen, ready for their arrival next Saturday morning.' Mrs Taylor holds the letter to her chest with one hand and smooths out its creases with her other. 'I wouldn't want to let Mr Compton down.'

'No, of course not,' I say. I tell myself to cut this woman some slack. She doesn't appear to be wealthy and I wouldn't want to take a paid job away from her. She has probably worked for the Comptons for many years, so I tell her that she is very welcome to come over to the house whenever she is free and we make arrangements for her to come on Friday afternoon. She tells me, more loudly than necessary, that she has some guests staying this week and the hotel is almost full, so she will be very busy until then. Clara's further dig in my ribs tells me that this information is for her family's benefit, rather than mine.

'So, the master and mistress are coming over, eh? So they should and all. It's about time they came to see if you're all right,' says Clara when Mrs Taylor has said goodbye and settled herself in a pew close to the front of the church.

'Why haven't they said anything to me about their visit?' I say. 'And why have they asked *her* to make up the beds, instead of asking me?'

Clara shrugs. 'I don't know, but I can think of one good reason.'

'Like what?' I say.

'They don't know whether you're up to it,' she whispers. She glances down at my stomach. 'Changing beds isn't easy work, as you well know, but doing it when you're seven months pregnant, well, they might be being nice to you, caring for your welfare and stuff.'

'I doubt that,' I say. 'They don't care about my welfare, not one little bit.' I don't tell Clara that, although the Comptons won't give me a second thought, I know that they will want to protect my unborn baby. The baby that they have paid for. The baby that the horrible Reverend and Mrs Flynn are looking forward to receiving very soon. The baby that they will bring up as their own child, pretending to the world that they have been given a gift from God.

A sudden image of me handing over my baby, warm and sleepy after her feed, swaddled in a soft pink blanket, sends a stabbing pain to my heart and tears to my eyes. Clara sees them immediately.

'Hey, don't worry about it,' she says. She takes hold of my hand tightly. 'Mrs Taylor's all right. She likes to think she's something when she's not. But don't we all sometimes?'

I nod. 'Yes, I suppose so. It isn't her fault. I'm sure a letter is on its way to me,' I say.

'I'm sure it is,' says Clara. She squeezes my hand.

'So Mrs Taylor runs a hotel?' I say. 'What is it like?'

'Well, it certainly isn't a hotel for one thing. It's a bed and breakfast on Victoria Street that's all, but it's clean and she is good at her job, I'll give her that, which is why she has been working for the Comptons for years.'

'But what if she sees me without my coat? She'll see that I'm expecting.' Despite Clara's protestations that I should not be ashamed, I do not want to be the cause of gossip.

'Well, if you really don't want her to see you, then you need to be out when she comes. Have your coat on ready and go for a walk.'

'I will do,' I say. 'That's a good idea, thank you, Clara.' What would I do without Clara? I would be lost and alone with her and her family.

As the vicar appears at the pulpit and the organ music begins for our first hymn, I mouth another grateful 'thank you' to her and she gives me a warm kiss on my cheek and links her arm through mine as we stand and begin singing. Her arm remains there throughout the rest of the service.

Chapter Thirteen
December 1908 - Violet

The following Friday, my morning tea and breakfast, the quiet hour with my Advent candle that I usually look forward to, is filled with anxiety about the forthcoming visit from the Comptons. They are not due to arrive until tomorrow morning, but I am dreading it. Already, I am counting down the hours until they go home. I hope that they are only staying one night, but who knows?

I have made sure that all of my belongings have been transferred from the master bedroom to the small single room at the back of the house, where I have been sleeping for the past three nights. My suitcase containing the money is under the bed. In the absence of a wardrobe in that room, my dresses are neatly folded and are in the drawers of the large chest. My shoes are tucked away in the corner of the room and my book is on the bedside table.

The tiny room reminds me of my room at Compton Hall. Servicable. Impersonal. Dull. It is only across the corridor from the master bedroom, but it is another world away. A room fit for a servant, but not fit for a lady. There are no pictures on the walls, which are painted the colour of damp clay. The window is small and set high into the wall so that when I sit on the bed, the view into the back garden is out of reach. The tiny ceramic vase that I moved from the bookcase in the drawing room brightens the room a little. It sits on the top of the small chest of drawers. The delicate lavender leaves from the garden, which have now dried, add some much-needed colour, like a single orchid in the middle of a desert.

I am already missing the wonderful view from the bay window in the front bedroom. I have quickly become used to it and have enjoyed watching the swans glide graciously across the lake as I straightened the bed each morning. The changing beauty of the landscape, as it transitioned from autumn into winter, gave my day the tiniest sprinkle of joy. But I tell myself that the move into the back bedroom is only temporary. I will move myself back into the master suite as soon as the Comptons have gone home.

I have still not received any notice of their arrival from Compton Hall, which I hope means that the letter has been lost in the post, rather than the fact that nobody has bothered to tell me who is coming to spend the weekend here. I presume that Mr and Mrs Compton will sleep in their usual bedroom, but I have no idea who their guests will be and where they will sleep.

When I hear the knock on the front door, earlier than expected, I rush to put on my overcoat and hat before I answer it. Mrs Taylor doesn't hide her surprise as she looks me up and down, questioningly.

'Good morning, Mrs Taylor,' I say, standing to one side to allow her to enter. 'Please come in.'

'On your way out, or have you just come in?' she asks.

'I am on my way out actually.'

Mrs Taylor walks straight down the hallway, into the kitchen, and hangs her coat on one of the hooks by the back door. I forget that there are many people around here who know the house as well as I do. I'm slightly perturbed that she didn't come to the back door like she would if the master and mistress were home, but I'm not going to challenge her about it. At least she didn't let herself in with the key, and she had the decency to knock.

'But you haven't finished your breakfast, love,' she says. 'You don't need to go out on my account. You sit yourself down and I'll just get on with things.'

I lean over the table and blow out my Advent candle. 'No, really, I have had enough. I need to get out. There's an errand I need to do. There's something I need to collect from...' I pause, as I think of somewhere that I might be visiting, something that I might need to collect.

'Well, make sure you wrap up well, have you got a scarf?' Mrs Taylor perches on the edge of one of the dining chairs and unfastens her boots, pulling them off with a groan. 'It looks like snow. The hills are already covered with it.'

I am thankful Mrs Taylor hasn't noticed that I haven't finished my sentence. She doesn't seem to be a great listener. She spends the next few minutes gossiping about a young couple who have been staying in her hotel, who she doesn't believe are married, at least not to each other. They are far too amorous for a married couple, she tells me, as I clear away my breakfast pots and wash them quickly in the sink. I am about to tell her where the clean bedlinen is kept, but before I do, she tells me not to worry about anything and that she knows where everything is. I thank her and tell her that

I will be back in a couple of hours. I am relieved that she assures me that she is a quick worker and she will probably be gone by the time I get back.

I open the front door and am shocked to see that the garden and the path down to the road are blanketed in freshly fallen snow. I step out, tilt my face to the sky, and allow the powdery crystals to float onto my face. Within seconds, my coat is covered with flakes, although they quickly melt. I take Mrs Taylor's advice and dash back to the kitchen and grab my scarf, which I tightly wrap around my neck, tucking the ends inside the neckline of my coat.

I walk carefully down the path, my boots crunching the snow beneath me. When I reach the gate, I look back at the house. The severe stone facade is softened by the falling snow and it looks almost welcoming. It surprises me that the Comptons have never chosen to spend Christmas here. If I owned this house, I would love to wake up here on Christmas morning. I would never tire of throwing open the curtains of the master bedroom to reveal the magnificent view of the lake. Its performance never gets boring, as it puts on a daily glittering show for all to see. After breakfast, Ernest and I would walk to church in the snow with our children and come home to a welcoming fire and a huge roast goose.

I take my dreams with me as I walk through the gate and turn left towards the lake. As I close the gate behind me, a dozen sparrows shoot out of one of the tall oak trees, squawking and squabbling as they escape into the air.

The tree drops clumps of snow onto the ground, covering my recent footprints.

*

My walk around the lake is not as pleasant as I first imagined. I have always loved snow, but within half an hour, I am tired, cold and wet, and desperate to return to Lakeview Cottage. The increasing wind whips at my face with painful hailstones, as the gentle snow now turns to battering rain. I turn my back on the lake and trundle up the hill towards the centre of the village, where the overhanging shop canopies offer some slight shelter from the elements. I take my time looking into all of the windows and it isn't until the church clock strikes two p.m. that I remember I haven't eaten any lunch. I am almost faint with hunger.

I walk back towards the lake. I am tempted to shelter in The Lilac Tearoom which overlooks the pier, but through their steamed windows I can see that there are no vacant seats. By this time, my hat and coat are soaked through and I cannot bear to be outside any longer. Mrs Taylor should surely have finished by now, and if she hasn't, I will have to tell her that I have a headache and lock myself away in the back bedroom until she has gone.

But as I let myself into the front door and call out her name, I am relieved to receive no reply. An inspection of the bedrooms satisfies me that she has done her job well and she has gone home. Only then do I begin to relax. I am desperately hungry, so I gnaw at a slice of bread while I warm up some soup that I made yesterday from leftover vegetables and chicken stock. I am pleased with it; I seem to have picked up some good tips from Cook during my time at Compton Hall and I am just sitting down at the table to eat when I hear a commotion outside the front door. Shrieks of laughter, both male and female. I jump up and dash into the hall. The loud voices don't appear threatening, but I consider arming myself with the poker from the kitchen. Before I can do so, the door flies open and the party of three stagger inside, falling over each other and their luggage, which they deposit onto the floor. I can't decide if they are drunk or just giddy.

Amongst the flapping of coats and shaking of umbrellas, none of them seem to have noticed me standing in the doorway to the kitchen. I don't know two members of the party, but one of them is well known to me. Very well-known indeed.

Chapter Fourteen
December 1908 - Violet

'Ernest,' I say softly. Half of me doesn't want to be heard. If I slip out of the back door, I could run to Clara's house before he turns around and he needn't see me at all. But before I have thought any more about it, he turns and faces me. The surprise is evident on his face.

'Violet, what are you doing here?'

'Who is this?' says the lady. She takes in my wet, untidy hair, the ring of mud and rain decorating the bottom of my skirt, my bare feet. Then she stares at my swollen belly and grabs Ernest's arm, clinging to him possessively. 'You told me that there wouldn't be any staff this weekend.' She doesn't take her eyes off me.

Her jade green woollen coat, the latest style of hat, with flamboyant peacock feathers in green, blue, and brown, would have been more impressive if not for the adverse weather that had dampened it. Her red-lipsticked smile exudes sophistication.

I keep my eyes fixed on Ernest, waiting for him to introduce me. He has paled. He laughs nervously. I have never seen him so bewildered. His eyes dart between me and his elegant guest. 'Lucille, Frank, this is Violet. She's…'

I step forward, my head held high, and introduce myself as Mrs Compton's lady's maid. I have promoted myself from housemaid. Let Ernest challenge me, if he dares. 'Mrs Compton has requested that I look after the house whilst it lies empty. Let me take your coats and hats. I'll hang them up for you.'

'Oh, how delightful,' says Lucille. 'I fully expected to have to be self-sufficient for a few days. This is a joy.' She pulls two pins from her hat and hands them to me. Then, standing in front of the mirror on the wall, she carefully lifts her hat, and gently touches her hair until she is satisfied that it is all still in place. She is beautiful. Her deep auburn hair and green eyes are striking. I can see why Ernest would fall for someone like her. Who wouldn't be attracted to such a lady. She is like a vibrant summer flower, brightening a dull winter's day.

I take her hat and wait for her to unbutton her coat before I help her out of it. She doesn't thank me, but I don't expect her to.

'Take this will you?' The man called Frank holds out his hat and, as I don't have any free hands, he balances it on top of Lucille's coat, followed by his own overcoat. He pushes past me and makes his way towards the dining room. 'Ernest, where's that wine collection of your father's you were telling me about?'

Ernest is pulled into the dining room by Lucille. I can hear them opening the doors of the wine cabinet, glass clinking as bottles are lifted out and labels inspected.

I start to make my way upstairs, my feet moving as quickly as possible without falling over the mountain of wet hats and coats in my arms. As I reach the top of the stairs, I look down and see Ernest has dumped his coat on the newell post at the bottom of the stairs.

Despite the pounding of my heart and the tears waiting to fall, I tell myself to stay calm. I need to keep control of myself. Somehow.

Mrs Taylor told me that Mr Compton and his friends would be staying for the weekend. Clearly, she meant *Master* Compton, not Mr and Mrs Compton, which explains why I haven't been told. By the look on Ernest's face, he had no idea that I would be here.

If only I knew that Ernest was the expected visitor, rather than Mr and Mrs Compton, I could have been more prepared, although I didn't expect anybody to turn up today. Mrs Taylor said that they were coming on Saturday morning, so I still would have been here in wet clothes, my dress dirty from my walk. What must he be thinking? I must look a sight. Not that he would give me a second glance whilst Lucille was in his eye-line. I wonder whether he would still have come, had he known I was here. I would like to think that if he had, he would not have brought his female companion, for the sake of both of our feelings.

I don't know how I am going to get through this weekend. Will Ernest want to speak to me in private? I hope so. If he doesn't, I will be devastated. We haven't seen each other for almost three months, and it seems that, in my absence, he has already moved on. I desperately hold back the tears. I can't let my emotions get the better of me. I can't allow Ernest's guests to see me upset. Ernest would never forgive me. Keeping busy means not thinking. I must concentrate on the task in hand. One task at a time. Right now, I need to hang these coats and hats in the correct bedrooms. I haven't been told who will be sleeping where. Will Ernest and Lucille be sleeping together? Surely not. I decide that Lucille will sleep in the room usually used by Miss Mary. It is pretty and light. Its corner position gives it two windows which means that whatever time of day, it is bathed in light. The curtains are made from the most beautiful silk fabric, decorated with deep pink orchids, surrounded by elegant green leaves, and two matching cushions lie side by side on the bed. The room will suit her.

I hang Lucille's coat on the back of the door and leave her hat on the stool by the dressing table.

Frank will sleep in the room next door, a smaller room, but just as elegant, usually used by Ernest. In a moment of pique, I lay his wet coat on the bed, and rest his hat on top of it. The room feels cold, but nobody has given me orders to light the fires, so I leave it as it is.

Closing the door behind me, I pause on the landing, unsure whether to go downstairs and tidy away my soup bowl, or whether to lock myself in my room and stay there for the whole of the weekend. I presume the guests will be gone in a couple of days, but it is a couple of days too many for me to bear.

I decide to go to my room, the tiny maid's bedroom at the back of the house, with its single bed, uncomfortable mattress, and drab brown curtains.

I close the door behind me and turn the key in the lock. I don't care whether Ernest and his guests need anything. Like

Lucille said, she didn't expect anyone to be here, so they shall have to cater for themselves.

I sit on the edge of the bed, listening to muted laughter rising through the floorboards.

I watch the rain slipping down the glass in the window as I stroke my bump and tell my baby that her daddy is downstairs.

I get up and pick up the tiny vase from the chest of drawers. I pull at each of the delicate lavender petals in turn, dropping them to the floor. He loves me, he loves me not, he loves me, he loves me not, he loves me, he loves me not.

Hope sinks like a rock thrown with abandon into the lake.

Chapter Fifteen
December 1908 - Violet

The sun set more than an hour ago and I calculate that it must be past six o'clock. I have been up here for hours, trying to lose myself in my book, but being unable to concentrate. I have read the same page over and over again, but the story is failing to make an imprint in my mind.

I am hungry, but I am determined that I am not going to move until I hear that everyone has retired to bed. Only then will I venture downstairs and get myself some food. My stomach has been complaining noisily, but it will have to wait a little longer.

Suddenly I hear voices downstairs coming from the hallway, and then the front door slams shut. I deduce that they must have gone out. I open my bedroom door slowly, and seeing that the coast is clear, I tiptoe across the landing and into the master bedroom. Through the front window, I can see Lucille and Frank walking down the path away from the house. Lucille's arm is linked through Frank's. A torch is lighting the way through the darkness. I can't see Ernest.

'Hello, Violet.'

He is here, standing in the bedroom. I don't want to turn and face him, but I must. When I do, I can't read his expression. He is holding onto one of the bedposts, staring at me.

'Hello, Ernest.'

'What are you doing here?'

'I thought I heard the front door close, so I was looking..'

'No, I mean in this house. I didn't know you would be here. I would never...'

'Never what?' I say. 'Never have brought your lady friend here?'

'She is not my lady friend,' he says.

'Have you told her that? I think she thinks otherwise, the way she gripped onto your arm earlier.'

Ernest shrugs. 'She is like that with everyone. She's very friendly.'

I look over my shoulder out of the window again, but it's so dark outside that I am struggling to see anything except for Frank's retreating torch, bopping up and down as the two of them walk towards the gate.

'Where are they going?' I ask.

'To get some food. I said I would join them in the restaurant in a few minutes, I just wanted to...'

'I've never eaten in a restaurant,' I say. I have often wondered what it must be like to be served your meal on delicate china plates while a pianist plays Bach quietly in the corner. What a luxury. But my nerves would get the better of me; I know that I would embarrass myself and would spill something and cause the fresh white linen to be soiled irrevocably.

'Violet, why didn't you tell me that you were here?'

'I did. I wrote you a letter as soon as I heard you had left for Oxford, but Philip took it and gave it to your mother.'

'I didn't know that.' He sighs heavily.

'She told me that you mustn't be disturbed, that your final year at university was important.' Ernest's nod of agreement infuriates me. 'There are other important things going on, Ernest, not just your studies.' I snap at him.

'I know, I know.' He approaches me, slowly. 'How are you?'

'I'm fine, don't touch me.' I step back.

'Mother told me that you had left Compton Hall without serving your notice.'

'Did she?' I'm not surprised that Mrs Compton would do everything in her power to keep me away from her son.

'I never thought I would see you again.'

'How hard did you try?'

'I don't know what I could have done. Why are you being so aloof? Violet?'

He looks sad, but I don't know what to say to him. I sit down on the windowsill, but it's cold and draughty, so I get up and begin to move towards the door. 'I haven't seen you for over two months, Ernest. No, three months. You haven't written to me, or…' I wipe my tears quickly. 'And then you turn up here unexpectedly, with a new lady friend.' I don't want to cry. I want to be strong, although I know that I'm not. I need to leave the room, but he reaches out and grabs my arm.

'But I told you, I didn't know where you were,' he says, softly. He stands so close to me that I can smell him. Soap and expensive cologne.

I push his hand away from my arm. For a fleeting moment, he looks hurt. 'You've already said, but I'm sure that you could have written to me at Compton Hall, and asked that the letters be forwarded to my parents' house.'

He laughs. 'You know that my mother wouldn't ever have done that.'

'Yes, I do know that.' Logically, I know that Ernest doesn't have my home address, the one in Manchester. I know that he would have been in a difficult position and that he wouldn't want to anger his parents. Even so, I feel a need to punish him. I am so angry with him, for not being here with me, for not loving me enough to find me.

'But you're here. I am so pleased to see you.'

A gust of wind throws raindrops against the window. I wonder what state Lucille will be in by the time they reach the restaurant. I didn't see her carrying an umbrella. Precipitation isn't a friend of ladies who wish to dress to impress.

'I need to go,' I say. 'I haven't eaten all day, and your friends will be waiting for you.'

I leave him and go downstairs. The kitchen is in darkness, so I light the lamp, fill the kettle with water, and put it onto the stove. My bowl of soup is still waiting for me on the table, but now it is cold and unappetising. The fresh loaf of bread that was in the bread tin this morning has now gone. Only crumbs are left on the countertop, together with the remnants of a block of cheese. Left unwrapped, it is beginning to harden around the edges. I wrap it tightly in greaseproof paper and put it back in the larder.

'Yes, I'm sorry about that,' says Ernest. He has followed me down the stairs. 'We were all hungry. I meant to tidy the kitchen but…'

'Well, you don't need to, Master Ernest, you have a kitchen maid to do that for you.' I wipe up the breadcrumbs with a wet cloth, wishing that I could scrub away my feelings for Ernest.

'Violet, stop, please.'

'Stop what? Stop cleaning up? We'll have mice if the kitchen is left in this state.'

'No, stop being like this.' I can feel him watching me as I rinse the cloth under the running water. 'I told her that I wanted to be with you, you know,' he says. 'That day, when you told me that you were pregnant. I told Mother that day, and I told her that we wanted to be together.'

'Yes, you said that you would. But now?'

'Now?'

'Lucille?'

'Lucille is Frank's sister, and Frank has been a good friend at Oxford. A man needs a friend.'

'Of course.' And a woman needs a father for her child. I stop cleaning and sit down at the kitchen table. I'm too weary to stand any longer. I want him to go out so that I can scramble some eggs, and then go to bed.

'Lucille doesn't mean anything to me.' He pulls out a chair and sits opposite.

'Do I mean anything to you?' I didn't want to ask, but the words escape before I can stop them. 'It's okay, don't answer that question. Your pause tells me everything that I need to know.'

He rubs at his chin. He didn't have a beard when I last saw him. He seems older now. Much older, although it has only been a matter of months. He looks handsome and incredibly out of reach. His air of authority and prestige clothe him and even his badly creased shirt couldn't fool anyone into thinking that he was anything but a gentleman. And I am nothing but a maid. Suddenly I am surrounded by shame. It engulfs me, smothers me. I can't bear the way that he is looking at me. Is he forlorn, or is it pity that I can see in his eyes, those beautiful brown, hot-chocolate eyes that captivated me? I am unable to tell, but the fact that Lucille – beautiful Lucille in her expensive, fashionable clothes and impeccable breeding – is waiting for him in a restaurant only highlights the immense differences between us. I don't know how I could ever have imagined that we would be suitable for each other. Our lives are so far apart, we might have come from different countries. We speak entirely different languages.

'I'd like to be alone now,' I tell him. 'I need some food.' I rub at my belly, a reminder of his unborn child.

'Of course, of course. I shall leave you to…is there anything that you need?'

'No, thank you. I will take a walk to the bakery in the morning and get some more bread.'

'Yes, I'm sorry…'

'I'll get some for you and your friends too, and anything else if you write a list for me, but I am not here to wait on you. You know that, don't you?' I stand, holding tightly to the back of the chair. The table between us. He nods and an expression that I can't read flits across his face. He leaves and I finally hear the front door closing behind him.

*

I don't know what time they return. I must have been fast asleep, as I didn't hear them coming up the stairs and going to bed. I finally managed to fall asleep at some time after eleven, after reading my book in bed. The drawing room was too cold to contemplate and, although a fire had been lit in the dining room, I didn't have the energy to tackle the mess of dirty glasses, wine bottles, and plates that had been left in there, so that room, although the warmest in the house, was out of bounds. I poked at the fire and made sure the fire guard was safely in place before I closed the door behind me.

When I felt Ernest climbing into my single bed and wrapping his arms around me, I was sure that I was dreaming. But now as he kisses the back of my neck and tells me that he is sorry, I know that he is real. His breath smells of wine and garlic and I wonder where he has been and what he has had to eat. I made myself a plateful of scrambled eggs, but only managed to eat a couple of mouthfuls before I felt sick. I imagined him sitting in a dimly lit restaurant, laughing heartily with Frank and flirting with Lucille while the mother of his child was alone in a cold house, feeling nauseous.

'Shall we go into my bed?' he says, 'It's much more comfortable than this one.'

'Why don't you get into bed with Lucille?' I say.

'She isn't the type to sleep with anyone until she's married.' He's drunk, I know he is. Even so, his words feel like a dagger to my heart.

'Go back to your own bed, Ernest,' I tell him, even though I don't want him to leave me.

'I will, but I want you to come with me. Come on, they're asleep. They won't hear us.' He takes my hand and we both climb out of bed. As my eyes adjust to the darkness, I can see that he is naked from the waist up. I wrap my arms around his neck and he kisses me passionately and the months that we have been apart seem to melt away. I try to dismiss the thought of him kissing Lucille in the same way.

'The baby has grown,' he says, cupping my belly with both hands.

'Yes, she has. I think we're having a girl.'

'A girl? Really?'

'It's just a feeling I have.' I wish I could see the delight on his face, but the moonlight only permits me to see his outline. 'You know your mother wants me to give her to your aunt and the horrible Reverend Flynn?'

'What?'

'Yes, that's what I was trying to tell you in the letter when I wrote to you at Oxford from Compton Hall. Your mother wants me to stay here until I've had the baby and then give her to your aunt, to bring up as her own.'

'That's preposterous. You can't do that.' He waits for me to answer. But I don't. 'You didn't agree? Tell me you didn't agree. What did you say?'

'Well, I didn't want to, but…'

'Tell me you didn't agree,' he repeats. He steps back and I can hear the vase wobble on the chest of drawers as he backs into it.

'Ernest, you weren't there. Your mother told me that I had to leave you alone, that you had to finish your studies in Oxford. I didn't have a choice.'

'Of course, you had a choice. People always have choices.'

Not people like me, I want to say. 'Don't raise your voice like that, you'll wake Frank and Lucille.'

'I don't care. Why didn't you tell me?'

'I told you that Philip intercepted the letter before it was posted.'

'Not then. Now. Why didn't you tell me as soon as you arrived here? They have post boxes in Bowness. You knew where I was.'

'I know, I don't know.'

'Violet?'

He is waiting for me to explain. I think of the letters in the top drawer of the chest that Ernest is now leaning against. I have written three letters to him since I have been here but I haven't posted any of them. I have been too busy convincing myself that my dreams wouldn't ever become a reality. A gentleman would never marry a housemaid, not even an ambitious one. Not even a housemaid who wants to better herself and become a teacher. A pipedream, that's what Mr Compton would call it. I convinced myself that the only way Ernest would marry me is if he ran away, and denounced his family and his heritage, and I've always known that would never happen. Not when it finally came to it.

'You went to Oxford without speaking to me,' I say. It's easier for me to throw allegations than to defend myself.

'Mother followed me around like a shadow that day. I was packed and sent away before I had time to think. I always intended to write to you, but the next day, she told me that you had already gone.'

Now, I want to tell him that I am sorry I doubted him, and that I am overjoyed that he is here now. We can be together after all, when he has left university and he is making his own income. He doesn't need his father's money. We will be fine on our own. I want to tell him that this baby will have a wonderful life with us and that we will have more children, lots of children, in the future. But the lump in my throat prevents me from speaking. He has Lucille now. I don't want to hear him reject me.

'Plans have been made now,' I say.

'Well, I'll just tell Mother that you've changed your mind,' says Ernest.

'You can't do that.'

'Why? You're not serious about giving away our baby, surely?'

'Ernest, what do you think will happen to me when the baby is born? They won't let us be together. Not now you've got Lucille. Be realistic. I don't have a choice. At least the money will help me while I recover, until I get a job, get myself back on my feet. Then I can begin my teacher training. Maybe then…'

'The money? What money? Violet! What money?'

Ernest's fingers are digging into my arms. 'You're hurting me, get off!' He lets me go. 'Your mother gave me a hundred pounds.'

'A hundred pounds? For the baby?'

'It isn't what I wanted, you've got to understand that.' I'm crying now, but he doesn't offer me any comfort.

'I can't believe what you've done. You're…'

'Ernest, please.'

'Stay away from me.' As he opens the bedroom door, he

is temporarily illuminated by the bedside lamp in the master bedroom which casts a dim light into the landing. He doesn't look back. He closes the door behind him and I am once against thrown into darkness.

As I am closing my bedroom door, I think that I hear a door opening at the other end of the corridor, and I have a sense that someone is watching me, but in the darkness, I can't tell who it is.

Then I hear a sigh.

It's Lucille.

Chapter Sixteen
December 1908 - Violet

The following morning, I wake later than usual after a restless night. After my wash, I wind my unruly hair into a tight bun, dress in my maid's uniform, and stand at the top of the stairs, trying to decide what to do. I haven't worn this dress since the day Philip arrived unexpectedly in October. At Compton House, this dress represented hard work, tight schedules, orders, and discipline. Here it seems to be synonymous with surprise visitors; not the kind of visitors that bring joy, spending afternoons together chatting by the fire and eating too much sponge cake, but the kind that bring shock, tears, and unhappiness. The skirt is long and pleated at the waist, so it still fits me.

I decide to change it. I cannot bring myself to remind Ernest of my station within his family.

Back in my room, I rifle through my drawers for something more suitable to wear. I am no competition for Lucille, but that doesn't mean I have to look dowdy. I settle for a navy blue skirt which I have been wearing for church. Clara's mum gave it to me. It is bigger than my normal size and fits over my bump perfectly. I choose a duck-egg-blue blouse to go with it. The blouse isn't as decorative as the one Lucille wore yesterday, but I have hardly worn it and it is clean. Ernest used to like it. He told me once that it made the colour of my eyes sing. I wonder if he remembers.

As I dress, I spot the edge of my small suitcase underneath the bed. I push it further underneath with my foot. For a moment, I contemplate getting it out, packing all my clothes into it, and running away. That's impossible, I know. I have nowhere to go, other than back to my parents' tiny house and I am reluctant to do that. But then again, I am reluctant to stay in this house for the whole weekend. I cannot bear to see Ernest with Lucille and I certainly don't want to serve them. Like she said, they hadn't expected anyone to be here, so they wouldn't miss me. I am sure that Ernest would prefer me to be elsewhere. After his reaction last night, I am not sure that he will ever want to see me again.

But where would I go? I have enough money to be able to stay in a hotel for a couple of nights, but the thought of walking into the luxurious white hotel on the side of the lake fills me with dread. Everyone would be looking at me, I just know they would. I am not their usual clientele. I would stand out a mile amongst the elegant ladies and well-dressed gentlemen. Going to Mrs Taylor's bed and breakfast isn't an option, either, as she would expect me to stay here and look after Master Compton and his friends. She would ask too many questions that I wouldn't be able to answer.

I can't think properly at the moment, I am so tired. I need to make some breakfast for myself before I can formulate a plan.

I tiptoe softly down the stairs to the sound of silence, except for the gentle clink of cutlery against china. The group is breakfasting in the dining room and as I walk past the open door, I can smell fried bacon and toast. In the kitchen, I can see that in the frying pan on the stove there are two rashers of bacon and there are two slices of bread laid out on the countertop.

'Ernest insisted that we save you some breakfast.'

I turn to see Lucille standing in the doorway, holding the teapot in her outstretched hand. I take it from her. 'That's very kind of him,' I say.

'This tea has gone cold,' she says.

'I'll refill it for you and bring it through to the dining room.'

I expect her to rebuke me for not being up earlier. What kind of housemaid wakes up an hour after the guests? She fixes me with an icy stare. I want to ask her if there is anything else that I can help her with, but I would like her to leave and any conversation would only prolong her stay. She clings onto a white lace shawl which is wrapped around her delicate shoulders, folding the material through her hands again and again. My eyes are drawn to a sapphire stone in the centre of a brooch at the neck of her blouse. The stunning blue catches the morning sun. It must have cost a fortune and I wonder what man bought it for her.

'Ernest is very happy at university,' she says. She looks down at my bump. She frowns and I can see a thousand questions flicking through her mind, like the pages of a complicated book that she is struggling to understand.

'I am glad to hear it,' I say. 'Mr and Mrs Compton must be pleased.'

She nods. 'And he is very happy with me,' she adds. 'It won't be long before we are engaged.'

The teapot clatters to the floor. The lid snaps in half. The teapot handle breaks off and flies underneath the table. I dash to the sink and grab a cloth to mop up the spilled tea before it soaks into the floorboards.

'I'm so sorry. I don't know what happened there,' I say. I bend to pick up the broken crockery, but tears prevent me from seeing clearly.

On my hands and knees on the floor, I want to tell Lucille that Ernest should be mine. He was happy with me too, before his mother interfered and sent me here. But I can't find the words. They are lost in the depth of my emotions. I know she wouldn't believe that Ernest and I had a real relationship. One that was built on mutual respect, conversation, and shared laughter, rather than just sex. She sees me as just a maid, a lowly servant who is in the unfortunate situation of having fallen pregnant, and in her world, whether or not I get to keep the baby, does not mean that I get to keep the father of the child. He is free to marry someone else. Someone better. Someone like her.

When I scramble up, she has gone.

I sink down onto the rocking chair next to the stove and wish that I could stay here all day. I wish that the whistle of the kettle was just for my tea, not for Ernest's, or Frank's, and certainly not for Lucille's. I can feel the animosity that she has left in the kitchen. Its palpable weight has drained me suddenly. But I force myself to get up. I desperately search through the wooden dresser, pulling open the doors and shifting piles of plates to search behind him. Thankfully, I find another teapot, make fresh tea with shaking hands, and take it to them in the dining room. I balance the tray with the teapot and a fresh jug of milk in one hand and knock lightly on the open door with the other.

'Come in,' says Lucille. How quickly she has taken on the role of the lady of the house.

The jocularity from yesterday has gone. Ernest and his guests are quiet. I try to catch Ernest's eye as I place the tray on the table, but he is busy inspecting his empty plate. If I was doing my job properly, I would collect the dirty pots; I would ask them if they would like any more toast and I would ask Lucille if she would like me to pour the tea. Instead, I walk out and leave them to it.

My mind is made up. I need to leave.

Upstairs, I pack my suitcase with my book, a fresh change of clothes, some underwear, and a handful of pound notes. My instinct is telling me to take all the money with me, to walk away forever, and never come back. Squeezing myself and a baby into my parents' already overcrowded house would be a very tight fit indeed, but I know I would be welcomed. But I need some time to think. So I take the rest of the money, bundle the notes together, and stash them underneath my pillow. Then I tidy the bed, cover the pillow with the blanket, and tuck it in tightly.

I contemplate taking the three letters I have written to Ernest out of my top drawer and leaving them on his bed, or somewhere else where only he would find them. When he has read them, then he will know how much I love him and he will know that I want him to be my husband in the future when we are older, and when we both have jobs. By candlelight, late into the night, hastily scribbled words tell him of my plans to be a teacher. I have a God-given affinity to children and I know that they will love me and I will love them. I will model myself on my favourite teacher from school, Sister Catherine, who passed on her love of books and encouraged my thirst for learning. My letters tell him how I would love to build us a home that we can fill with lots of children and I beg him to speak to his parents and assure him that I will be a good wife.

A sudden gust of wind from the open window in the master suite slams the door shut, reminding me of Ernest turning his back on me last night.

Closing the drawer, I leave the letters where they are. I am resigned to sacrificing my firstborn to the horrible Reverend Flynn and his wife.

I creep down the stairs, taking my suitcase with me. I tiptoe through the hallway, and into the kitchen. My overcoat is still a little damp from yesterday's rain, but at least the inside is dry. I shrug it on and fasten the two top buttons. It will no longer fit snugly over my bump. I pull on my hat, button up my boots, and leave the house through the back door. I know that Ernest will see me walking down the path, as the dining room faces out towards the front, but there is nothing I can do about that. My desperation to leave is so acute that nothing will stop me unless he rushes out and begs me to stay.

Chapter Seventeen
December 1908 - Violet

Without consciously planning my journey, I find myself at the house where Clara works, the home of Mr and Mrs Douglas. I have seen the young couple a few times in church and around the village and Clara has told me that, despite their partying ways and over-consumption of alcohol, they are lovely people, so I have no hesitation in knocking on their front door.

As soon as the door opens and I see Clara's smiling face, I cannot stop the tears and I drop my suitcase and fall into her arms, sobbing onto her shoulder. She strokes my back and lets me cry while we stand together in the hallway. After a few moments, she lets me go, picks up my suitcase from the floor, closes the front door behind me, and ushers me into the kitchen, where a large rosy-cheeked middle-aged lady is seated at the kitchen table, peeling potatoes.

'Edith, this is Violet, a good friend of mine.'

'Hello, love. Oh dear, what's to do? I hope you have a good reason for those tears. They're not brought on by some man, are they?'

'Here, sit down,' says Clara. She pulls a chair out for me and I sit opposite Edith, whose warm smile invites me to talk.

'Well, you could say that,' I say. 'I'm being over-sensitive. I'll be fine in a little while. I just wanted to see a friendly face. I hope you don't mind me calling round?'

'Of course not,' says Clara. 'You know you're welcome any time. Although it's best to pop round to the back door if ever the master and mistress are at home.'

'They won't be back until this evening,' adds Edith. 'Make yourself comfortable. A trouble shared is a trouble halved. Clara, is that kettle on?'

'It's on, Edith, don't worry. It never has a chance to go cold while you're around, does it?'

'Get away with you, you cheeky bugger.' Edith laughs and throws a potato peeling at Clara. It floats to the floor, far away from its intended victim. Clara picks it up and places it on Edith's head, causing her to scream and burst into childlike laughter. I can't help but smile. The thought of Mrs Meadows and the camaraderie of the warm kitchen at Compton Hall could very easily bring fresh tears to my eyes if I allowed it. I blink rapidly and concentrate on the pattern on the wooden table until the painful nostalgia has passed.

'Lucky for you, I made an early start this morning and the bed is changed, the fires are made up and the dusting is virtually done, so I've got time to have a sit-down,' says Clara. She places a mug of steaming tea in front of me and shovels two spoonfuls of sugar in before I can protest. She stirs it violently. 'So, what have they done?'

'What have who done?' asks Edith.

'Who?' asks Clara.

Edith taps Clara on her arm and waits until she faces her before she speaks slowly and loudly. 'I said what have who done?'

Sometimes I am guilty of forgetting that Clara is hard of hearing; she has become so good at lip-reading that I am never sure whether she has heard me or whether she has expertly read my lips.

'Violet's master and mistress are visiting the house this weekend,' Clara tells Edith. 'Lakeview Cottage, you know, the big one overlooking the lake.' She turns back to me. 'What have they done to upset you?'

'It isn't them,' I tell her. 'Mr and Mrs Compton aren't the visitors. It's Ernest.'

'Ernest?' Clara's hands shoot to her face. 'No!'

'Who's Ernest?' asks Edith. 'Ahh, is he…?'

She looks down at my bump as I slip my coat off. I can't hide it anymore. There's no point in trying. 'Yes, Ernest is the father.' I can feel my cheeks turning pink as the confession is announced to the world. I am meant to be keeping it a secret. I promised that I would, and apart from telling Clara, I haven't told anyone else. But now it's too late. The truth is out. I no longer care who knows.

'It's been awful, Clara,' I say, trying to hold my tears at bay. 'He said that he wasn't expecting me to be there, so it was a shock for us both, but it wasn't the reunion that I had envisaged. Not by any means.'

'What did he say?' Clara's tight lips tell me that she's angry and I love her for her loyalty.

'It isn't so much what he said.' I take a sip of my scalding tea. How can I tell her that Ernest is furious with me because I have taken money from his family for our baby? I have sold our baby because I didn't have enough faith in him, and now he doesn't want to have anything to do with me. Not that I blame him. How could he still love me after I have done something so despicable?

'He brought a lady friend with him,' I say.

'A lady friend? Who is she? Just the two of them in an empty house for the weekend?'

'No, no, her brother is there too. And they didn't share a bed.' I don't know why I feel the need to protect Lucille's honour and Ernest's reputation as a gentleman. 'But she's beautiful, Clara.' Fresh tears flow down my face as the realisation that I have lost the battle to keep Ernest's affections hits me forcefully. Lucille is a worthy opponent.

'You're beautiful, Violet,' says Clara. She leans across the table and takes my hand. 'Anyone would be lucky to have you in their lives.'

'Aye, I'll agree with that. You're a lovely little thing,' says Edith. 'I'll bet she's not as pretty as you. Look at that gorgeous black hair of yours, all shiny.'

'But you have a beautiful soul, too,' says Clara. 'I wish you could see yourself the way others see you, the way I see you.'

'Thank you, both of you,' I say. 'But she is perfectly suited to Ernest and I know that she will be welcomed by his family, if she hasn't been already. She's a proper lady. Not like me.'

Clara lets go of my hand and sits back in her chair, arms crossed over her chest. 'So what did Ernest say? Did you get an opportunity to speak to him?'

I nod and tell them both about Ernest creeping into my bed last night. I tell them that he didn't stay for long, he just cuddled me and then went back into his own room. I miss out the segments of the story where we argued because Clara would want to know what we argued about. 'I think Lucille saw him leave my room in the middle of the night. She was quite frosty with me this morning. The whole group had an air about it, I don't know why. I don't know if they had cross words, or if they were all just suffering the effects of last night's wine. So I packed up my suitcase and came here.'

'You did right, love,' says Edith. 'You keep out of their way until they've gone.'

'You can stay with us,' says Clara.

'I knew you would invite me, thank you, but I can't impose. I'll stay at a bed and breakfast. I have seen a few along this road and they look nice.'

'Yes, they are nice, mostly,' says Clara. 'But why waste your hard-earned money?'

Hard-earned? Those innocuous words stab my heart. My baby gives me a small kick from the inside and my hand instinctively goes to my belly. I sip my tea and listen to the scrape, scrape, scrape of Edith's knife against the potato skin.

'So what's she like, this Lucille?' asks Clara.

'Posh. Poised. Expensively dressed.'

Clara tuts. 'I know the sort.'

'I'm sure she is very nice,' I say. 'I don't know anything about her, but to be fair to her, if she's in love with Ernest, I can see that she would have been shocked to see him emerging from my bedroom last night, and by now she must have put two and two together and concluded that there is a very high chance indeed that this baby is his.'

'You're not the first and you won't be the last,' says Edith.

I wonder what her personal experience is, of love, of babies, of life.

'She said they will be engaged soon, Lucille and Ernest.'

'And do you believe that?' asks Clara. 'I don't. I think she was only saying that to hurt you.'

'Do you? I am trying to see things from her perspective,' I say. 'I mean, if you can understand someone else's point of view, it always helps, doesn't it? But I'm struggling to put myself in her shoes. If I was a lady, with a handsome man to offer me security and love, I certainly wouldn't see a housemaid as someone to worry about, so why would she tell me they were getting engaged if it weren't true?'

'You have a point,' says Clara. 'Women like her don't need to worry about anything, except clinging onto their privileges. But maybe a pregnant housemaid is a little more of a threat.'

I shrug. 'She's the one who will get to walk down the aisle with him. She's won.'

'Yes,' says Clara. 'A big wedding in the village church, looking forward to a nice easy life as the wife of a wealthy man. She'll never experience the back-breaking work of people like us. That's why we need to carry on the struggle, Violet. The sooner we women get the vote, the better. We can't live like this for much longer. Things have to change. Life is so unfair for women like us.'

'You have never spoken a truer word, Clara,' says Edith.

I am barely listening. My mind is occupied with thoughts of Ernest and Lucille; their future wedding; our wedding which will now never be; the letters that I should have sent to him. I contemplate rushing out of here now, racing down to Lakeview Cottage, grabbing the letters, and forcing them into Ernest's hand. I could stand in front of him and wait until he has read every word, until I am sure that he knows how much I love him. I could ignore the glares and rising temper of Lucille and tell Ernest that the only thing that matters is me and him.

But instead, I sit here and listen to Clara and Edith.

Chapter Eighteen
December 1908 - Mary

Ernest returns from his weekend trip to Cumberland, exhibiting his fury like a storm, fierce and unyielding. I am sitting on the chaise-longue in the hallway with my book, which I often like to do after lunch when the sun is in the perfect position in the sky to cast warming sunbeams through the glass on either side of the door, when I hear him stamping into the house. He throws the front door open so hard that it crashes against one of the plant pots, causing the tall parlour palm and soil to be flung across the floor. The previously spotless floor of the hallway is now blighted with soil, fallen leaves, and ceramic fragments.

'Mother!' he shouts. 'Mother, where are you?'

I had been excited to greet my brother and to hear about his Michealmas term at Oxford, but when I see his temper, I ignore him and stay quiet, just like I do when Father's mood brings a dark cloud over the house.

Barrow rushes into the hallway. I can see him contemplating which disaster he should deal with first; the rescue of the overturned plant, or the angry son.

'Where's Mother?' Ernest asks Barrow.

'The library, sir,' says Barrow obsequiously.

Ernest acknowledges my presence in the hallway with a slight nod of the head. As soon as he begins to run up the stairs to the first-floor library, Barrow shouts for one of the housemaids to clear the mess in the hallway quickly *before the master sees it.*

I can feel, as well as hear, Ernest's feet marching down the corridor to the library before he barges into the room and slams the door closed behind him. I drop my book onto the chaise-longue and rush up the stairs. I am tempted to listen with my ear pressed tightly to the library door, but I know there is a creaky floorboard somewhere around here. I can immediately hear the raised voices of Mother and my beloved brother, but I can't quite make out what they are saying through the thick walls and the solid oak door, so I return to my bedroom and wait. I know that my brother will come and find me eventually and will tell me what is troubling him.

I hate to hear him so angry and upset.

Sometime later, Ernest knocks on my bedroom door. By now, the sun has set and I am sitting in the armchair underneath the lamp, trying to keep my mind occupied with some embroidery before dinner. When I see Ernest's stricken face, I drop my needlework to the floor and run to him. We cling to each other until I can feel him eventually relax. When we pull away, I see that he has been crying.

'Violet is at Lakeview Cottage,' he says.

We sit side by side on the edge of the bed and I am thankful that he isn't looking directly into my face. I have never been able to keep secrets from my brother, but he will be devastated if he finds out that I have known all along.

'What do you mean? How do you know?' I asked.

'I've just been there and I saw her. Mary, it was hideous. We travelled on the train from London...'

'We? Who is we?'

'My friend, Frank, and his sister, Lucille.'

I know Frank. He has been to Compton Hall a number of times since Ernest started at Oxford. He is raucous and brash and I tried to avoid him whenever he visited. I tell Ernest that I didn't know that he has a sister, and I get the feeling from the rising colour in Ernest's cheeks and his sheepish look that he and Frank's sister are more than just friends. 'What is Violet doing there? Does Mother know?' I ask.

'Yes, of course, she bloody well knows. Who do you think arranged it?'

'I don't know. Don't shout at me, Ernest, I am as confused as you are.' I hate lying to my brother and I silently pray that he will forgive me if he ever learns the truth.

'Sorry, yes, I apologise. But I'm so bloody angry. Mother sent her away to Bowness so that she could be in hiding whilst she had the baby.'

I'm not sure what to say. I could say that Mother probably thought she was doing the right thing to avoid a scandal, but appearing to be on Mother's side isn't wise. I know that Ernest had liked Violet very much, maybe even loved her, and Violet's sudden disappearance made him desperately sad. His letters from Oxford told me how he wished things could have been different. I bite my tongue and wait for him to continue.

'She's different, Mary,' he says. 'She isn't like a regular servant. She's clever and witty and I love spending time with her. At least, I used to.' He swipes at his eyes with the back of his hand. 'I am the most naive man on earth, I must be, but I thought that when I told Mother and Father that Violet was expecting a baby they would allow us to marry.'

'Oh Ernest, really?'

'Yes, I admit I expected them to be not too pleased about it, but I thought that if they got to know her, as a person rather than a member of staff, they would come to love her too. How wrong I was. I thought he was going to hit me, Mary. I honestly thought that Father was going to lash out. Mother sent him out of the room, and then rather than assuring me that she would placate him and everything would be all right, she told me to go and pack my bags and leave for Oxford, even though the term wasn't due to start for another few weeks.'

'She told me that you had chosen to go back early. I was rather upset that we didn't get time for a proper goodbye.' I remember the morning when Ernest left. His usual good humour and excitement about returning to Oxford weren't there. He was quiet and morose at breakfast. That was before I knew about Violet, about Mother's plan to shoo her away, to separate the young lovers, so I put it down to the fact that he was entering his final year and that, at last, the frequent parties had to come to an end and he had to do some serious studying if he wanted a chance to pass his final exams.

'No, I hadn't chosen it all,' says Ernest. 'She just wanted me out of the way so that she could send Violet off to Lakeview Cottage before I had the chance to speak to her.'

'It's a terrible situation, Ernest, and maybe Mother should have told you where Violet was, but don't you think that she is doing a nice thing by allowing her to stay in our beautiful house? I mean I have heard gossip about other households where the staff have been dismissed and sent away without a penny. Violet isn't doing too badly if you compare her situation with those other poor girls.' As soon as the words are out, I realise how incendiary they sound and I wait for Ernest's temper to flare again. But maybe if he can see that Mother isn't all bad, maybe if he could see her point of view, and see that she was being kind and charitable and doing what she thought was in the best interest of all concerned, then maybe the peace and equilibrium can return to the house. I have always looked forward to Christmas and a feud between my brother and my parents is not in my festive plans.

Ernest bends forward, his elbows on his knees, and rests his head in his hands. I stroke his back and tell him that everything will work out in the end, it always does. He sits up.

'Mother isn't some angelic philanthropist, Mary,' he says. 'She isn't doing this so that she can look after Violet and give her somewhere pleasant to stay.'

'I just thought…'

'Violet has her own family, for goodness sake. She isn't some pauper who needs to be rescued. Do you know why she did it? I'll tell you why she did it. So that she could steal our baby and give it away to Aunt and Reverend Flynn.'

Yes, I know, I want to tell him. I have known for weeks and I have wanted to tell you, my darling brother, so that we could stand up to our parents together. A united force. I want to tell him how I have struggled with the knowledge, alone and unsure, and how it has made me desperately unhappy. 'What do you mean? Is that what Mother just told you?' I say.

'Violet told me,' he says. 'Whilst Mother was lying to me, telling me that Violet had run away, behind my back she was making an agreement with her to allow her to stay in Lakeview Cottage. Then she would take the baby from her and give it to the Flynns, in return, for a hundred pounds. And do you know what's worse, Mary?'

I shake my head. What could possibly be worse than this?

'Violet, the woman I thought I loved, went along with it. She agreed to sell our baby. Can you believe it? You know the Flynns have wanted children for years?'

I nod as the tears fall down my face. 'I don't know what to say, Ernest,' I say.

'It's shocking, isn't it?' he says. He stands up and walks over to the fire. He throws a shovel full of coal onto the dying embers and stabs at the pieces of coal with the poker, nudging them and moving them around until they catch fire and begin to burn. I watch him silently. 'I'm not staying for dinner,' he says. 'I need to go for a walk.'

'But Ernest, it's dark.'

'I don't care. I cannot stand to be in a house where the servants are gossiping about me.'

'Nobody is gossiping about you.'

'I wish that were true,' he says. 'Mother told me that Philip very kindly drove Violet to the train station. He knows all about it apparently, the pregnancy and everything. Violet herself told me that she wrote me a letter, explaining

146

Mother's despicable plan, and that she asked Philip to post it for her, but he gave it straight to Mother.'

'Did he read it?'

'I don't know. But I asked Mother who else knows about where Violet is and she admitted that Cook knows too. And she actually justified that by saying that she asked Cook to make Violet a cheese sandwich to take with her on the journey. So if Cook knew, you can guarantee that everybody knew. Everybody except me.'

'I didn't know,' I lie. My fingers are tightly crossed underneath my legs. 'Does Cook know that Violet is expecting?'

'Mother says she doesn't, but I don't know whether I can believe anything she says anymore. She said that the servants were told that Violet is keeping the house for us, cleaning and scrubbing it, ready for the summer. What a load of hogwash, who would believe such a story?'

'It does seem rather far-fetched. Nobody has done that for us before.'

Ernest then tells me he has to go and clear his head. He plants a kiss on my cheek and leaves. Later, as I enter the dining room for dinner, Barrow tells me that Mother has a headache and has asked for a small bowl of soup in her room. Father is busy in his study.

So I eat alone.

Chapter Nineteen
December 1908 - Violet

It is Monday morning, but have no idea whether Ernest and his friends have finally gone. Last night, I walked into the village with Clara from her parents' house and saw that Lakeview Cottage was in darkness. We walked up to the front door and knocked on it loudly. Nobody answered. I wasn't confident that they had left, and I could not hide my unease from Clara, so she insisted that I should stay with her for one more night, to be sure, as there was a possibility that they were still here.

'They might have simply gone out to that swanky restaurant again. How awful would it be if we bumped into them again?' she had said. 'Surely you don't want to see Ernest flaunting his new love interest in your face?'

Her questions had worried me and she hurried me back to the safety of her family home for another night.

I couldn't have been made to feel more welcome at her house. Not just by Clara, but by her whole family. Her mother hugged me tightly and assured me that I would be welcome any time. I wasn't sure what Clara had told her about who the father of my baby was, but she seemed to understand that I wanted to stay out of Ernest's way whilst he was visiting Lakeview Cottage. I felt so comfortable in

Clara's house that I did not worry about any awkward questions that may have come my way. No judgement seemed to exist in Clara's family.

On the first night, when it was time for bed, Clara climbed into her small bed beside me and we lay side by side talking into the night. I was squashed against the wall and Clara was half hanging out of the side. She put her arm around my shoulders and asked me to rest my head on her chest, saying we would have more room that way. Reluctantly I did and when we eventually fell asleep, I slept for a solid seven hours, comforted by her friendship and love.

Breakfast the following morning was a noisy affair and it felt good to be in the bosom of a family once more. Billy chatted to his dad about the jobs for the forthcoming week, Clara's mum bustled about checking everyone had enough toast, enough butter, enough tea. Clara, in between bites of toast, told me that she would love to go to London one day, to attend one of the suffragette marches. She wanted to carry a banner and shout slogans. She told me about her visit to Manchester in the summer and the mesmerising talk given by Mrs Emmeline Pankhurst in Heaton Park.

'We need to fight for our rights, Violet,' she said. 'Times are changing and one day there will be equality between the sexes, but until then, we need to fight.'

'That's twice you have said the word 'fight', Clara,' said her dad. 'Why do women have to be so violent in their words? It isn't ladylike.'

A cloud descended over Clara's face. 'You don't understand, Dad,' she said.

'I understand perfectly well, young lady, but men and women are not equal and they never will be.'

Clara's mum topped up her dad's tea from the pot and stood behind him, smoothing the rising tension in his shoulders with pacifying strokes. 'Clara's young and passionate. Let her be.' She winked at me, which told me that she was on Clara's side but that she was trying to avoid a political argument erupting at the breakfast table.

'Clara, darling, I love the passion in you, but you need to let this go,' said her dad. 'Let Mrs Pankhurst travel up and down the country on her thankless mission, if she wants to, but you don't have to follow her.'

Clara silently seethed for the rest of the meal.

After church on Sunday, as she and I walked to the lake, handfuls of breadcrumbs in our pockets for the ducks, Clara told me that attending the rally in Manchester had changed the way she sees the world and that she was desperate to join Mrs Pankhurst on her suffrage movement. 'The more of us who join, the easier it will be to win,' she said. Her eyes ignited with fervour as she relayed the events of that day. 'There were thousands of women there, Violet. Thousands of them. Can you imagine it? I felt the air crackle with, I don't know what it was, emotion, excitement. And quite a bit of anger. Women are angry, Violet, and so they should be. We have been second-class citizens for too long now.'

'Aren't we always going to be second-class citizens?' I said. 'Even if we get the vote, that won't make us equal to men, and we are never going to be equal to people like the Comptons.' I remembered my train journeys from Skipton, sitting in third-class carriages while women like Lucille stretched their legs and drank tea from delicate little cups in the first-class carriages. Their position in first class was guaranteed to them simply because of their fortunate birth.

'No, Violet.' Clara stopped walking and turned to face me. 'This isn't just about women being equal to men, it's about us being equal to everyone. I am as good as any man, aren't I?'

I told her that, of course, she was and that I could understand what she meant. In reality, I cannot see how things can be any different. Some people have money, some don't. Men work in prestigious jobs, make decisions in business, they hire and fire workers. Women don't.

She tried to explain that if women could vote, we could change the world. Women would make political decisions in the way that men had for millennia. But I didn't believe it. How could it be true? Someone like me would never be equal to someone like Lucille, Mrs Compton, or Miss Mary. Even if Mrs Pankhurst got what she wanted and I was allowed to vote, I couldn't see how it would change my life. I couldn't see how I would be any better off, financially or socially. I hadn't been so lucky as to be born into a family like the Comptons. I would never have enough money to build my own factory like Mr Compton had done, and I would never have the respect that Mrs Compton commanded, simply because of her position as his wife. I wanted to tell Clara that women would never be equal to men, her dad was right. And I would never be equal to Lucille. But I bit down on my tongue. I didn't want to contradict her. I didn't want to talk about politics. I just wanted a peaceful walk by the lake. I wanted to feed the geese and the ducks and enjoy the tranquillity of the water gently splashing onto the shore. I wanted to concentrate on the beautiful nature surrounding me so that I didn't allow thoughts of Ernest to run rampant in my mind.

'I'm going to go to London,' said Clara. 'Whether my dad agrees with it or not, I'm going to go.' She threw some breadcrumbs towards a small flock of ducks. Two swans hurried out of the water, flapping their terrifying wings, until the ducks meekly yielded to their fierce neighbours. 'I am not going to allow a man to tell me what to do, even if that man is my father. One day, when I've saved enough money, I'm going where all the action is and I'm going to join in.'

'Join in with what?' I said.

'I'm going to be a proper suffragette,' said Clara. She smiled and grabbed my hand. 'I'm going to march down the streets and shout and scream and make a fuss until we are given equal rights.' I couldn't help laughing. Her smile was infectious. 'Come on,' she said. She pulled me away from the lake and began skipping along the shoreline.

I skipped alongside her, our entwined arms swinging, laughing, and asking her to slow down. 'You daft apeth,' I said when she stopped, both of us gasping for breath. 'It's a good job it's a dreary day and there aren't many people to stare at us. You'll get us thrown into the loony bin at this rate.'

'There will be lots more people staring at us when we're marching in London,' she said.

She let go of my hand and stood in front of me, staring into my eyes. She looked as though she was about to say something and I expected her to carry on chatting about Mrs Pankhurst and her followers. But suddenly, she grasped my face with her hands and planted a kiss on my lips.

'What are you doing?'

She laughed. 'Stop worrying, nobody's looking. What are you frightened of?'

I didn't know what to say, so I shrugged and told her I was frightened of nothing.

We sat on a bench facing the lake, where she told me more of her plans. By this time next year, she wants to be in London. She told me she has visions of renting a small flat or a room in a big house and working in one of the big fancy stores, Harrods or Marshall and Snelgrove. I smiled and told her that I expect it would be a nice place to work, being surrounded by luxurious clothes all day. What I didn't say was that in reality, serving women in those stores was no different to serving women in their own houses. Clara wants to escape a life of service as much as I do. But then she explained about the prospects. If you worked hard, she said, you could become a department supervisor or even higher, you could become one of the managers. The sky was the limit, she said. I told her that with her ambition, she should be able to go far. She replied that it was Mrs Pankhurst's ambition that would allow us *all* to go far.

Then she asked me to go with her to London. Without waiting for my response, she told me that she had been thinking of how wonderful it would be to live together. She would go to work whilst I stayed at home and looked after the baby. 'You're not my husband, Clara,' I told her. 'You can't take on the responsibility of caring for me and a baby. It's out of the question.' She looked wounded and I was instantly ashamed. I felt as though I had trampled on her precious dream. She said that she wanted to help me, as a friend, because I couldn't expect to live on my own, surely. When she asked me what my plans were after the birth, I told her that I didn't know, which is true. I said that I would probably go home to Manchester and live with my parents. She nodded and looked crestfallen.

I haven't yet told her that my baby will be given away. Whilst she lamented the stigma and challenges of single parenthood, and how societal expectations and moral judgements had to change, I had visions of my baby being held by Mrs Compton's sister, crying for her mother and wriggling to be free of a stranger's clutches, looking for a breast, rejecting the rubber teat of the bottle. I felt uncomfortable, hot, panic-struck, and once again, on the edge of tears. I wanted to confide in Clara and tell her what I had agreed to, but I was frightened of her reaction and how she would judge me.

Now, as I gather my suitcase and offer my thanks to Clara's parents for letting me stay with them for the weekend, I am exhausted and can't wait to get back to Lakeview Cottage and its quiet solitude. I never expected that I would look forward to returning to that place, but it seems that absence makes the heart grow fonder of old, grey mansions as well as people. After two nights of sharing Clara's single bed, I am looking forward to sleeping in the master bedroom again, where I can stretch my limbs. When I get back, I will strip the beds, clean the kitchen and the dining room, which I know will have been left in an abysmal state, and then settle down in front of the fire with my book until bedtime.

I do not want to speak to anyone for the rest of the day and I do not want to think.

Clara has exhausted me with her constant chatter about change, and women's rights, and fights, and protests. I have enough to worry about at the moment. I am facing each day as it comes and I am not thinking about the future and, for now, that's how I want it to stay.

I kiss everyone goodbye and begin my walk back to Lakeview Cottage. It doesn't take long and within fifteen minutes, I am letting myself in through the front door. The house smells different. Of unpleasant men, sweet perfume, and bawdry. I decide to leave the front door open so that the stale cigar smoke and alcohol fumes can gradually float away. In the dining room, I throw open the sash window, too, and begin the task of restoring the room to its previous state. I gather the wine glasses and carefully carry them into the kitchen to be washed and polished dry. Then I stack the plates and soak them in a bowlful of hot, soapy water in the sink. After Ernest had been thoughtful enough to leave me a couple of slices of bacon in the pan, I would have expected him to have cleared away the plates. At least, he could have soaked them in the sink. Dried egg and bacon fat isn't easy to remove after it has been sat there all day. But I could imagine Lucille simpering at his side and reminding him that there was a maid in the house who would clean up after them. Ernest's ego, together with Frank's pontifications, wouldn't have allowed him to disagree with her.

Thankfully, there doesn't seem to be any damage to Mr and Mrs Compton's dining table. Any scratches in the mahogany that Mrs Compton might find will be put down to me, there is no doubt. There are a couple of red wine stains on the table cloth but I will soak it overnight and do my best to get it clean. I am almost thankful that I have something to keep me occupied.

Upstairs, despite the cold wind blowing through the house, I open the windows in all the bedrooms. If I work quickly, I won't feel the cold. As I lift the pillows and pull the sheets from the bed where Ernest slept, I feel a little disappointed that there is no letter waiting for me. I had hoped that he would have left one underneath his pillow for me to find. I tell myself that I am stupid to expect one and that I must put Ernest Compton out of my mind. He isn't the one for me. This is just a short chapter of my life which will be over soon. The rest of my book has yet to be written. So I gather the bed linen and take it down to the kitchen to be washed tomorrow.

It is approaching dusk by the time my jobs are finished. I'm tired and hungry, but there is one final task that I must complete before I can relax. I go into the maid's room at the back of the house to recover the letters that I wrote to Ernest, together with the remainder of the money from Mrs Compton. I know there is only me in the house now, but I feel better knowing that my personal items are safely hidden in the bedroom where I will be sleeping, back in my suitcase under the bed.

I pull the drawer open, but it is empty. I pointlessly run my hand through the space. I can clearly see that the drawer is empty. I pull open the next drawer, and the next one, and the next one. I search desperately amongst my folded clothes.

My letters to Ernest have gone.

I twirl around, skimming the room with panic. I notice that the blanket covering my pillow has been moved. The change is subtle, but my housemaid's eyes are trained to notice such things. I lift the blanket, and then the pillow. It is as I suspected. The money has been taken, too.

All I have left is the ten pounds that I took with me to Clara's.

Chapter Twenty
December 1908 - Violet

After a fruitless search of the house, I am now absolutely certain that my money and the letters I wrote to Ernest are no longer here. My emotions have surged from being confused, to being distressed, to being angry. Now I am enraged and wrathful. Of course, there are only three people who could have taken them - Ernest, Lucille, and Frank. But, from what I could see, Frank spent most of his time drinking wine and being consumed by his own frivolity, so it is unlikely that it was him. What motive would he have? Ernest and Lucille, however, both have a motive to hurt me. Neither of them knew what I had concealed in the chest of drawers and under my pillow, which means that they would have had to go searching for something, anything that they could find. Lucille would have wanted to find evidence that Ernest and I were lovers. My letters to him would have been the exact proof she was looking for. The money would have been an unexpected bonus.

I conclude that it must have been her.

Then again, Ernest knows that I have agreed to take money from his mother in return for the baby, so maybe he took it out of spite, or maybe he is hoping that without the money, the transaction (I hate to call it this, but what else is it?) will not take place. But he doesn't know that I have already been given the money, does he? I didn't tell him any of the details. He would likely assume that the money and the baby would change hands simultaneously. Would he embark on a search of my bedroom, the tiny bedroom that he would have no reason to visit unless he knew that I would be there, to chance upon the money? I don't think so.

I am so confused.

I would hate to think that Ernest would hurt me like this and it is easier for me to believe that it would have been Lucille.

I blame myself. I should not have been so stupid as to leave such a large amount of money lying around. But then again, it was hidden. Who would have thought that someone would search under my pillow? I could not have taken it all with me as walking around outside with a large stash of pound notes in a suitcase is not a wise thing to do either. I should have been able to trust that three extremely wealthy people in the house wouldn't steal my money. They don't need it. All three of them have enough of their own. The fact that one of them has taken the money, knowing my station in life, makes me livid.

I can't decide which is worse. If Ernest took it, I can safely assume that he did it to hurt me, knowing that it was probably payment for his child. If Lucille took it, I can safely assume that she did it to hurt me too, knowing that I am not wealthy. She doesn't know where the money is from. It could be my inheritance, the lifetime savings of an elderly grandmother, and yet she chose to take it from me, knowing that it would take years for me to save that amount. In fact, I would probably never be able to save that amount of money again. People like me don't have savings. Wages are often spent before the week has ended.

But what can I do about it? Shall I tell Mrs Compton? Shall I tell Ernest? Could I accuse Lucille and risk tarnishing her good name when I don't have any proof?

I feel rejected and abandoned.

I need to be with my family.

I need to go home.

I take out my pen and notepad and begin a letter to my mother.

Dear Mum,

I hope you, Dad, Thomas, Rose and Bridgett are well. I miss you all so much. I can't bear to not see you at Christmas, so I am going to book a train ticket and come home. I hope that won't disrupt you too much?

My plans have changed and I am free now. I do not have to work at Compton Hall after all. I know that Christmas is only four days away, and I hope that you receive this letter in time. If not, then it will be a lovely surprise when I land on your doorstep, won't it?

I will see you very soon,

With lots of love,

Violet xx

With the letter safely tucked away in the front pocket of my coat, I begin the walk to the Post Office. When I get there, there is a long queue and Mrs Davis, the postmistress, is deep in a conversation with a lady at the front of the queue, discussing her recent grandson and how well he is doing, apparently almost walking and he isn't yet a year old.

Nobody else seems to mind. The Christmas spirit is alive and well amongst the local residents, and generally, women love to talk of babies. The proud grandmother turns around and smiles to the waiting queue behind her. One of the other ladies tells her that children are such a joy, especially at this time of the year. Everyone seems to agree with her.

I should be in the Christmas spirit too, I know. I should be happy and carefree, looking forward to the festivities; Carol singing at church on Christmas Eve, mince pies by a warm fire and my mother's amazing roast goose that she saves for months to buy. Instead, I find myself tapping my feet and tutting and throwing scowls around the small shop, which nobody seems to notice.

Eventually, it is my turn and I buy a first-class stamp for my letter.

'Christmas post can't be guaranteed,' says the postmistress with a look of smug satisfaction. 'On account of the weather.'

I look out of the window and can see nothing but clear skies, but I don't challenge her. For some reason that I cannot explain, I tell her with a forced smile that my letter isn't important and does not need to arrive before Christmas. My fingers are crossed behind my back and I say a silent prayer as I walk out of the shop that she is wrong in her prediction that those light and fluffy clouds are full of snow.

I begin to cross the road.

'Whoa, watch out, miss!' A loud shout brings me to my senses and I step back just in time to miss horses hooves clattering past me. I grip my belly with both hands and shout that I am sorry. The rider wouldn't have heard me above the noise. Two ladies walking past stop to stare. They don't offer any help. None is needed, but I wonder if I was dressed like Lucille and wearing a wedding ring whether it would have been a different situation. Of course, it would. I stare back at them until they lower their eyes and walk on.

I trudge a mile up the hill to the train station, where I buy a ticket for Wednesday 23rd December to take me to Manchester. From there, I will have just a short walk home. To my family, to people who love me.

Cheered that I have made the right decision, and with my train ticket safely tucked away in a pocket inside my bag, I take my time walking back to Lakeview Cottage, stopping in various shops along the way. For Dad, I buy a slab of Kendal Mint Cake, a delicious brittle confectionery that will satisfy his sweet tooth. In the haberdashery, I choose a pair of knitted gloves for Mum, the colour of a summer sky. I can no longer afford to splurge on the leather ones, thanks to the thief who has taken my money. For Thomas, I buy some cufflinks, and a book each for Bridgett and Rose - Adventures of Sherlock Holmes and Little Women. When my shopping is done, I call at Clara's parents' greengrocers to tell them that I will be going home for Christmas and ask them to pass the message to Clara. They had invited me to have lunch with them on Christmas Day, so I apologise for any inconvenience I have caused by withdrawing at such late notice. Clara's mum tells me not to be so silly and comes from behind the counter to hug me and wish me Merry Christmas. Her strong maternal arms confirm that going home for Christmas is the right thing to do.

I need my mum.

Chapter Twenty-One
Christmas 1908 - Violet

I arrive at London Road Station in Manchester just after one o'clock, two days before Christmas. The post mistress' prediction about the snow was accurate. When I left Windermere, the town was covered with a glittering white blanket, pulled tightly over the hills of Cumberland, and stretched as far as Manchester. It is getting deeper and deeper by the minute and I wonder whether she was right about the delivery of letters being delayed. My mum will welcome me with open arms whether she has had advanced notice of my arrival or not, but I can't help thinking about Ernest and whether I should have written to him instead. I have a feeling that I am wasting time spending Christmas with my family when I should be following my heart and trying to repair my relationship with my baby's father at Compton Hall. I should be hammering on the door and insisting to be let in, whether or not I am welcomed by Mr and Mrs Compton.

But then I am reminded about the missing money and the fact that it could have been Ernest who took it. If that is true, then what more proof do I need that he no longer loves me? If I had an opportunity to speak to him and he insisted that he was innocent, would he question Lucille about whether she had taken the money and my letters? I would, of course, if I were him. But in truth, it's unlikely that a gentleman of Ernest's standing will accuse a lady such as Lucille.

It's too late now. I have made my decision. I am here in Manchester. I will be surprised if I ever hear from Ernest again. I resolve not to dwell on what he may or may not be doing, as there is absolutely nothing I can do about it now.

As I exit the station, I fall in love with Manchester all over again, as I do every time I arrive home. It looks pretty with the covering of snow hiding the dirty streets. The newspaper seller on the street corner, the magic man doing card tricks in the middle of a circle of amazed onlookers, and the young girl selling matches all feel so familiar. It makes me wonder why I ever left in the first place. I should have stayed with my family and found local employment, rather than being tempted away to Yorkshire to the grandeur of Compton Hall. The promise of accommodation, a smart uniform, and a good wage were too much for me to resist. Home was feeling smaller and smaller by the day and I was desperate to escape, to have my own bed, my own room. What a snob I had been.

On London Road, the comforting smell of roasted chestnuts mingled with the ever-present smell of fish and chips makes me hungry. I stop at the chestnut stall and dig around in my pocket for some coins. I find a penny and buy a bag of warm chestnuts which I can share with my mum when I get home. The vendor is young and overly friendly. He winks at me and doffs his cap.

'Eating for two are you, love?' he says as he hands the bag to me. For a moment, I had forgotten that I had to break the news to Mum and Dad about my unplanned pregnancy and my stomach flips with anxiety. I nod and force a smile. 'You take care now,' he says.

I put the chestnuts in my coat pocket. Holding my coat closed with one hand – it is now too small and I'm unable to fasten the buttons - I pick up my suitcase with the other and begin the walk towards home. I turn right onto Newton Street. The huge factory buildings on either side of the narrow street sap most of the daylight and cause a wind tunnel. The snow billows in my face, forcing me to walk with my head down. I pick up my pace, as much as the weight of my growing belly and my suitcase will allow, but halfway along the street, I need to stop to catch my breath. I rest in the doorway of The Bull's Head, a temporary respite from the bad weather. The snow is heavy now, thick flakes thundering down, reducing visibility to just a few yards. I'm not far from home, but I need a short break.

As I am resting against the wall in the pub's sheltered doorway, the door flies open and the landlord pushes a man out onto the street, shouting that he will be welcomed back when he 'sorts himself out.' The man stumbles but somehow manages to stay upright. Obscenities fly from his mouth, but the landlord is no longer listening. The pub door is closed. The man takes a cigarette from the top pocket of his jacket and rests it between his lips while he pats each of his pockets in turn, presumably searching for matches. He looks up at me.

'Now then, what do we have here?' The man isn't wearing a hat and within seconds, his head is covered with snow. It quickly melts and runs in rivulets down each side of his face. He squints his eyes, as though trying to focus his vision. 'What's a nice young lady like you doing in a place like this?'

'I'm on my way home,' I reply. I shouldn't engage him, but I know that if I ignore him, it is likely to fuel his temper even more. I pick up my suitcase and step out onto the pavement.

'Not so fast,' he slurs. He steps towards me, but in his drunken state, I am able to avoid him and manage to walk past and continue my walk. 'Oi, where are you going, you hoity toity little…'

'Jack Turner! Leave that young lady alone. Look at the state of you. Does Barbara know where you are?'

'Ahh, shut up. Stop mithering me, woman. What's it to do with you, any road?'

The voice is familiar. I smile to myself. With my back to her, Mum doesn't know it is her eldest daughter being harassed by this man, and yet here she is, standing up to him, supporting someone she assumes is a stranger. I turn around and see her. My love for her races through my veins and causes a lump in my throat.

'Mum. It's me.'

'Violet! Is that you? Come here, come here! Move out of the way, Jack. This is our Violet. She's come home for Christmas.'

'And she's brought you something, by the looks of things,' says Jack.

My mum's eyes flash to my belly, but the shock only rests on her face for a second, before her smile returns. I drop my suitcase and fold my arms around her. 'I'm sorry, I'm so sorry,' I whisper into her ear. I don't want to cry in front of this man, who is watching us closely, no doubt eager to rush back home with the news that William Pearson's daughter, the clever one who went to work in that posh country house, has come home with a bun in the oven.

'Get out of my way and go home, Jack,' says my mum. 'I need to get our Violet inside. A woman in her state needs to be kept warm.'

Jack offers to carry my suitcase, but my mum tells him that we can manage, thank you very much. He steps into the road to let us pass. He touches his head, and then looks bemused to find that the cap that he was about to lift has been lost.

My mum carries my suitcase home.

*

As soon as we are home and we have hung our coats on the rack behind the front door, I follow Mum into the kitchen. She fills the kettle with water, puts it on to boil, fills the teapot with tea leaves, and gets two cups down from the dresser before she finally asks me when the baby is due. I am unable to read her expression. It seems to be a mixture of disappointment and concern and something else. Fear? I'm glad that it is just us two in the house. Bridgett and Rose won't be home from school until four thirty and it will be after five by the time Dad and Thomas get here.

'It's due in the middle of February,' I say.

'Lent,' she says.

I shrug my shoulders and nod at the same time. I'm not sure when Easter will be next year, but to admit that seems irresponsible.

'I'm sorry, Mum. I know I've already said that, but it was a mistake,' I say.

'I should bloody well hope so. An unmarried girl doesn't get herself into that position on purpose.'

'No, of course not. But I mean, getting involved with Ernest was a mistake, too. I thought he loved me though, otherwise, I wouldn't have done it. He told me that he did.'

Mum raises her eyebrows. 'He said that, did he? Hang on a minute, Ernest you say? Isn't Mr and Mrs Compton's son called Ernest? Don't tell me that baby belongs to Ernest Compton?' I don't reply. 'Bloody hell, Violet.'

She pours the tea and carries the cups to the table. We both sip out hot tea and allow the seriousness of my situation to sink in.

'I don't suppose that lot will allow him to marry you?'

I shake my head. 'No. Mrs Compton told me not to have anything to do with him. She said that he needed to concentrate on his studies. This is his final year at Oxford.'

'Well, good for him,' says Mum sarcastically. 'God forbid that a man's life would be ruined by his thoughtless actions. It's always the women that have to pay for such things.'

'Will Dad be cross with me? Please tell him not to be cross with me.' The thought of my Dad thinking less of me, loving me less, brings tears to my eyes.

'Violet, love, don't you worry about your dad. I'll handle him. Would you like me to tell him for you?'

'I would, but I think he might notice as soon as he walks in.' I rub my round belly and we both burst into unexpected laughter.

'Have I ever told you about when me and your dad got married?'

'Yes, 1889. The year before I was born.'

'That's right, but do you know what month we were married?'

'I don't think I do. I always presumed that it would have been in the summer,' I say.

'Because most people get married in the summer.'

'Yes.'

'We got married on 21st December 1889. In fact, it was our wedding anniversary two days ago. We never celebrate it. There's always too much going on at this time of the year. It seems self-indulgent, somehow.'

Mum waits while I do the mental arithmetic before she confirms that she was three months pregnant on her wedding day. 'Your granny and grandpa had a huge strop at me when we told them, but they soon calmed down when your dad told them that he intended to marry me anyway, baby or no baby. It was a lovely wedding day when all said and done.' She gazes wistfully into her tea and I wish that I could have the same conversation with my parents that she had with hers. I wish Ernest was here with me now, sitting at the kitchen table drinking tea, waiting for Dad to get home so he could ask for my hand in marriage. Then we could plan our wedding and be legally bound together before the baby was born.

'But you love each other, don't you, you and Dad?' I ask.

'Of course we do. Why ever would you ask such a thing?'

'I just wanted to make sure that you were together for love, and not because of me.'

'Well, you don't need to worry about that. Are you hungry?'

'Yes, a bit,' I tell her. 'I forgot, I bought us some roasted chestnuts. They're in my coat pocket.' I retrieve them and find that they are still warm, they were so tightly wrapped. I take them back to the kitchen and pass the bag to Mum. She opens it and stuffs a chestnut in her mouth quickly, telling me that they are her favourite thing.

'Mum?'

'Yes, love.'

'Thank you.'

'What for?' she asks, with a mouthful of chestnut.

'For not having a strop, like your mum and dad did with you.'

'I can't speak for your dad, but you know what he's like. It would take a bomb to shake up his calm disposition.' She laughs and takes another chestnut from the bag. 'It will be fine. We will take care of you both. It might be better if we switch rooms, so that me and your dad have the smaller one. You will have more room in the front bedroom with the girls. Thomas doesn't mind the box room.' She stood up and began clearing the table of the tea things. 'They will be home soon. I've got some nice ham for tea. We can have sandwiches or potatoes, roasted or boiled?'

'A sandwich will be fine, Mum, thank you.'

I watch my mum as she works and wonder when will be the right time to tell her that there will be no need to swap bedrooms because I won't be keeping the baby.

Chapter Twenty-Two
Christmas 1908 - Violet

'What does it feel like, Violet?' asks Bridgett. 'Does it hurt when it kicks you?'

We are lying in bed. Bridgett is on the top bunk. I am lying beneath her in the bottom bunk and Rose is in a single bed at the side of us, the bed that used to be mine, before I moved to Compton Hall. Bridgett's head hangs over the side of the top bunk and I can almost touch her long pigtails. I am trying to sleep but my sisters' constant questions will not allow it. I know that I shall get no peace until I have told them everything they want to know.

'No, it doesn't hurt,' I reply. 'The baby is only tiny. Imagine a newborn baby kicking you, it wouldn't hurt, would it?'

'No, I don't suppose it would,' she says.

'But it will hurt when it comes out, won't it?' asks Rose. 'I don't want to think about it. It's disgusting.'

'Shut up, Rose, what do you know about how a baby is born?' says Bridgett.

'I know more than you!'

'Girls, please don't argue. A baby can sense the atmosphere in a room, you know. If it hears you being mean to one another, the baby will come out red-faced and bad-tempered,' I tell them.

'Like Mrs Wilkinson next door,' laughs Rose.

'Yes, and I don't want a baby as bad-tempered as her, thank you very much,' I say.

'What are you going to call it?' asks Bridgett.

'I don't know,' I say. 'Either Margaret, after Mum, or William, after Dad.'

'That's boring,' says Rose. 'Call her Rose.'

'Or Bridgett,' says Bridgett.

'That's enough questions for now, thank you very much. Can we get some sleep? I've had a long journey today and I'm tired.' I fake a yawn, which in turn causes both girls to yawn. I can't bear any more questions about the baby when I know that I won't be the one who is choosing her name. I won't get to choose the colour of the blanket that covers her in her cot, or even the colour of her first hat and bootees. If I allow myself to dwell on such details, the kind of details that I know Bridgett and Rose are excited to discuss, then I will never stop weeping. The pain of having to lose her is growing each day, but I know that I must lose her. For her sake, if not for mine.

My mum and dad's reaction to the news of my pregnancy could not have been any more supportive and I know, without a doubt, that she would have a relatively good life with us, in this tiny house, filled to the rafters with her family and as much love as we can cram in. But Reverend Flynn and his wife can give her a better life. As well as the material comforts such as a clean, warm home and a table always groaning with food, they can send her to the best school, buy her a pony, and throw lavish parties for her birthdays. She will have a wardrobe full of pretty dresses and she can spend the summer at Lakeview Cottage with the Comptons.

But more important than all, they can give her the best chance in life. The kind of chance that she deserves. I don't want my daughter to have to work in the mill at the bottom of the road. I don't want her to work in a shop, standing on her feet for ten hours a day, running after demanding customers, and putting other people's needs before hers. I don't want her to work as a housemaid and for her hands to be dry and sore like mine, or for her back to ache after a long day of toil.

By the time she is sixteen, maybe Mrs Pankhurst's suffragettes will have won their fight. Women will have the vote. Things will change. The future will be different. For her, at least.

But what about my future? I also need to do what is best for me. Without another man's child, I might stand a chance of finding love with someone. I could marry and have more children and be happy. More than anything in the world, I want to be happy and I say a silent prayer that one day I will be, as I wipe the tears that fall down my face.

As soon as Bridgett and Rose are quiet and I am sure that they are asleep, I climb out of bed and tiptoe downstairs. Mum and Dad are still up, drinking tea in front of the fire in the living room. Thomas is out courting with Victoria Grainger.

'Mum, Dad, can we have a chat?'

'What is it, love?' asks Dad. The look of concern that clouded his face when he first saw me this evening is still present. 'Come on, sit with me.'

I sit next to Dad on the small sofa and he shuffles up to be closer to me so that our legs are touching. I watch the fire for a moment, delaying the inevitable conversation. 'I should have told you earlier,' I say.

I don't know where to start. The pregnancy was meant to be kept a secret. Forever a secret. I regret coming home now. I should have been brave and stayed at Lakeview Cottage, then I wouldn't have to tell my parents that they are not going to be grandparents after all, despite the fact that they are just coming to terms with the idea. How can I tell them what I have agreed to do? How can I tell them that I took money from Mrs Compton, but that it has now gone missing and that after she stops paying my wage, as soon as the baby is born, I will be penniless until I have recovered from the birth and am able to find a job, so I will need to move back home for a little while. But just me. Without the baby.

'Spit it out, Violet,' says Mum, with a hint of impatience.

'Mrs Compton's sister has offered to take the baby and bring it up as her own.' I don't know how else to say it. I could have been more gentle, perhaps. The hurt on my parents' faces tells me this is a shock to them, the second enormous surprise of the day, but Mum told me to spit it out, so I did.

'There's no need for that, love,' says Dad. 'You'll be fine here, the two of you.'

My mum doesn't say anything for a moment, and I wonder what she's thinking. Would she agree with me that her grandchild would be better off with another family? Or

174

does she agree with Dad that we will be fine here, living on the edge of poverty with little prospects of improvement?

'We have given you everything you needed, haven't we?' she says.

'Of course, yes, of course, but…'

'Did you ever want for anything when you were growing up? I did my best, didn't I?'

'Oh Mum, of course, you did.' We are both crying now.

'But the Comptons have money, is that it? You want to give away your baby to someone who has money, even though this woman, this sister whoever she is, won't be the child's real mother?'

'I don't *want* to give my child away, no,' I say. I am trying to keep my tone on an even keel. I have never raised my voice to my parents, but my anxiety and panic are rising, along with my voice. 'This isn't what I want at all. Not any of it.'

'And what about Ernest?' says Mum. 'What has he got to say about all this? Or has he washed his hands of you both?'

'Now then, now then,' says Dad. 'There's no point in us falling out about it, is there? We need to make the best of a bad situation, that's all. Everything will be fine.' He pats my knee and takes a drink of his tea. 'Like I said, you can both live here, you and the baby.'

'But what about me? Where would I work? Where would I live? I can't live here forever.'

'Of course you can,' he says.

'No, Dad.' I take a deep breath. I don't want to shout. The walls in these houses are so thin. 'I want to be married, don't you see? I might not marry Ernest, but I want to be loved and

175

have this.' I wave my arms around the room, 'I want my own house and a husband.'

'You will have that,' says Mum.

'Who will have me, Mum? Which man will take on another man's child?'

The fire crackles and spits. A burning piece of coal falls from the grate onto the stone hearth. Dad leans forward, picks up the shovel, and shovels the coal back into the fire, where it burns with all the others.

'Do you want some tea?' asks Mum. 'There's some in the pot, still.'

Dad puts his arm around my shoulder and their sudden kindness makes me cry. I sob into Dad's shoulder while Mum pours me a cup of tea. When I feel calmer, I tell them that Mrs Compton has been kind, given the circumstances, and that she sent me a beautiful blanket to wrap around my legs in the drawing room, as it can be cold even when the fire is lit, and she has arranged for one of the best doctors in the land to care for me. I tell them that she has offered to pay my wages until the baby is born, but I don't tell them about the hundred pounds. The cost of my baby. There is no point now, as the money has been taken.

Mum says that she couldn't have asked for more for me and says that top medical care is hard to come by and is very expensive. She tells me that I'm lucky to have a good doctor and she reassures me that I'll be fine. She blinks away the tears. She thinks that I don't notice, but I do.

We don't discuss how difficult it will be for me to hand over the baby, how it will tear at my heart and my soul, and how my parents will miss out on their first grandchild. I concentrate on the fact that my baby will have the best upbringing that money can buy.

As Mum disappears into the kitchen to fill the teapot with more hot water and Dad adds yet more coal to the fire, I begin to feel claustrophobic. The tiny house, the place that I called home for sixteen years, suddenly feels too small. I find myself wishing that I was on the train, journeying back to Cumberland, back to the space and freedom of Lakeview Cottage.

Chapter Twenty-Three
Christmas 1908 – Mary

Ernest has decided he would like Lucille to spend Christmas with us and, given the circumstances, Mother readily agreed. She told him she couldn't wait to meet the young lady and that it was a splendid idea. Thankfully, Lucille's raucous brother, Frank, has other plans so he won't be gracing us with his presence for the festivities.

Lucille arrives at Skipton Train Station just after noon on the day before Christmas Eve. I spot her immediately, even though we have never met. Lucille's luscious hair, the colour of amber, shimmers like that of a siren. One side is pinned with a delicate hair slide decorated with pearls. Ernest told me that Lucille has always attracted attention and today is no exception. Heads are turning to watch as she strides along the platform towards where we are waiting.

Ernest greets her with a warm kiss and introduces her to me. She gives me a wide smile and shakes my hand, somewhat reservedly. I can see that she is one of those women who never welcomes the presence of other good-looking women. I have met her sort before. The sort who is never particularly polite to other women at parties, and can sometimes be overtly rude. She looks me up and down surreptitiously to determine whether my beauty will usurp her position as the natural, and expected, centre of attention. Within seconds she quite obviously decides that I am no threat and kisses me on each cheek, telling me how happy she is to meet Ernest's wonderful sister, whom she has heard so much about.

Ernest, seemingly oblivious, picks up her two small suitcases, one in each hand, and carries them to the car, where Philip is waiting. Ernest passes the suitcases to Philip and, after opening the back door of the car, he climbs into the front seat. I contemplate asking him what he is doing. Surely he wants to sit in the back with Lucille? But she doesn't seem to mind, or if she does, her expression doesn't show it, so I sit next to her.

'How was your journey?' I ask as we set off.

'Very nice, thank you,' says Lucille.

I laugh. 'Look, if we are to be friends, you need to be truthful. I can tell you are being the gracious guest, who would never complain, but what you mean is that it was extremely long and tiring, and probably quite cold in the train carriage, and now you feel as though you need a lie down in a dark and quiet room?'

Lucille laughs and links her arm with mine. 'It doesn't matter how long the journey was. I'm here now,' she says. 'I managed to get on all the right trains at the right time, but I must admit that I am very much in need of a cup of tea.'

'Have you travelled all the way from Oxford this morning?' I ask.

'Goodness me, no. I have been staying with an Aunt and Uncle in London for a few days, since we got back from Cumberland actually.'

'How lovely.'

'Yes, it's the best. They have a delightful house and it's so convenient for the London social life. Ernest has been, haven't you, darling?'

'Sorry, what?'

Lucille taps him on the shoulder and he turns around. 'I was just saying, Aunt and Uncle's house in Bayswater is just perfect for visiting London, isn't it?'

'Oh, yes, it is,' he says. He turns back to face the front.

'They give the most amazing parties. Champagne cocktails, delicious canapes, the lot. In the summer, they hired a band and we danced in the garden until daylight. You should come to the next one.'

'Oh, I don't know…'

'No, really, Aunt and Uncle are the most terrific hosts. Everyone is made to feel welcome, isn't that right, Ernest?'

'Mmm? Yes, yes,' Ernest mumbles over his shoulder.

I tell Lucille that her family sounds wonderful and I would love to meet them one day. She chatters excitedly about the various get-togethers they have had until we finally reach Compton Hall. Now Ernest no longer has the excuse of the noisy car engine, and he will have to show Lucille some attention, whether he wants to or not. She seems to be the kind of delicate flower that will only bloom under delicious scrutiny.

*

I am warming to Lucille. She is vain and self-absorbed, but she is young. I am sure that the Lucille of today will be different to the Lucille in ten years. What is youth for if not for being self-absorbed?

That being said, I still have my doubts about my brother's love match. Last week, during those horrible few days when Compton Hall seemed to be filled with cross words and angst, Ernest told me that he was planning to propose to Lucille, and I suspect that he has brought her here to prove to our parents that he is capable of choosing a suitable wife. Whether they deem her to be suitable remains to be seen. Mother loves her already, I can see. But whether she loves her for herself or because she isn't Violet, I am not sure. Father, on the other hand, is a harder nut to crack. I could see him observing Lucille over his bowl of soup at lunchtime, but he didn't say much.

It is quiet in the library now. Father is working in his study, Mother is in the drawing room writing a letter, probably updating her sister about our exciting and vivacious visitor, and Lucille is resting in her room after her long journey. It is just me and Ernest.

'Lucille seems very nice,' I say, hoping to open the conversation about how she makes him feel.

'Yes, she's a nice girl,' he says.

I want to tell him here and now that I am concerned that he isn't in love with Lucille and that if he is planning to steam ahead with his proposal to her this week, then he should wait. Love, especially the new kind, when your heart beats faster, when smiles constantly play on your lips, is meant to make you happy, yet Ernest seems far from happy. I want to urge him not to make another silly mistake by choosing the wrong woman again, but I can't find the appropriate words. I don't want to add to his sadness by having a difficult conversation. I had put Ernest's profound melancholy of the past week down to the fact that he is worried about Violet and their unborn child, but now that Lucille is here, shouldn't he be happier?

Deep down, I know that Ernest has chosen Lucille in the hope that she can help blot out the painful memories of Violet, rather than because she is the love of his life, someone whom he cannot live without. I have to admit that Lucille's outstanding beauty, her bright green eyes and auburn hair, are utterly captivating, but marriage is based on more than that, surely? It has to be.

'It's good that you and Frank are best friends, too, is it not?'

'Yes. If you weren't courting James, I would have said that he would be a good match for you,' he says.

The thought of that gives me shivers, but I force myself to laugh. 'James met me first, I'm afraid.' Ernest doesn't reply. 'Are you happy?' I ask him after a few minutes of silence. 'With Lucille, I mean.'

'Is anyone truly happy, Mary?' he says, with a shrug of his shoulders.

'Yes, I am happy with James,' I tell him. 'He makes me very happy indeed, and I miss him when we're not together.'

'I am sure Lucille will make me happy,' says Ernest, in a tone that makes me feel that he isn't at all sure. Then he opens the newspaper and holds it high in front of his face. The conversation is over.

His mood is understandable. His relationship with Mother is teetering on the edge of collapse and Father is refusing to get involved and mediate. He admitted to me last night that he hasn't completely forgiven Mother yet, but he is trying to. He desperately wants to, he told me, but all he can think about is Violet.

'I am sure she is keeping well,' I said.

'I want more for her than that,' he said. My heart broke for them both in that moment. I could see the torment on Ernest's face. 'I wish I could write to her and tell her that I love her and that I should never have left her room that night. I should have held her all night and in the morning, I should have introduced her to Lucille and Frank as my girlfriend, not the maid. I should have told Lucille that Violet's baby is mine.'

As I watch him now, I can see that he is still tormented by the fact that he hasn't managed to make it up with Violet. I imagine what would happen if he went into Father's study and told him that he wanted to be with Violet. Wouldn't it be wonderful if our parents gave their blessing? He could write to Violet immediately and tell her he knew she was doing what she thought was best for the baby. He could explain to her that, although he didn't agree with her decision to give the baby to the Flynns, he understood why she had made it. Then all would be well.

'Ernest?'

He lowers the newspaper onto his knee. 'Yes?'

'Are you absolutely sure you are doing the right thing?'

'I don't see that I have many options.'

'You do…'

'No, I don't. I'm sorry, but you need to drop this subject now. I'm going to ask Lucille to marry me, and that's that.'

'Even though you love someone else?'

'Yes, even though I love someone else.' He takes a deep breath. 'Violet would never have me now, not if I begged her on my knees.'

'Why ever not?'

'Because I stole her money.'

'What money?'

'I presume it was payment for the baby. I found it and got angry. I had written her a letter and had gone into her bedroom while she was out, to put it somewhere safe. I guessed that her nightdress would be under her pillow, so I planned to put it there, face up, so that she could see her name on the envelope in my handwriting and she would see the love heart that I had drawn next to it. I thought that would be quite romantic.'

I nod. 'Yes, it sounds as though it would,' I say.

'But when I lifted the pillow, I saw a stack of money and instantly changed my mind. I took it and left the room, slamming the door shut. I couldn't control my anger, I'm afraid. It erupted like a volcano.'

'She'll understand, won't she? You can send it back to her. Write her another letter.'

He shakes his head. 'It's too late. I threw the money in Mother's face when I arrived home.'

I start to cry. Oh, how I wish it could be summer still. That wonderfully warm summer we have just had, before everything in my family began to unravel like a dropped ball of wool, when Ernest was still happy, before he became angry, and when the tight bond between mother and son was yet unbroken.

Chapter Twenty-Four
January 1909 - Violet

Christmas passed in a whirl and is over too soon. Christmas Eve was spent chatting by the fire and eating too many mince pies. Mum kept the kettle constantly on the boil and I drank so much tea that I had to tell her to stop. The baby was already kicking my bladder like a football, forcing me outside into the backyard in the snow to use the lavatory more often than was comfortable. In the afternoon, Rose and Bridgett built a snowman under the front window and gave him two pieces of coal for his eyes and a long carrot for his nose. Dad donated one of his old cloth caps to sit on his head. I judged him to be the best snowman in the street when the girls came back inside with red noses, freezing cold hands, and huge smiles on their faces.

At midnight, the family went to Mass, but I stayed at home, telling them that I felt a headache coming on and it wouldn't be wise for me to get cold. Mum nodded and I could tell that she was glad that she wouldn't have to endure the pitying stares from her friends and neighbours at church. Having a daughter being pregnant out of wedlock was everyone's worst nightmare. There but for the grace of God.

On Christmas Day, we exchanged gifts after a breakfast of warm porridge. Everyone loved the gifts that I had bought for them and Rosie and Bridgett soon disappeared into the bedroom, to begin reading their books snuggled warmly under the bed covers. Dad, who is usually so fastidious about being washed and dressed early, even on Saturdays and Sundays, told them that he would grant them the luxury of not having to be dressed until the afternoon. I sat by the fire in the living room and chatted with Thomas about his new girlfriend. He told me that he was serious about her and he was going to save up for a ring so that he could ask her to marry him soon. I hugged him and told him that I was genuinely pleased that he had found someone, and he said that he hoped I could meet her before I went home. He passed me a handkerchief and I told him that my tears were tears of happiness for him. I told myself that Christmas Day was not the day to be worrying about my own future; I was lucky to have such a beautiful family and I was tremendously grateful for them.

Dad then ushered Mum out of the kitchen, with a warning that if she interfered with his preparations, he would not be pleased. He poured her a glass of sherry from the bottle Thomas, Rose, and Bridgett had bought her as her gift, and made her sit on the sofa with me and Thomas. He then disappeared back into the kitchen to baste the goose and turn the roast potatoes over in the oven. I had to laugh at Mum's look of concern. Thomas kissed her cheek and told her to put her feet up and enjoy her sherry. Mum protested and said that it didn't make sense for a man who only cooks once in a blue moon to be in charge of the most important meal of the year. Dad popped his head around the door and told her, as he does every year, that she deserved to put her feet up and that everything in the kitchen was ship-shaped. She took a sip of her sherry and told him that she would relax if he could promise her that he wouldn't burn the carrots like he did last year. Dad threw the tea towel at her and she immediately rolled it into a ball and threw it back.

Their gentle raillery and the obvious love between my parents reinforced that I was making the right decision by handing my baby over to Mrs Compton's sister. As much as it would break my heart, I would be doing myself a disservice if I didn't give myself a chance to experience the kind of love that my parents have and the kind of love that Thomas has found with Victoria.

I am now back at Lakeview Cottage with mixed emotions. I know that the next time I see my family will be after the birth and I will miss them terribly, but being back at Lakeview Cottage at least means that I can see Clara again. I have missed her more than I thought I would. When Billy dropped off my box of groceries this morning, he told me that Clara has 'never shut up' talking about me, and if he didn't know better, he'd say that she was smitten. He passed on a message that Clara would call to see me after she has finished at the Douglas' house, which will be around dinner time as the Douglas' are away again, so she is only working a half-day. But as it's a bright and sunny day, I decide to take a walk to meet her. Mum sent me back with one of her coats, which thankfully is bigger than the one from Miss Mary and fastens with plenty of room over my bump, so I put it on, together with a warm hat and my new pair of gloves (a Christmas present from home) and leave the house.

The snow from last week has disappeared, except for a sprinkling on the top of the distant hills, but there are patches of ice in places, so I take my time walking down the driveway and then up the hill to Windermere, to the Douglas' house. I have only been walking for five minutes or so when I spot Clara in the distance. I wave to her and her face lights up with a smile. She waves back and begins to run towards me and I can't help myself from frantically waving my arm up and down and mouthing to her that she must slow down. The pavement is icy and I am terrified that she will slip and fall. I cover my eyes with my gloved hand, as I can't bear to watch, but within seconds, she is in front of me and we are hugging like long-lost sisters.

She pushes me away and holds me at arm's length. 'Let me look at you,' she says. Then she pulls me towards her again and kisses my cheek. 'I have missed you so much,' she whispers into my ear. I can feel myself blushing, but I don't know why. It is just Clara. 'Happy New Year to you.'

'Happy New Year to you, too,' I say.

'You look so good and this has grown.' She pats my belly and bends down to talk to it. 'Hello little one, I hope you are well inside there.'

'Clara, stop!' I am embarrassed about what people will think but she laughs and dismisses my concerns.

'You have a new life inside there, Violet,' she says. 'You should be proud of that.'

Mrs Compton's words ring loud and clear in my mind. *'Don't flaunt your pregnancy, Violet. In fact, try not to let anyone know. The less people who know, the better.'*

I shrug my shoulders. 'I'm not proud of it, Clara. How can I be? It isn't as though I have a husband to share the baby with.'

'You can share it with me,' she says. 'It will be years before Billy has any children and I can't wait to be called Aunt Clara.'

'You'll make a great aunt,' I say. I force a smile.

'What is it?' Clara peers at me with concern. 'Have you seen Ernest again? Has he upset you?'

'No, I haven't seen him and I haven't heard from him. I don't care about him anymore. He is yesterday's news.'

'I don't believe that. I know something is bothering you,' she says. She cups the side of my face with her hand and wipes a tear as it trickles down my cheek. 'I can always tell when something is wrong.'

'I need to talk to you,' I say. 'Come back to the cottage with me.'

*

Back at Lakeview Cottage, I make us some tea and cut two slices of my mum's Christmas cake which she made especially for me.

'Have you eaten any dinner?' I ask Clara.

'I had some soup earlier. Edith always makes too much, so I'm quite full, but I still have room for some cake. This looks delicious.'

'My mum made it. She's been making them for years, but this year, she made two and gave me this one to bring back here. She said she feels sorry for me being here all on my own.'

Clara takes a huge bite of cake. 'You're not on your own, you have me,' she says. Crumbs fall from her mouth and drop onto the floor. 'Sorry, sorry, I'll pick them up.'

'I'll clean up later,' I tell her. 'Let's go and sit down in the drawing room. I made the fire up earlier, so it should be lovely and warm, and much more comfortable than sitting at the kitchen table.'

'Did you tell your mum about me?' asks Clara.

'Yes, of course. She was pleased that I had found a friend, and I told her how kind your family has been to me and how I couldn't manage without you. Here we are, shall we sit here, in front of the fire?'

'Can we sit by the window?' asks Clara. 'This view is simply wonderful. If I lived here, I would sit here all day.'

She sits on one of the chairs by the window and places her cup of tea on the small side table. She keeps hold of her plate and takes another bite of cake. I haven't touched mine. I sit down opposite her. I put my teacup and my cake plate on the window sill next to me.

'Is the cake nice?' I ask.

Clara nods enthusiastically. 'Yes, it's lovely. I can tell that your mum hasn't been shy with the brandy. But you don't want to talk about cake, do you? What is it? I know something is bothering you, something other than the fact you haven't heard from Ernest.'

'Please don't hate me, Clara.'

'What?'

'I said please…'

'I heard what you said, but why would I ever hate you? I love you, Vi. I would never hate you.'

'Even if I told you that I have done something abhorrent?'

Clara frowns at me. She shakes her head. 'Abhorrent is a strong word. I can't imagine that you have done something

190

so bad. You're a good person. Whatever could you have done?'

I take a sip of tea, which I struggle to swallow.

'Oh my goodness, don't tell me that you have killed Ernest. Or did you kill that haughty Lady Lucille? Did you push her down the stairs? Is her body hidden underneath the sofa?' Clara laughs and jumps up, bending down to examine the floor underneath one of the sofas for dead bodies.

'Clara, stop it.' I can't help laughing. 'This is serious, please sit down.'

'I'm sorry,' she says. 'I'm all ears.' She eats the last of her cake and licks her thumb and forefinger.

'I'm not keeping the baby after it's born,' I tell her.

'Oh.' She looks up at me and wipes her fingers on her skirt. 'You're not?'

I am struggling to fathom the look of disappointment on her face. I feel a surge of anger. I am not her sister. The baby isn't going to be her niece. She does not have the right to look so sad. I want to tell her that I am not a child playing at house, playing with a doll that will lie quietly in its tiny pram until I decide to play with it again. The burden of disappointment from my parents is already weighing me down. All I want from Clara is support. I don't want to lie to her any longer, but I am worried now that I shouldn't have told her the truth. I should have simply carried on as usual, pretending that the baby was mine to keep, and then when it is born and the Comptons take it (rather I should say *her,* as I know the baby is a girl) away, I could disappear one night, back home to Manchester, and I wouldn't ever have to explain anything to Clara.

191

'I can't, Clara. I don't have a job, and when the baby's born, I won't have anywhere to live.'

'You said that you were going back to your parents' house in Manchester.'

'Yes, I have that option, but their house is tiny. It would never work out in the long-term.'

'Is that what they said, that you can't stay at home?'

'No, not at all. My parents have been very supportive, but I don't want to live there.'

'Why? If they are supporting you…'

'Because I want to have my own place. I want to be loved, don't you see?'

'You are loved.' Clara looks confused. 'Your parents love you, your brother and your sisters. And me. I love you.'

'I mean, I want to be loved…'

'By a man? By Ernest?'

'Yes, by a man. Maybe my chance with Ernest has gone, but someone else will love me.'

Clara shakes her head and I can see that she doesn't understand me at all. 'What about London?' she says. If you don't want to stay with your parents, you can stay with me, I told you that.'

'Oh Clara, I can't come to London, with or without a baby. I don't know anyone there, apart from you, obviously.'

She taps her fingers on the side of her saucer and blinks rapidly. When she speaks, her voice is heavy with emotion. 'Where will the baby live then? Don't tell me that you are going to abandon it in a children's home, are you? Those places are hell on earth.'

'No, no, of course not,' I say. 'It will live with Ernest's family.'

'Ernest?'

'Well, not with him exactly. His mother's sister is going to bring the baby up as her own. Mrs Flynn. She is married to a vicar, but they don't have any children and they have been married a while, so…'

'But that doesn't mean she has to take your baby, just because she doesn't have one of her own. I hope they haven't bullied you into this, Vi. Have they bullied you, Ernest and his mother?' She is shouting now. She slams her teacup down on the table.

'No, Clara, they haven't bullied me, honestly.'

'So it was your idea?' She stands. She is staring at me. I have never seen her so angry.

'No, it was Mrs Compton's idea, as a matter of fact, but I agreed to it.'

'I see.' She stomps over to the fireplace, her hands outstretched to the flames.

There is no point in telling her that, not only did I agree to give my baby away, but I agreed to sell her. The money has gone now. Clara would hate me if she knew the whole truth. I can tell by the look on her face that she hates me now anyway.

Chapter Twenty-Five
January 1909 - Violet

'Clara, there's a car driving up the drive. Look.'

Clara rushes over from where she is standing in front of the fire and leans on the back of my armchair to peer through the window. 'That's Doctor Bradbury's car,' she says. 'He lives on the same road as our shop, a bit further up the hill. He's the only person I know, apart from Mr Douglas, who has a car.'

'Mrs Compton said that she would arrange for a doctor to see me, but the baby isn't due for another six weeks or so,' I say. 'I don't want to see him, Clara.' I don't know why, but I am suddenly frightened.

'Don't worry,' says Clara. 'He's a nice man. He's been our family doctor since before I was born. He's probably just come to check that you're all right. I'll tidy these pots away and then I'll go, leave you alone to chat to him.'

'Clara, are you angry with me?' I clasp her hand. 'I need you, please don't be angry.'

She takes a deep breath, and I know I am asking too much. She is angry, she is disappointed and she is probably very confused. But I can see that she is trying to hide it.

'I'm not angry with you, no,' she says.

I know she is lying. 'Are you sure?' I ask.

She pulls her hand away and starts to collect the plates and cups.

'I'm not angry with you,' she says.

'Then please don't leave me. I don't want to be on my own with a strange man,' I tell her.

'Okay, I won't leave you,' she says.

I am so scared. Thoughts of the birth itself often spring into my mind but I dismiss them as something that will happen at another time, far into the future. Something that I don't have to worry about for now. The presence of a doctor makes it seem too real.

Clara stacks the two small plates and the cups into a pile and carries them into the kitchen, leaving me to watch the car as it slowly moves along the driveway towards the house. When it stops outside the front door, I see that the doctor is not alone in the car. Mr Compton is sitting in the front passenger seat, and Mrs Compton is in the rear seat. I run into the kitchen and grab Clara's arm. I need her to face me, to make sure she hears what I tell her.

'Clara, the master and mistress are with him. In the doctor's car.'

'About bloody time,' she says. She seems completely unperturbed by their impromptu visit. 'You've been here on your own for months and they haven't checked on you once. Have they even written you a letter, asked how you are?'

'They haven't, but Miss Mary sent me a blanket. This one, look.' I pick up the blanket which is strewn across the back of one of the kitchen chairs.

Clara shakes her head, dismissing the gift. 'I don't know why you're having anything to do with them, Vi. Honestly,

I don't. Stuck-up posh people like them get everything they have ever wanted, everything handed to them on a plate, while people like us work our fingers to the bone to give it to them. When I get the vote, I'm going to vote for a woman to run the country. Mrs Pankhurst is a great leader. I'm going to vote for her.'

I don't have time to listen to Clara's political rants. I don't agree that posh people have everything handed to them on a plate. Ernest told me how hard his father has worked to build his factory and it is thanks to men like him that hundreds of other people are in employment. It is true that his wealth and all of his properties, including the huge mill in Skipton, will be handed down to Ernest, and the family is certainly not living a life of poverty, nor will they ever, but from what Ernest has told me, his father has worked extremely hard all his life.

'Clara, they're knocking on the front door.'

'Well, let them in, silly.'

'What? Now?' I look at the dirty pots next to the sink, the Christmas cake in the middle of the table, the knife left out next to it, surrounded by crumbs, like recalcitrant children reluctant to go inside after a day of playing out.

'Go and let them in. I'll clean the kitchen. No doubt they will want a cup of tea, so I'll put the kettle on for you. Go, go.' Clara pushes me out of the kitchen and into the hallway. I brush non-existent dust from my dress, pat my hair, and open the door.

'Mr Compton, Mrs Compton, how nice to see you,' I say, opening the door wide and standing to one side to let them in. They don't seem to have brought any luggage with them, although it could still be in the car. It occurs to me that I shall have to rush upstairs, change the bed, and move my things out of their bedroom before they notice. I presume they will be staying overnight.

'Good afternoon, Violet,' says Mrs Compton. She enters the hall somewhat gingerly, shy almost, as though she is a visitor to someone else's house. 'How are you?'

She stares at my pregnancy bump and I know that she is concerned for the baby's welfare, but good manners dictate that she asks about mine too.

'Very well, thank you, ma'am.' I curtsy and give her what I hope is a welcoming smile.

'Violet, this is Doctor Bradbury,' she says.

'Pleased to make your acquaintance, sir,' I say, with another curtsy.

Doctor Bradbury nods and removes his hat before stepping inside the house. Mr Compton follows them both, but doesn't acknowledge my presence. I close the door behind them and offer to take Doctor Bradbury's hat and coat.

'Doctor Bradbury is an old family friend,' explains Mrs Compton. 'He collected us from the train station. I thought it would be a good idea for you to meet him, and give him a chance to examine you, prior to the birth.'

'Don't look so terrified, dear,' says Doctor Bradbury. He takes off his coat and folds it over my outstretched arm. 'I simply want to listen to the baby's heartbeat and check its size.'

Mr Compton wanders into the dining room and I hear him opening the drinks cabinet. 'Where are my bottles of Bordeaux?' he bellows. 'Have you moved them, girl?'

'No, sir,' I say. I have visions of Ernest and Frank gulping bottle after bottle without a care for Mr Compton's expensive wine collection.

A loud crash comes from the kitchen. I wince at the obvious sound of crockery falling onto tiles and wonder what Clara has smashed.

'Is someone else here?' asks Mrs Compton.

'My friend, Clara,' I say. 'I'm sorry, ma'am. She is cleaning the kitchen.' A flash of irritation shows on Mrs Compton's face. 'You know her, I think, Doctor Bradbury,' I add quickly. 'Her family owns the greengrocery.'

'Yes, I do know them,' says Doctor Bradbury. 'Nice family.'

'I'm sorry, ma'am,' I say again. 'I didn't think you would mind if...'

'Never mind that,' shouts Mr Compton, emerging from the dining room. 'What's happened to all my wine?'

'Oh, darling, you know that Ernest spent the weekend here with some friends.' She walks over to her husband, who is on the edge of anger. 'Here, let me take your coat. Ernest has every intention of replacing your wine. He told me so himself.' Mr Compton is somewhat pacified and hands his coat to his wife, who passes it to me. 'Violet, can you organise some tea in the drawing room?'

'Yes, ma'am,' I say.

Mrs Compton leads the doctor into the drawing room. Mr Compton returns to his drinks cabinet. I hang the doctor's and Mr Compton's coats on the hooks by the front door and then cautiously open the kitchen door, afraid to see what Clara has broken. Thankfully, I discover that it is only one of the plates, not the teapot. I close the door behind me and rest my back against it.

'What's happened to all my wine?' Clara raises her nose in the air and mimics Mr Compton's voice.

'Stop!' I rush over to her and put my hand over her mouth and we snigger like schoolgirls.

'They want some tea,' I say. I carry the clean teapot over to the tea caddy and spoon three teaspoons of tea into the pot before putting the kettle on to boil. 'Should I offer them some of my mother's cake?'

'Absolutely not,' says Clara. She picks up the cake and hides it behind her back, still sniggering.

'Give it here,' I say, laughing. 'You're going to get me in trouble if they hear us laughing.'

Clara gives me the cake. I fold the greaseproof paper around it and place it in the cake tin on the dresser. 'You'll have to help me to eat it then,' I say. 'I'm big enough without adding to my waistline.' I suddenly feel inexplicably sad. Whether it is the sight of Mr and Mrs Compton, or meeting the doctor, or hearing Ernest's name, I do not know. 'Clara, did you hear what Mrs Compton said, about Ernest replacing the wine?'

'Yes, he's so mean, isn't he? Not allowing his son to have a bottle or two.'

'Yes, but that isn't it. It means that she knows that he was here.'

'Yes, I suppose it does. But why wouldn't he tell her that he was coming? It is his family home after all.'

'Yes, but he can't have told her before he came, otherwise she would have told him that I am staying here. He had no idea, and I could tell by the look on his face that it was a shock to see me. He must have told her afterwards. That would have been a very difficult conversation indeed. I wonder what he said about me.'

'About seeing you again?'

'Yes, that would have been a shock to her, given that she told him I had run away and she didn't know where I was. I don't think she ever expected us to see each other again. Did I tell you that she told him that I had left Compton Hall and that nobody knew where I was?'

'No, you didn't,' says Clara. 'She lied to her own son? What a horrible woman she is.'

'Yes. Just trying to protect him, I suppose. She doesn't want him lumbered with a child at his age.'

'At his age? He's plenty old enough to have a child. He's a grown man, Vi.'

'I know he is. Rather, I should have said that she doesn't want him lumbered with *my* child.' I blink away tears. 'I can't wait for the day when I'll no longer cry about him. Will I ever get over him, Clara?'

'Yes, you will. That day will come sooner than you think,' says Clara. 'He's isn't worthy of your tears. None of them are.' She wipes away my tears with her thumbs. 'Don't let them see you have been crying.'

'I won't. I wonder what Mrs Compton thinks about Lucille. Do you think they have met?'

'He probably wouldn't have told her about Lucille,' says Clara.

The kettle boils, preventing me from asking Clara to elucidate. When the tea is ready, Clara tells me that she should go home and she slips out of the back door. I carry the tea into the sitting room and place it on the low table next to one of the sofas. Mr Compton has managed to prise himself away from his diminished wine collection and is seated on one of the sofas, puffing on a fat cigar. Doctor Bradbury is next to him. Mrs Compton, still wearing her hat and coat, is sitting opposite them. Her fur stole has been draped over the arm of the sofa, where her arm rests, gently stroking the dead animal's fur.

'Would you like me to pour the tea, ma'am?' I ask.

'No, thank you, Violet, I will do it.'

'Would you like a slice of cake or something more substantial to eat?'

'No, thank you. We had lunch on the train.'

'Bah! It was barely enough to feed a child,' says Mr Compton. He tips his head back and expels smoke upwards, like steam from an engine.

'My mother made a Christmas cake, if you would like…'

'No, Violet,' says Mrs Compton, directing her forceful response to her husband. 'But thank you,' she adds in a more gentle tone. 'Doctor Bradbury has lots to do, I'm sure, and I wouldn't want to delay him.' She smiles at me. It is halfway to an apology, I suppose. I am used to her being impolite; I don't need her to say sorry for the way she speaks to me.

'Where's the vase?' barks Mr Compton.

'What vase, dear?' asks Mrs Compton.

'I'm asking the girl.' He points to the gap on the top shelf of the bookcase. 'The vase. Have you broken it?'

'No, sir. I've taken it upstairs. I'm sorry, I'll bring it back down.'

'It doesn't matter about that now,' says Mrs Compton. 'Shall we get on?'

'Violet,' says Doctor Bradbury. I turn to face him. 'The examination will only take a moment. Would you like to do it here, or upstairs?'

Neither, I want to scream at him. Here in front of Mr and Mrs Compton, or alone upstairs in a bedroom? No, no, no. 'I'm not sure,' I say.

'Don't look so worried, dear,' he says. 'It will take a few moments, that's all.'

I look to Mrs Compton for guidance but she is engaged in pouring the tea. Mr Compton is puffing on his cigar and watching billows of smoke float around his head. The doctor stands and as he approaches me, I find that my feet are pinned to the floor in terror. He places a warm hand on my shoulder and directs me into the dining room.

'Sit down here, Violet,' he says, pulling one of the dining chairs away from the table. I perch on the edge of the chair. He disappears into the hallway and then reappears carrying a large black leather bag. I have no recollection of seeing the bag when he first came into the house, but he could have retrieved it from the car while I was making the tea. He closes the door behind him. 'If you would like Mrs Compton here as a chaperone, just say.'

I nod. 'Yes, please.'

He goes out and returns followed by Mrs Compton, who stands by the door; the reluctant bystander. The doctor fumbles in his bag and lifts out a stethoscope.

'This is called a stethoscope,' he says. 'It will enable me to listen to the baby's heartbeat.'

'I know what it is,' I say. 'My sister wants to be a nurse and she has a book with drawings showing all the instruments that doctors use.'

'How interesting,' says Doctor Bradbury. 'How old is your sister?'

'Fourteen, sir. She's called Rose.'

Mrs Compton coughs and any connection that may have been made between the doctor and I is broken. Doctor Bradbury kneels in front of me and explains that one end of the stethoscope will be placed on my tummy and he will hold the other end to his ear, and then he will move it around until he picks up the baby's heartbeat. He places his hand on my bump. He doesn't hurt me and I tell myself not to be daft. I watch the doctor's face as he concentrates, occasionally closing his eyes, as if to help him hear the tiny heartbeat. After a few moments, he gets to his feet.

'I'm afraid I can't hear anything, Violet,' he says.

'Is the baby dead?' asks Mrs Compton. Her hand shoots to her neck.

'The baby's not dead, doctor. She kicks me all the time,' I say.

He smiles. 'I am pleased to hear it, but I would like to check, if you wouldn't mind lifting your skirt.'

'Lifting my skirt?' I'm appalled and clutch the fabric of my skirt to my legs.

'Oh, get on with it, Violet,' says Mrs Compton. 'The doctor has seen everything before. It isn't as though he's asking you to stand in front of him naked.' Her composure has returned and she is back to her normal disagreeable self.

I turn my back to Mrs Compton, which is just as well, as she wouldn't like the look I want to throw her. Doctor Bradbury smiles at me again. 'You don't need to be afraid, Violet, but it will be easier for me to hear the baby if I could put the stethoscope directly on your skin.'

My face blazes with embarrassment as I lift my skirt. The doctor kneels in front of me and I try not to flinch at his cold hands. I wish that I had chosen to be examined in the bedroom, where I could be lying comfortably on the bed. I also wish that I hadn't chosen to have Mrs Compton in the room. I can tell what she's thinking - that I shouldn't be ashamed of allowing a man to be so close to me, when I have already been too close to her son.

I keep my eyes focused on the front window and the bare branches of the trees being buffeted by the winter wind. The lake in the distance looks black and icy cold. The passenger ferry is moored to the pier and only a few people are taking walks along the promenade. The temperature seems to be dropping rapidly and ice crystals are beginning to form around the edges of the window. I will have to close all the curtains soon, even though it isn't yet dark, to keep any heat from escaping.

'There, all done,' says the doctor. 'I'm happy to report that the heartbeat sounds strong and healthy.'

I could have told him that the baby was healthy. I told him that she kicks me, but he clearly needed to check for himself, to justify the fee that he would no doubt charge the Comptons for today's visit.

'When would you calculate the baby to be due, doctor?' asks Mrs Compton.

'From what you have told me and looking at the size, I would agree that Violet is almost eight months pregnant. That's right, is it not, Violet?' asks the doctor.

'Yes, sir.'

'The baby will be born in the second or third week of February.'

'Very well,' says Mrs Compton.

Doctor Bradbury advises that as my time for confinement approaches, I shouldn't be left alone. Perhaps a friend could stay with me? Mrs Compton says that of course, she wouldn't like to think of me being alone. She tells me that they are staying at a hotel overnight and that they shall be busy tomorrow, so they won't see me again before they return to Compton Hall. I have absolutely no desire to see her again, so I wish them a safe journey and thank them for arranging for Doctor Bradbury to see me. We say our goodbyes and Mrs Compton tells me that I may close the door behind them, to prevent the house getting cold; there is no need to wait for them to drive off.

As soon as they have gone, I flop down on one of the sofas, exhausted. The room smells of cigar smoke, which is annoying as it reminds me of Ernest's visit. I can't bear to be in the room any longer. I would rather sit at the kitchen table until the smell has dissipated. As I get up, I notice what looks like a brown envelope hidden behind one of the cushions on the opposite sofa: the sofa where Mrs Compton was seated. I lift the cushion and find that it is indeed a large envelope. There is no stamp, no postmark, and no address. The name *Violet Pearson* is handwritten on the front.

I take the envelope into the kitchen and, curiosity getting the better of me, open it immediately.

Inside there is a pile of pound notes, tens and fives. I count them out carefully.

One hundred pounds.

Chapter Twenty-Six
January 1909 – Mary

Ernest chose New Year's Day lunch to announce to the family that he and Lucille are to be married. He asked her at the stroke of midnight. He stopped her in the hallway and on bended knee, he held out a small blue velvet box in his hand. The rest of the party were standing outside on the lawn, watching the fireworks light up the sky from the village green, and sipping champagne. She told us that she had thrown her arms around him and squealed, but she had managed to keep the secret until the following day.

Over lunch, as we all clinked our wine glasses and congratulated the happy couple, Lucille offered her right hand to anyone who wanted to admire it and asked each person if they agreed it was the most beautiful ring they had ever seen. I pretended I was overjoyed that my brother had found someone he could be happy with. I tried to catch his eye across the table, but he was avoiding me.

Since then he has kept himself busy and Lucille has glued herself to his side, making it impossible for me to speak to him privately.

I am trying not to worry about it. I tell myself that even if he doesn't love Lucille now, he will do, given time, I am sure of it. And by the time Violet's baby is born and has been given to Aunt and Reverend Flynn, Ernest will be safe and settled back in Oxford again, so he won't have to see it. His life will become a whirl of long dinners with Lucille and her family, parties, and studying. He won't have time to think about anything else. I hope that by the time his wedding and honeymoon are arranged, (Lucille mentioned something about a July wedding, as her favourite roses will be in bloom then) Violet will be a dim and distant memory. In the future, Ernest and Lucille can have children of their own.

It is Lucille's last evening with us. Tomorrow she and Ernest will return to Oxford.

'It's been the most wonderful Christmas ever,' she says. She lifts her hand for the hundredth time today and gazes at her engagement ring.

'I must admit, your ring is truly beautiful,' I say.

'Yes, isn't it? I simply love sapphires and diamonds. Your brother does have good taste.'

I am not sure whether she means in his choice of ring or his choice of bride. I look over to where Ernest is sitting on the armchair nearest the fire. 'Did you know that Lucille loves sapphires, or was it a lucky guess?' I ask him.

He shrugs. 'A lucky guess.' He smiles at Lucille. She doesn't seem to be aware of its lack of warmth. 'I'm going to leave you two lovely ladies alone to talk about weddings and such like.' He stands and stretches. I know my brother, a night owl who generally doesn't sleep until the early hours of the morning, especially if we have company, and I know that he is far from being tired. It is only just gone ten thirty.

'You're not going to retire to bed yet, are you?' I ask him.

'Not yet, no,' he says. 'I'm going to take advantage of the fact the grown-ups are already asleep and I'm going to raid Father's study. I know exactly where he keeps his most expensive brandy.'

'You can bring us some, too, if you like.' I say. But he has gone.

Lucille looks crestfallen. I don't know her well enough to decipher what she is thinking and I am afraid to ask, fearing it might lead to tears. She looks perilously close to them. However, I have a nagging suspicion that Lucille believes Ernest wants to be alone so that he can think about Violet, rather than because of his penchant for fine brandy. I can see the hurt in her eyes, despite the ring on her finger.

'Do you think Violet's parents called her Violet because of the colour of her eyes?' she says.

'Absolutely not,' I say. I hope I am saying the right thing. 'All babies have blue eyes at birth, don't they, for a day or so?'

'Even the ones with brown eyes?'

'I'm not sure,' I say.

Lucille is nursing her third glass of wine and seems on the edge of an alcohol-induced emotional breakdown.

'I hate her, you know,' she says. 'Violet. I hate Violet.'

'I don't know her well enough to form an opinion,' I say. 'To me, she is just one of the servants.' I am too ashamed to add that I should have spoken to her more. Violet and I are a similar age and she had been in the same room as me on plenty of occasions; dusting and cleaning whilst I was reading or writing letters. But no words had been exchanged between us, except for the day when I called her into my bedroom to give her one of my coats. It was the least I could do. I rarely converse with any of the servants, except to give orders. Ernest's kind heart must have seen her differently.

'I don't know her, either,' says Lucille. 'But I hated the way Ernest had looked at her. That weekend we were at Lakeview Cottage, it was awful. He is besotted with her. I could see it in his eyes then and I can see it in his eyes now. He doesn't look at me the way he looked at her.'

I don't know what to say. I cannot disagree. I know Ernest has been very much in love with Violet. Even after that weekend, when Violet had confessed to him that she had accepted Mother's offer to sell the child, Ernest still loved her.

'Ernest loves you very much,' I say. I hope I am saying the right thing to make her feel better.

Lucille flashes me a smile. Her high cheekbones and her perfectly straight teeth, her poise and her elegance, all add to her beauty. 'But I know that he loves her more,' she says. 'I can sense it. And she is carrying his child. How do I compete with that?'

'You don't have to,' I tell her. 'If Ernest had wanted her, despite our parents' objections, he would have chosen her. He is his own man and he makes his own decision.' I know that isn't true.

'But I helped him to make the decision,' says Lucille. She tips the last of the wine into her delicate mouth and stares into the empty glass.

'What do you mean?' I ask.

'I burned the love letters.'

'What love letters?'

'She had written to him. I found three letters in the top drawer of the chest in her bedroom. I went snooping when she was out. Don't look at me like that, Mary. I am in love, and love makes you do stupid things. Sometimes, dishonourable things.' Lucille takes the wine bottle from the table and empties the remaining contents into her glass. She takes a large gulp.

'What did they say, the letters?' I ask.

'I only read one of them,' she says. 'I can't remember, just words of love. Pages and pages of love. I couldn't bear it. I screwed them up and threw them onto the fire. I watched them burn, and then the following day I persuaded Ernest to leave the house before she got back, so he couldn't talk to her.'

For a moment, I don't reply. I don't know what to say. I can't judge Lucille's actions when I have never walked a single step in her shoes, but I wonder what would have happened if Ernest had found Violet's letters before Lucille; before he had discovered the money. What would have happened if Ernest had chosen to put the letter he had written to Violet in the top drawer of the chest, rather than underneath her pillow? He would have found her letters then. He would never have seen the money. Things would be so different. Maybe he would have forgiven Violet for her rash decision to take the money from Mother if he knew how deeply she loved him.

There are many maybes, but there are a couple of things I know for certain. One is that our parents will not give Ernest their blessing to marry Violet, and the other one is that Ernest has now convinced himself that Violet will never speak to him again, not after he took her money.

I finish my wine and tell Lucille that it is time for bed. I am suddenly exhausted.

Chapter Twenty-Seven
January 1909 - Violet

It has been wonderful having Clara stay with me this past week, and knowing that she has permission, if not blessing, from Mrs Compton makes it so much nicer. The doctor called again yesterday and repeatedly told me that everything was progressing as he would expect and that I have nothing to worry about. Clara is taking his advice to 'sit and rest as often as you can' to the extreme and is treating me like an invalid. But she has a heart of gold and I am happy for her to look after me. This is probably the only time in my life when it will happen, she told me, so I need to make the most of it.

When she is at work at the Douglas' during the day, I sit with my feet up in the sitting room, reading or sewing. Clara pointed out my swollen ankles to Doctor Bradbury and although he said that they are quite normal, he agreed with Clara that I shouldn't be on my feet too long and I certainly shouldn't be going for long walks. So when the weather allows, I put on my coat and hat and take gentle strolls around the garden.

Last night, as Clara was dishing out some beef stew that Edith had made for us at the Douglas' house, and I was cutting two large slices of bread to dip into the delicious gravy, Clara asked me if I was still sure that giving my baby to Mrs Compton's sister was the right thing to do. I was shocked and asked her if she thought that I had changed my mind, but I hadn't yet told her. She looked hurt, again, and I apologised and told her that I think about it every day, and every day I wonder if I am doing the right thing.

An image of the horrible Reverend Flynn flashed into my mind. Despite being a man of the cloth, I have never seen him exhibit the kindness and compassion you would expect of a Christian man. He is surly and rude to most people, and especially to the staff at Compton Hall, and particularly to his wife. I cannot imagine that he would treat his daughter any differently.

Sometimes, it worries me that my baby won't have the love that she would have from her 'real' family. From my family, the Pearsons. But then I remember that the Comptons are her family. Even if Ernest and I were married, my daughter would still be subjected to encounters with the horrible Reverend Flynn, although to a much lesser extent, of course. His wife is nice though. She's a soft, loving lady, from what I have seen and from what Ernest has told me, and she will bear enough love for two people, so I am happy (as happy as I can be) that my child will be well cared for.

I told Clara that I hadn't changed my mind, no. I reminded her that my baby will have the kind of wonderful life that only the Comptons can give her.

'That's rubbish, Violet,' she said. 'I'm sorry, but I know you have said that before, and I can't hear that argument again.'

'I don't mean they will love her more,' I explained. I have told Clara that I think the baby is going to be a girl.

'I know, you mean she will have a nice life because they are rich. The Comptons are her family anyway. Surely they wouldn't allow Ernest's firstborn child to be poor. They would send you money for her, wouldn't they, if she lived with you?'

'Of course they wouldn't. Why would they do that? The baby is illegitimate. I would be out of sight and out of mind, and so would the child,' I said.

'I don't agree. Once they meet the baby, everyone will fall in love and …'

'Clara, please.' Her constant protestations made me weary and I had to ask her not to mention it again. 'I've made my decision and you have to trust that I have made the right one, for me and for the baby.'

Clara nodded. 'If you insist,' she said. 'I just want what is best for you, that's all.'

'And what is best for me is to put this horrible episode of my life behind me and move on. One day, I hope to fall in love and have more babies.'

I watched tears fall down her cheeks. She wiped them away with the sleeve of her dress. 'Ignore me,' she said. 'I worry about you, that's all.'

But as we ate our meal in silence, I couldn't help thinking that her tears were the result of something else, that she wasn't crying just for me. She was quiet for the rest of the evening. I hardly noticed because I was concentrating on reading a new book and was immersed in its story, but when we agreed that it was bedtime, and I went around the house checking that the front and back doors were locked and that all the lamps were off, it occurred to me that Clara hadn't been her usual chatty self all evening. I berated myself for not noticing sooner, but I have found that losing myself in a book for a couple of hours helps to keep my mind off the imminent birth, which I am terrified about. Clara gave me a half-hearted hug goodnight at the top of the stairs.

'Clara, please tell me what's wrong,' I said.

'Nothing,' she said.

I held onto her hand and demanded that she tell me, otherwise, I wouldn't let her retire to bed. 'I know that you're not simply worried about me. Something else is bothering you.'

'You said you can't wait to put this whole sorry episode of your life behind you,' she said.

'Well, can you blame me? I mean, I loved Ernest, I still do, I suppose, but I didn't expect to get pregnant before I was married and I didn't expect him to meet someone else.'

'But if you hadn't got pregnant, and you hadn't come to stay here for the winter, you would never have met me.'

'That's true.'

'But when you *do* put this behind you…'

'Oh Clara, is that what's bothering you? You think that when the baby is born, I'm going to leave you and never see you again?' She nodded. It occurred to me that the oppressive sadness that burdened me was also a heavy weight for Clara, although for different reasons. 'Don't cry, please. I didn't mean it like that. You're my best friend, Clara, and I love you. Come here.'

She fell against me and rested her head on my shoulder. 'I love you, Violet. More than anything.'

We stayed there for a long time while she cried and it was my turn to stroke her back and tell her that everything would be fine, rather than her doing that for me. When we broke away, she wiped away the remnants of her tears. I told her to sleep well and not to let the bed bugs bite, as my mum used to say. She didn't laugh.

I turned away and walked towards the master bedroom, leaving her to sleep in Miss Mary's room. I had a feeling that she was still watching me, but I couldn't bear to see her sad face, so I went into my bedroom and softly closed the door. As I lay in bed, I couldn't help thinking that the way she told me she loved me was the way that Ernest had said it. Not the way that one of my sisters would say it. I tried not to dwell on the fact that she might love me in a way that I cannot reciprocate.

After an hour of not being able to sleep, I got out of bed and knocked on her bedroom door.

'I am still awake,' she said. I opened the door. She moved to the other side of the bed and I climbed in beside her. I didn't know what to say. We held each other for a few minutes, both of us crying for different reasons.

'You know what hurts me the most, Violet?'

'I think so, yes,' I said. 'I'm sorry that I don't love you *in that way*. But I love you dearly as a friend, you know that, don't you?'

'Oh you daft sod,' she said.

'Why are you laughing?'

'Because if I didn't laugh, I'd bloody well cry myself stupid,' she said. 'It's not me I'm crying about. I know you're not like me, and that you want a husband. I'm crying because you don't realise how loved you are. There are so many people who love you. Not for who you might be in the future, not because one day you might have a better job, a better coat, and more than one pair of shoes. They love you right now. For you.' With the last two words, she poked me in the chest twice, to emphasise the importance of her message. 'Do you know how amazing you are?'

'I don't know, not really.'

'Yes, you do,' she said. 'Think about it. You're beautiful, yes, but there is so much more to you than that. Your face shines with kindness and gentleness. Look how you treated Mrs Taylor when she said she had been asked to come over and make up three beds for the Comptons' visit. You could so easily have refused to let her in the house, but you walked the streets in that horrible weather so she wouldn't lose her pay. You treat people with compassion and warmth. You are a rare and precious diamond, Violet Pearson.'

'Do you really think so?'

'I know. Trust in yourself. You have so much to offer, and the world is a better place with you in it. Believe in yourself as much as others believe in you, and you'll find the strength to achieve anything you set your heart on. You don't need the likes of Ernest to make you feel loved. You are loved already.'

This morning, Clara was back to her bright self and went off to work with her usual springy step. Before she went, she carried one of the dining chairs outside for me and I am sitting at the front door, wrapped up in my hat and coat, enjoying the view of the lake below. The ducks are particularly noisy this morning, protesting loudly at a couple of small children who insist on running between them while they are trying to rest in the weak sunshine. The nanny is distracted, enchanted by a newborn in a large pram and each time her face disappears behind the pram's hood, no doubt smothering the baby with kisses, the children take advantage and scatter the ducks once again. I am sure that I wouldn't allow my child to do that. I would teach her that having respect for nature is a quality she must be proud of. Be kind with your actions and gentle with your words, I'd tell her.

I hold my bump and can feel the baby moving inside. I know for certain that when she is born, I won't be able to let her go. Clara is right, I am surrounded by love. But that won't help me when I am up against the Comptons. It doesn't matter how much I want to keep the baby, they will take her from me. I know they will.

Chapter Twenty-Eight
January 1909 - Violet

My back began to hurt from the moment I climbed out of bed this morning. I have had a restless night, tossing and turning and waking at regular intervals throughout the night to use the lavatory. Thank goodness that Lakeview Cottage is a modern home, with one fitted indoors. I now have a new respect for people like my mother. Visiting an outside lavatory in the middle of the night is not pleasant for anyone, and it is certainly not an easy task for a woman who is heavily pregnant.

I didn't tell Clara about my painful back before she left for work. There is no cause for alarm. As she does every morning before she leaves, she told me to rest, and I told her that I intended to. I had planned a morning reading my book outside and watching people at the lakeside, but I am unable to get myself comfortable on the hard chair. Even with two cushions behind my back, I can't quite find the right position.

I decide that a morning in bed will be a welcome treat. I go back inside and make myself a pot of tea and arrange the tray with the pot, a cup, a jug of milk, and a couple of shortbread biscuits that I baked a few days ago. I carry the tray carefully, as I can no longer see where I am putting my feet, but as I reach the bottom of the stairs, a sharp pain around my middle takes my breath away. I pause, balancing the tray with one hand and clinging to the bannister with the other hand. I can feel another pain coming, so I place the tray on one of the stairs and sit down next to it to rest until it has passed. But after that pain has passed, another one arrives in quick succession and I wonder whether this is what it feels like to be in labour. I can't be in labour yet, surely? The baby isn't due for another three weeks, at least. She is too small to come now. The house is too cold for her. I consider getting up to make a fire, just in case, but another pain tells me that kind of physical activity is out of the question.

I take deep breaths as each pain brings with it a new swell of rising panic. What on earth am I to do? I don't know what to do. I can't possibly have my baby on my own. I begin to pray, to ask God to send someone to help me. To send Clara home from work early, to send the doctor on an unexpected visit. Anyone. Please God. I wipe the sweat from my brow with trembling hands.

As I recover from another wave of pain, I remember that my groceries are due to be delivered today. It is Friday. Billy will be here soon. He always brings the box of groceries to the back door, so I try to stand, but my legs are weak and seem unable to carry the weight of my tightening belly. If I can't get to the kitchen, how can I attract his attention? He won't be able to hear me shouting from here in the hallway.

Another wave of pain brings uncontrollable tears. I sob with pain and fear and inconsolable sadness, letting each bout of pain dig its excruciating nails into my belly. I deserve to suffer. I lie on the hallway floor and give in to the punishment that my body is doling out to me.

*

'How long have you been here, Violet? Violet. Can you hear me?'

Is that Clara? It sounds like her, but somehow different. I can't open my eyes. The pain is too much to bear.

'Shall I go and get Clara?' says a man's voice.

I open my eyes slowly. Billy and Clara's mum are both on their knees, one on each side of me. Clara's mum is close to my face, stroking my damp hair away from my face. Billy passes her a wet towel. It is cold and I clamp my eyes shut again as she holds it to my forehead.

'Violet, darling, we need to get you up. Can you stand up?'

I don't know if I can. I don't reply, but I beg her with my eyes to take this pain away.

'Here, Billy, hold her under her right arm. I'll get the left. Ready? One, two, three, lift.'

'Where to now, mum?' asks Billy.

'Try and get her upstairs,' says Clara's mum. 'Don't cry love, everything will be fine, don't worry.'

'My baby,' I whisper, as I take each step one at a time. I don't know where the tray of tea and biscuits has gone and I wonder whether the tea will be cold now. I have no idea what time it is, but my mouth feels as dry as dust and a mouthful of tea would be very welcome.

'Your baby's on its way, love. Don't worry,' says Clara's mum.

'It's too early,' I manage to tell her. 'I've got three weeks or more yet.'

'Well, your waters have gone, so there's nothing we can do about it.'

She steers me into the nearest bedroom at the top of the stairs, which is the one that Frank slept in when he stayed here. Ernest's childhood bedroom. I don't have the strength to argue with her. I have an overwhelming need to lie down, so the sight of the bed is very welcome. Clara's mum instructs me to hang onto the bedpost while she pulls the covers down and plumps the pillows.

'Here, climb in,' she says.

I flop down on the pillow and gratefully close my eyes. I hear her telling Billy to go and get Clara, and to bring Edith, if she is there. I am wondering why she doesn't tell him to bring the doctor, but when Billy has gone - I can hear his racing feet thundering down the stairs and straight out of the front door - Clara's mum tells me that the doctor is away for a few days. He has gone to the seaside to stay with his sister and her husband.

'But don't worry, I know what I'm doing,' she assures me. That's the third time she has told me not to worry and I wonder whether she is telling herself, rather than me. 'I'm going to pop downstairs to boil up some water. Where do you keep the spare bedding and towels?'

'Each room has its own collection,' I tell her. 'In the bottom drawer of each of the chests. And there are more towels in the kitchen dresser.'

She disappears downstairs. Within minutes, she is back and without a word, she pulls down the sheet, lifts my dress, and removes my undergarments. I don't have time to be embarrassed before another pain overtakes me, causing me to cry out. Clara's mum dabs at my head again with the damp towel, before wiping it across her own. Her cheeks are red. Her face filled with anxiety.

'I'm sorry,' I say. 'I asked the baby to wait until the doctor was back from the seaside, but she's a stubborn little madam.'

She laughs. 'Babies generally are. They always want their own way and will scream and scream until they get it.'

I don't know how long has passed, but eventually Clara and Edith burst into the room.

'Now then, what have we got here?' says Edith. Her sleeves are rolled up, ready for work.

'It's almost time,' says Clara's mum.

'Jolly good,' says Edith. 'I've had four bairns of my own, Violet, and I've delivered countless others, so you're in good hands.' I tell her thank you and then grip Clara's hand as another pain comes. Edith moves to the end of the bed. 'When you feel the next pain, I want you to push into your bottom.'

I am not sure what she means, but my body takes over and I do as I am told, and amid the shouts of encouragement from Clara, her mum, and Edith, my daughter is finally born. Edith wraps her in a towel and places her on my chest. There is blood and mucus everywhere from the afterbirth, but all I can focus on is hearing my baby cry. And there it is. The most beautiful sound in the world. I kiss the top of her head and when I look up, everyone in the room is crying and Clara's mum is squeezing Edith so tight, it's a wonder she can breathe.

Chapter Twenty-Nine
January 1909 - Violet

Edith has gone home. It is just me and Clara's mum in the room. Clara is downstairs making some toast. She insisted that I should have something to eat and I have to admit that I am as hungry as a miner after a long shift.

'Shall we try and put her to your breast, Violet?' Clara's mum says.

I agree, knowing that the baby will need as much sustenance as she can get. She is small, but otherwise, she seems healthy. She has ten fingers, ten toes, and the most beautiful face anyone has ever seen. Her mop of dark hair is just like her father's, but Edith told me that she is likely to lose that over the next few weeks before more hair grows back.

The baby latches onto my breast easily and begins to suck. I rest my head back against the pillow and close my eyes.

'Look what I've got,' says Clara, coming back into the bedroom carrying a large plate of hot buttered toast. 'There's enough toast here to feed the five thousand, so tuck in,' she says. 'You too, Mum. You both look worn out.'

She passes me a slice of toast and I take a bite, allowing the melted butter to dance on my tongue. 'This is the most delicious thing I've ever eaten,' I tell her.

Clara kisses me on the cheek and then leans over to stroke the baby's hand. She smiles when the baby's tiny fingers grasp hers tightly. 'She doesn't want to let go,' she says. 'She loves her Auntie Clara. Please don't let her go.' She whispers the final words into my ear so that her mother doesn't hear. But she does.

'What do you mean, don't let her go?' asks Clara's mum.

Clara wipes a rogue tear from my face and then one from her own. 'Nothing, Mother,' she says.

'It's okay, Clara,' I say. 'We can tell your mum.'

'Are you sure?' asks Clara.

'Tell me what?'

'This baby isn't mine to keep.' The words catch in my throat. 'I promised that I would give her to Mrs Compton's sister, to bring up as her own child.'

I can't tell what Clara's mum is thinking. Would she have done the same thing if she had a child out of wedlock when she was my age? Or is she judging me for being a horrible person, for abandoning my child when she has only been in this world for a couple of hours? I am not sure. I listen to the rain as it relentlessly pounds against the glass of the bedroom window. Each drop a melancholic note of despair. The wind, drumming through the trees, adds a mournful howl to the saddest symphony I have ever heard. I cry, along with Mother Nature.

'But now you have changed your mind?' asks Clara's mum.

'Yes! Yes, I have. How did you know?'

'I'm a mother myself, Violet.' She strokes my hair. 'It's a mother's love,' she says. 'Once you feel it, there's nothing in the world that is going to come between you and your baby.'

'I feel as though I'd fight to the death anyone who would attempt to come between me and her,' I say. Both women gaze at me and my baby and I'm so filled with love that I could burst. 'I can't let her go,' I say. 'I want to keep her. Please don't make me give her up.' My tears quickly turn to rasping sobs.

'Nobody will make you, Violet. You don't have to let her go,' says Clara's mum. 'You can write to Mrs Compton and explain that you have changed your mind. She and her sister can still see the baby, can't they, if they want to? I am guessing that Ernest Compton is the baby's father, and that's why you wanted to avoid him when he came to stay here the weekend before Christmas?'

'Yes, he is.'

'Okay, so that means that Mrs Compton is her grandmother. She's a reasonable woman, isn't she? I am sure she will want a baby to stay with her natural mother.'

I shake my head. 'She wants the baby to go to her sister.'

I am frightened to admit that they will turn up here, bundle her up, and take her away. Before I have poured their tea, they will be in their fancy car, wheels spinning on the gravel drive, taking my tiny daughter with them. After all, we have an agreement. We have a contract. It may not be a legal contract, but I remember Mrs Compton's words that if I don't abide by my side of the bargain, she will tell the police that I have stolen the money from her. Of course, I would deny it and I would tell them the truth and offer to give the money back, but if they had a choice between me and her, who would the police believe? A lady, a pillar of the community, or a jobless housemaid, a slut who has thrown herself at their son and tried to trap him with an unexpected pregnancy? I can see how it will play out. I will be arrested and my baby will be taken away from me.

I ask Clara and her mum to sit down on the edge of the bed and while they eat their toast, I tell them the whole story. I tell them that I was offered money in exchange for the child and that I accepted the sum of a hundred pounds. I tell them that I negotiated payment up front before I came to Cumberland. Neither of them bat an eyelid. They simply listen and encourage me to continue.

I tell them about the weekend when Ernest came to visit with Lucille and Frank, and that afterwards I searched Ernest's bedroom, underneath his pillows and under the mattress on his bed, hoping that he had left me a letter telling me how much he truly loved me. But there was nothing. I tell them that I had written to him three times, but each time I hadn't posted the letter, as I was afraid of the rejection that would undoubtedly come my way, and that when I went to get the letters from where I had left them in the drawer in the back bedroom, I discovered that they had been taken.

'And the money from Mrs Compton had gone too,' I say. 'I left it underneath my pillow, but by the time I got back from your house, it had gone.'

'That's terrible,' says Clara's mum.

'Who took them, do you think?' asks Clara. 'Ernest, or that Lucille woman?'

'I don't know,' I say. 'But I haven't heard from Ernest since then.'

'Oh well, that's made your mind up,' says Clara's mum. 'If he has got himself a new lady friend, there isn't much you can do. You need to move on. And if he has taken the money, whether he has kept it or given it back to his mother, you don't owe them anything.'

'That's right,' says Clara. 'You don't need to feel guilty about keeping the baby. You're under no obligation to hand her over. She's yours.'

'I know that,' I say. 'And I think I am moving on. Slowly, but surely. But there is more to the story. Do you remember when Mrs Compton came to see me at the end of last month and she brought the doctor to see me for the first time?'

'Yes, I do,' says Clara.

'Well, after she had gone, I found an envelope underneath the cushion where she had been sitting, and when I opened it, I found a hundred pounds in cash. She must have known that the money was taken from me and she replaced it. I've got it here. It is nestled in my suitcase underneath the bed in the master bedroom.'

'Bloody hell, Vi, you're rich,' says Clara.

'But don't you see,' I say. 'If I'm keeping the baby, I will need to give it back to her.'

'You are not,' says Clara. 'You are going to need that money. Children are expensive. Don't worry about it for now. Everything will sort itself out.'

I wish that I had Clara's optimism.

'I have no idea how I will cope,' I say.

'You will cope,' says Clara. 'I will help you. I want to help you. Remember what I told you last night? Believe in yourself and you can do it. You are loved.'

'Of course, you are loved, Violet, dear,' says Clara's mum, as though the obvious has been right there in front of me this whole time.

Chapter Thirty
January 1909 - Violet

The first two days after the birth have flown by in a blur of feeds, nappy changing, and fitful snoozes. This morning, I woke up covered with cold sweat, thanks to the nightmare about my baby being dragged out of my arms by a group of strangers. I fought and fought, but I wasn't strong enough and I could only stand and watch as she disappeared out of my life. But she is still here. She is still with me. Nevertheless, I lean over the side of the bed to check, and there she is, fast asleep in the beautiful wooden basket Clara's dad made for me. Clara told me that on the day my baby was born, her dad had stayed up for hours, sawing and banging into the early hours of the morning to create somewhere for her to sleep, and the basket was safely delivered to me the following morning on the back of his cart. Anyone seeing the delivery, safely covered by hessian sacks, would have assumed that the grocer and his old chestnut mare were merely delivering groceries.

I have named the baby Maggie after my mother. Maggie Pearson. Not Compton. Not Flynn. She will have my family name. I stroke the delicate down of her soft face. I still can't believe that she is mine.

She murmurs and cries a little. Before she disturbs Clara, I pick her up and put her to my breast for her first feed of the day. I rest on the pillow, holding her tight, never taking my eyes off her face.

The bedroom door opens slowly and Clara's head peeps in.

'Good morning,' I say. 'Sorry if we disturbed you so early.'

'I was awake,' says Clara. 'I heard her cry, so I thought I'd see if you wanted a cup of tea.'

I laugh. 'You should know by now that you don't ever have to ask, Clara. I'm like Edith and her tea. The answer will always be yes.'

Clara laughs and goes downstairs. By the time she arrives back, Maggie has finished her feed and, wearing a clean nappy and a clean gown, she falls asleep in the middle of the bed. Reluctant to disturb her and put her back in her basket, and because I feel much more relaxed when she is next to me, I cover her with the white blanket that Mrs Compton bought for me. I wonder if this will be the only gift from her grandmother that she will experience.

'What would you like for breakfast?' asks Clara, as she puts the tea tray on the bedside cabinet. 'I can make you some porridge, or would you prefer some toast? There are plenty of eggs, too.' She walks over to the window and draws back the curtains. Pale morning light seeps in.

'Don't you need to get yourself to church, Clara? I can make some toast for myself later.'

'You cannot. You need to stay right where you are for a few more days. You know you're not out of the woods yet?

231

Edith says that you need to take care of yourself and I am going to make sure that you follow her instructions.'

'Thank you,' I say. 'But tomorrow, you need to work. I am worried that you will lose your job if you don't go back.'

'Mrs Douglas hardly notices if I'm there or not, but I am sure that she certainly doesn't want me to pass any germs to her. She is happy to avoid anything that will prevent her from partying with her friends.'

Clara's mum had been to see Mrs Douglas on Friday, after Maggie was born, and had told her that Clara had a terrible fever and would not be able to work until later in the week. Mrs Douglas was apparently happy for Clara to stay away and said that they would manage very well without her.

'Is Edith okay?' I ask. 'I'm worried that she will struggle without you.'

'Yes, she's fine,' says Clara. 'I will chat to her in church later. But my mum said that she saw her in the shop yesterday and she said that you and the bairn are the most important things. She said that she can manage for the rest of this week. Her niece offered to help with Mrs Douglas' laundry and do a couple of hours of cleaning, if necessary.'

'Edith won't tell anyone about the baby, will she?'

'No.' Clara shakes her head forcefully. 'I'd trust her with my life. But you know that we don't have much time in this house, don't you?'

I nod. 'I know. Is Doctor Bradbury back from visiting his sister yet?'

'I don't know. But I would imagine he would be back today, which means that he could call and see how you are at any time.'

'Oh, don't say that Clara. He wouldn't, would he? He saw me only last week.'

'I don't know, but if Mrs Compton has asked him to keep an eye on you, then who can tell?'

I have been expecting this day to come. The day when I have to leave Lakeview Cottage. Now that my baby is here, I know that I can't possibly part with her, although I haven't yet allowed myself to think about what I will do. I can't envisage the next stage of my life. It is too frightening to contemplate. I feel as though I have been at Lakeview Cottage for so long that I have begun to see it as my own house, even though I know it isn't. However much I would love to live here and bring my child up here, I know I can't. I am here merely as a temporary custodian.

I gaze out of the bedroom window. The view to the lake is even more beautiful from upstairs and, through the leafless trees, I can see the early morning winter sun glimmering on the water. I love this bedroom and I wish it could be mine forever. I have fallen in love with Bowness and its beautiful lake. The clean air; the comforting snow-topped hills that seem to wrap their protective arms around us; the little shops packed to the rafters with everything you could wish for. I love them all. The warm and friendly locals will be impossible to leave behind. Yet I know that I must leave, and soon. If I am to keep my baby, I can't let Doctor Bradbury see me. I can't let Mrs Compton know that the baby her family is waiting for has already been born. She will take her from me without a backward glance, and I will never see her again.

'I need to get up, Clara,' I say, pushing the bedclothes away from my legs. 'I need to leave.'

'Not today!' She holds me back and covers my legs with the blanket. 'You're not well enough, and you can't take a tiny baby outside in this weather. The sky might look blue, but it's freezing cold out there.'

I relent and stay in bed. 'What are we going to do? We need to stop the doctor from calling. Should you tell him that I have a dreadful cold? I could have caught the same pretend germs that you have.'

'I suppose we could say that, but I'm not sure that would stop him from calling,' says Clara. 'In fact, that will give him a reason to come and check on you. Who's that?' Clara rushes over to the window and I kneel up on the bed, trying to get a better view of the figure wrapped in a dark coat, head down, walking towards the house. 'It's okay. It's only Mum. I'll go and let her in.'

While Clara is out of the room, I visit the bathroom. Initially, I feel fine, but after a few steps, I feel dizzy and lightheaded and hold onto the wall as I walk. By the time I have finished in the bathroom, Clara and her mum are waiting for me in the bedroom.

'How do you feel, love?' asks Clara's mum.

'I felt a little dizzy, but it's gone now, thank you,' I tell her. 'I'd like to get dressed, I think.'

'Why do you want to get dressed? I can bring you everything you need,' says Clara. 'It's no trouble, you don't need to get dressed yet.'

'I do, Clara,' I say. 'I can't explain why, but wearing a dress, rather than my nightdress, will make me feel more relaxed. Ready for anything. And if I have to run out of the house, then I'm prepared. I won't stand a chance if I have to run outside in a flimsy nightdress. I need to make sure that Maggie is always dressed and warm, too.'

Clara explains to her perplexed-looking mum about our fear that Doctor Bradbury will come over and see me unexpectedly and, as soon as Mrs Compton knows that Maggie has been born, she will be taken away from me. Clara's mum says that she understands completely, but the best thing I can do for the baby is to make sure that I'm fit and strong enough to care of her. She says that even if the doctor called right now, this very second, it would take a day or so for the message to get to Mrs Compton. Doctor Bradbury would have to send a telegram. He wouldn't be able to leave his patients and drive to Compton Hall, not after he has just had a few days away. So, we don't need to panic. She assures me he is unlikely to return from his holiday and come to Lakeview Cottage immediately. He will very likely go to church this morning, and then tomorrow he will have patients to see. He probably won't call until tomorrow or the day after that.

Clara's mum talks sense and I feel a little calmer. However, I tell her and Clara that I need to make preparations to leave and that I would like to get dressed and slowly and carefully pack my suitcase. Then, at some point tomorrow, I can get the train to Manchester. I expected Clara to be upset when the subject of me leaving was ultimately raised, but I am shocked at so many tears. She sits on the edge of the bed and rests her hand on Maggie's tiny chest.

'I will miss you so much, both of you,' she says.

'I'm not going a million miles away,' I say. 'You can visit me often, every month. You will be Maggie's aunt as much as Rose and Bridgett are.' My comforting words are not comforting enough and Clara dashes from the room, sobbing, telling us that she needs to wash her face and blow her nose.

When she returns, Clara's mum holds out her arms and Clara walks into them. The two of them hold each other tightly and I know just how Clara's mum feels. She will be feeling Clara's sorrow just as much as Clara is. Even though it is a normal part of life, something that none of us can avoid and must endure, I vow to myself that I will keep Maggie free of pain, physical and emotional, as much as I can.

'Violet,' says Clara's mum, over her shoulder. 'Why don't you and baby Maggie move in with us for another couple of weeks or so? That way you can relax while you fully recuperate, and then when you're ready to go to Manchester, you and the baby will be stronger and fitter. You don't have to worry about anyone hearing her cry, the walls are so thick and once the door to the shop is closed, nobody will hear a thing.'

I tell her that it's a great idea and thank her for her kindness. The truth is that I'm not ready for the journey to Manchester yet. Another two weeks will make so much difference and the baby will be that much stronger. During that time, I can write to my mum and ask her to come to Windermere Station to meet me and then we can travel back together. She can even bring Rose and Bridgett with her. The girls will love the adventure. I can pay for all the tickets. I have plenty of money. I will ask my mum to buy me a new hat and coat and to bring it with her. I don't want to take the coat that I have been wearing all January, the one that people have seen me wearing. I know that a fresh coat won't mean nobody will recognise me, but it will diminish the chances, especially if we wait until after dark. I am sure there will be a train out of Windermere in the evening, and it is dark from five o'clock. I tell myself that the journey is almost without risk.

As the plan begins to form in my mind, I instantly feel better. We decide that we will make the move to their house immediately after church. Clara's mum says that Clara's dad and Billy will bring the horse and cart and between us, we will be able to manage. As though she can read my mind, she tells me not to worry about the convoy that might attract attention. She will send the men back first and then she will walk home with the baby, wrapped tightly underneath her coat. She will walk the long way, not up Lake Road, but up the quiet back streets. Before I can voice my objection, she says that I need to hold onto Clara's arm, and if anyone sees me, they won't see anything suspicious, they will simply see two friends out for an afternoon stroll.

Clara and her mum dash off to church and I begin to pack a small bag, which takes me no time at all. The rest of the morning is an anxious wait to see who gets to the house first, Clara's family or Doctor Bradbury.

Chapter Thirty-One
January 1909 - Mary

We are having breakfast in the morning room when the telegram arrives. I spot the boy as I look out of the window. He cycles up the long drive towards Compton Hall on his rickety bicycle. The stones on the gravel path present him with a challenging journey. I watch his thin legs push against the stirrups. His flat cap is pulled low over his eyes, protecting his face from the sharp needles of rain. The sleeves on his too-small jacket reveal wrists as thin as a newborn fawn's spindly legs.

I sip my tea from a delicate china cup. Mother spreads homemade marmalade onto crisp slices of light brown toast. Father ignores us both as he flicks through the morning's newspaper. I hear the doorbell ring, followed by Barrow's footsteps in the hall. Then mumbled voices. I watch as the boy cycles away, his job done.

'A telegram, Sir,' says Barrow, a few minutes later. He holds a silver tray in his right hand. The telegram sits in the middle of the tray like a ticking time bomb, waiting to bring the news that we have all dreaded.

'What is it?' asks Mother. 'Is it the baby? Is everything all right?'

'Give me time to read it, woman,' barks my father.

Mother puts her head down and concentrates on smearing more marmalade on the already overladen toast. She blinks rapidly and pursues her lips. I hate it when my father speaks to Mother like that, especially in the presence of the servants. Barrow's face remains poker-straight and emotionless. He has heard everything before; family arguments, private conversations, sharp words, and clipped tones. Whether he respects his master more or less for the way he speaks to his family is anyone's guess.

'I knew it!' shouts Father. He thrusts his chair back and storms out of the room. He leaves the dining room door open behind him and I can hear his angry footsteps crossing the tiled floor of the hallway towards his study. A moment later, the study door slams closed.

'Read it to me, Mary,' says Mother. 'I don't have my glasses on. Quick. Quick.'

I have already read the words to myself. Father had left the telegram facing upwards on the tablecloth and I could see it was from James' father, Doctor Bradbury.

'That will be all for now, Barrow, thank you,' I say. The butler gives a tiny bow and leaves the room, closing the door behind him. I pick up the telegram and read it out loud to Mother, word for word.

VIOLET HAS GONE STOP TAKEN ALL BELONGINGS INCLUDING BABY GIRL

I watch as the colour drains from Mother's face. I run around to her side of the table and put my arms around her.

'Are you all right, Mother? Here, have a drink of tea, have you put sugar in?'

She doesn't reply, so I spoon in two teaspoons of sugar, stir rapidly, and hold the cup to her mouth. She takes a tiny sip, holding onto the cup with shaking hands, and then waves the cup away. I expect her to cry, to weep and wail and bemoan the loss of the baby that was due to be delivered to the family. But she simply stands up, smooths down her skirt, and tells me to ring for Barrow. We are going to Lakeview Cottage, she informs me. First thing in the morning. She wants to speak to Doctor Bradbury herself and find out what is going on.

I ring for Barrow whilst Mother paces the floor, mumbling to herself and wringing her hands, and I instruct him to arrange for a telegram to be sent to Doctor Bradbury telling him to meet us at the cottage as soon as he can on Wednesday. Then I ask him to send another telegram to the greengrocers asking for a small box of vegetables and half a dozen eggs to be delivered. I suspect we are likely to be there for a couple of days, I tell him. I ask him to ask Cook to prepare a selection of sandwiches for the journey, and a lemon cake if she has time. Barrow says that he is sure she will have time and he will see to everything. He tells me that he will instruct Philip to prepare the car.

Barrow asks Mother whether Mr Compton will be travelling with us and whether he would need some clothes packing, but before Mother can reply, I ask him to go and speak to Father and ask him.

Barrow bows and leaves the room for the second time, after glancing over at Mother who is continuing her pacing, with a worried look on his face.

I don't know why I am so surprised by this turn of events. Wasn't it obvious all along that Violet wouldn't stick to her side of the bargain? What mother willingly hands over her baby to another family, if she has a chance to keep her?

I wish I could talk to James, but at least I will see him tomorrow. I wish I could talk to Ernest. I consider telephoning the university and asking them to pass a message to him that he should come home, but there is nothing he can do. I try to occupy my mind with the arrangements for our travel, but I don't care about cake or any other food. We are not going on a picnic, although I know Mother will feel better if provisions are properly arranged, whether or not anyone has the stomach for them. I wish I could tell Barrow to disregard all my instructions. I want to tell him that we aren't going anywhere, we have changed their minds. Cancel the telegrams. Cancel the packing. Cancel the food. I don't see the point in travelling to the other side of the country to find that the house is indeed empty; the telegram on the table tells us so. Doctor Bradbury had surely seen for himself. But Mother will want to speak to him and get to the bottom of what has actually happened to Violet. Maybe she is hoping the doctor will know where she is.

Mother assures me that she is fine, so I drag myself upstairs and begin to pack a bag. I can call for one of the maids to do it, but I want to be alone.

To think.

To plan.

To consider my brother.

I seem to be the only person in the family who cares about what Ernest wants. Nobody has considered how difficult it would have been for him to see his child regularly - his daughter: the telegram told us that the baby was a girl. I doubt Mother has given him a single thought. How awful it would be for him, with his child being part of our extended family, but never being able to sit his daughter on his knee and smother her face with kisses and tell her that daddy loves her.

Ultimately, this might be the best thing for him. The fact that Violet has gone means that we can all move on. We need to accept that the ridiculous notion of Aunt and Reverend Flynn being given a baby who doesn't belong to them will now never happen.

Chapter Thirty-Two
January 1909 – Violet

By the time I arrive at the greengrocer's, I am exhausted. I have leaned so heavily on Clara's arm throughout the walk from Lakeview Cottage, she must be exhausted, too. The street is dark. The gas lamps struggle to shine through the low cloud and drizzle, but I am thankful for the inclement weather. The sudden drop in temperature has hurried people indoors, to their fires and their warm drinks, to their families and loved ones.

Clara leads me down a ginnel at the back of the shop and up the stairs to the flat above. Clara's mum is already here. She is holding Maggie, hugging her swaddled body as she rocks her back and forth.

'We've made it,' says Clara. She takes my coat and tells me to sit by the fire.

'Is she all right?' I ask Clara's mum. I peer into the blanket and can see that my beautiful daughter is peacefully sleeping.

'Nothing to worry about,' says Clara's mum. 'I'm enjoying myself here. It has been years since I've rocked a baby to sleep. Do you want her?'

Of course, I want her. I need her. My breasts ache for her. 'Don't disturb her,' I say, reluctantly. 'She's enjoying herself there, I can tell.'

There is a sharp knock on the door and my heart misses a beat. I jump up, knocking over a small side table.

'I'm sorry, I'm sorry,' I say.

Clara's dad rushes in from the tiny kitchen. 'It will be Edith, that's all. Don't start. Nobody knows you're here, except her.'

I put the table back on its legs.

'Now then, missy, don't you be doing any strenuous work,' says Edith. Clara has let her in. 'You've just had a baby, or have you forgotten.' She takes hold of my arm and pushes me back into the chair. 'How you feeling?'

'I'm very good, thank you,' I say. 'Thank you for helping me, Edith. I couldn't have done it without you. Without any of you.'

'Get away with you,' she says. She kneels in front of me and puts the flat of her hand on my forehead. 'I can't feel any fever. Have you felt all right, in yourself?'

'She felt a bit dizzy this morning,' says Clara.

'That's to be expected. You've lost a lot of blood, so you need plenty of rest until your body makes more. Do you understand? No dashing about and moving furniture and the like.'

I laugh. 'Yes, of course.'

'Good, now off to bed with you. Come on. Bed.'

Clara leads me and Edith into her bedroom. A lamp is lit at the side of her bed, giving it a welcome orange glow. The wooden basket that Clara's dad made for Maggie is at the foot of the bed. It is already padded with clean blankets and looks as cosy as a mother's hug. The scene brings a tear to my eyes. Clara pulls back the top blanket and the cotton sheet underneath it. She pats the bed. 'Do as Edith says.'

'Where are you going to sleep?' I ask.

'I will sleep in one of the chairs in the living room. Don't you worry about me.'

Edith helps me to undress and hands me a clean nightdress and I am thankful to finally get into bed. Clara's mum brings Maggie and gently lies her in her cot. The baby murmurs like a kitten, but settles again.

'I'm going to get you something to eat and a nice big mug of tea with plenty of sugar,' says Clara. 'Are you having one, Edith?'

'No, thank you, love. I'm going to go,' says Edith. 'I'll pop back when I can tomorrow and check on you.'

'Edith,' I say as she turns to go. 'Don't tell anyone where I am, will you?'

'You can rely on me,' she says. She taps the side of her nose.

Within minutes, I am asleep. I haven't felt as relaxed as this since before I left Compton Hall all those months ago.

Chapter Thirty-Three
January 1909 – Mary

Despite Mother's obvious distress, Father has refused to come to Cumberland with us, citing 'business difficulties' as a reason why he couldn't for once in his life put his family first. So my mother and I are travelling by ourselves. Mother didn't want a maid or Mrs Meadows to accompany us.

Philip isn't generally prone to conversation and on this occasion, I am pleased that the time in the car is mostly spent in silence. So far, Mother has refused to speculate on where Violet has gone and who she is with until she has seen Doctor Bradbury. All she has said as we journeyed over the Yorkshire Dales and into Cumberland was that Doctor Bradbury had let her down. She asked him to keep an eye on Violet and he had allowed her to run away, she said. I wanted to tell her that Violet was a grown woman, not a child, and she hadn't 'run away', because she wasn't being held captive. She had made her own decision. But I remembered that Violet had agreed to sell the child, and although I don't know anything about the law, didn't that mean they had a contract? I have often heard Father talk of business contracts. But surely agreeing to sell a baby couldn't be the same? Babies weren't commodities to be bought or sold. Not knowing what the legal situation is, I kept my mouth closed and my thoughts to myself.

We arrive at Lakeview Cottage early afternoon, after a three-hour drive. It seems as though the last of the daylight has virtually gone, although the day isn't yet done. The house is cold and dark. I ask Philip to light the fire in the drawing room, but Mother tells him not to bother. I follow her into the kitchen, which is slightly warmer, having benefitted from the afternoon sun.

Philip lights the stove and I make us some tea. After forcing down the remaining sandwiches that Cook had made for us that morning, Mother retires early to bed, blaming a headache, so I spend the evening reading in my bedroom, a thick woollen blanket wrapped tightly around my legs. I contemplate walking up the hill to the Bradbury's house. I know James will be delighted to see me, but I am too tearful to face him. I need some time by myself, with only my jumbled thoughts for company.

After a while, I wander downstairs into Father's study and search his desk for some paper and a pen, determined to be the first to tell Ernest of the situation. But once I have the pen in my hand, poised over the paper, I find that I cannot find the words to tell him in a way that wouldn't break his heart, so I close the lid on the desk.

I warm some milk on the stove and take it back to bed.

*

The following morning I tiptoe into the drawing room to pull back the curtains. I am surprised Mother is already up, although she isn't yet dressed. She is perched on the edge of one of the sofas, her winter house coat wrapped tightly around her waist. Her long grey hair tumbles down her back. She is clutching a small white vase. Her middle finger strokes the delicate handle on the side.

'I found this next to my bed,' she says. 'Violet moved it upstairs. She must have taken a liking to it.' She looks up to the empty space on the top shelf of the bookcase where the vase usually lives. 'It's a pretty thing, isn't it? I can see why she would like it. I bought it from one of the new gift shops in Windermere in the summer. Do you remember, dear?'

'Yes, it is beautiful,' I say.

'What a wonderful day that was. We had lunch on the lawn and stayed outdoors until it was almost dark, do you remember?' She stares into the cold and dusty grate, as though her memories are in there, dancing amongst the unlit coals.

'Yes, I do remember that day,' I say. The Bradburys came for dinner and I remember that Ernest, James and I all went for a walk to the lake after our meal. Ernest very kindly gave us some space to be alone, but after ten minutes or so of Ernest walking ahead of us, I called him back. I love my brother's company as much as James'.

I prise the vase from Mother's fingers and place it on the side table. 'Let me do your hair for you, Mother. Stay there, I'll go and get your hairbrush.'

I run upstairs for my mother's hairbrush which she keeps on her dressing table. I grab it quickly and dash back down the stairs. Mother is where I had left her, a silent, empty shell of the person she had been at the same time yesterday before the telegram had torn her world apart.

I should have insisted on a fire being lit last night.

'Your aunt will be devastated,' says Mother when she sees I have returned to the room. 'She was so looking forward to having a baby of her own. And a girl, a precious girl would have been so loved.'

I want to tell her that the baby girl *will* be loved. She will be loved by Violet, too, and it is only right that she is brought up by her own mother. The ideal situation, of course, would be if the baby girl could be brought up in Compton House by Violet and Ernest together. As a couple. As a married couple. But I know that is not a consideration. Ernest told me about the discussions between him and our parents. Violet was not good enough for him, they had said. She isn't a lady. Her family is not 'connected' and she would never be accepted into society. You might say those were kind, almost tempered, words. At least Mother didn't tell Ernest what she had told me, that he couldn't possibly marry Violet because they didn't want her uncouth, bad-mannered, working-class family at the wedding. Ernest would have been devastated.

As I brush and plait Mother's hair, I silently pray that God will look after Violet and her baby and that He will send her health and happiness, wherever she might be. I pray for acceptance to be sent to Ernest and for compassion to be sent to my parents.

By the time Doctor Bradbury arrives at Lakeview Cottage, it is ten-fifteen in the morning. Mother is washed and dressed, has eaten a small breakfast of porridge, and has regained her composure.

Dark clouds have gathered over the house and the threat of a sudden storm of torrential rain has forced us to light the fire. There is a sudden chill in the air. Mother and I are settled in front of the fire in the drawing room.

'I think the doctor is here,' I say. 'I can hear a car.'

Mother doesn't respond.

'We have a visitor, ma'am.' Philip stands in the hallway, peering into the drawing room. 'I shall get the door.'

I watch Mother's scowl as it develops. There is no smile to greet her guest. The initial shock which she has carried about for the past twenty-four hours like a heavy suitcase is replaced by anger, all of which is directed at the doctor as soon as Doctor Bradbury walks through the door. She jumps up and marches into the hallway.

'Where is she?' she demands.

'I don't know, Phyllis,' says the doctor. 'I came to see her on Sunday afternoon, a routine visit to check on her welfare, just as you asked, and found the house empty.'

'When did you last see her?'

'A week ago,' said the doctor. 'I told you that I would check on her weekly from now until the birth, and I kept to my promise. There was nothing else I could have done.'

The doctor removes his coat and hat and Philip takes them from him and hangs them on the coat hooks at the bottom of the stairs. I ask Philip to make some tea and when he has brought it to us, to stay in the kitchen while we have a private conversation with the doctor. I know that Barrow can be trusted, but I am not sure about Philip. He has wily eyes, cunning as a fox, and will report back to the rest of the servants, as sure as eggs as eggs.

I follow Mother and the doctor into the drawing room. The doctor declines Mother's offer to take a seat; instead, he stands with his back to the fireplace, standing over us, imposing his assumed superiority. I wonder whether he would have done that if Father was with us. After Philip delivers the tea and closes the door behind him, the doctor explains that he had been away for a few days visiting his sister, but he had made seeing Violet a priority upon his return. He says that he hadn't announced his visit to her, but he expected to find her at home, it being Sunday afternoon. He had knocked on the front door for a while and, having got no answer, he had walked around to the back of the house and had knocked on the kitchen door and had peered in at the window, but he was sure that the house was empty.

'Did you ask around the village?' Mother says.

'Yes, of course,' says the doctor.

'That girl who was here, her friend, did you ask her?'

'Clara. Yes, I did,' says the doctor. 'I went to the greengrocers immediately and asked to speak to Clara. At first, I was told she wasn't home, but then she appeared in the doorway.'

'What do you mean? She was hiding from you?'

'Possibly, yes. It is to be expected.'

'What did you say to her?'

'I told her that nobody was answering the door at Lakeview Cottage and asked her if she knew where Violet was. I made out that I was worried about her.'

'What did the girl say?'

'She told me that Violet had given birth to a girl a few days ago and had run away with the baby. I suspect she knows where Violet is, although she denied it, of course.'

At that, Mother slams her fist onto the arm of the sofa. 'She can't deny it. I will demand that she tells me. We must go there now. Mary, get Philip.'

'I will drive you,' says Doctor Bradbury.

'Very well, let's go then,' says Mother.

They both leave in the doctor's car. Their tea goes cold, untouched on the side table, next to the ceramic vase. I sit in the silence and wait for their return, which comes sooner than I expected.

I know as soon as I see Mother's face that the news is not good. The doctor doesn't stay. I greet Mother at the door. I want to ask her how the visit has gone, whether she has news of Violet, but I am afraid of the answer. In any event, I find that Mother isn't in the mood for talking. Before I say anything, she shakes her head and simply says that Violet has gone.

Chapter Thirty-Four
January 1909 – Mary

The expected delivery from the greengrocers never arrived. I assume that the long-standing relationship between my family and the local business is now over. I can't imagine that they will be asked to deliver to us again, and I can't imagine that they will want to. Last night, after Mother arrived back from her visit to them and sequestered herself away in her bedroom, I told her that I needed some air and walked into the village for some bread, cheese, and milk. The larder was already stocked with tea, although in all honesty, I was desperate to open one of Father's precious bottles of wine. I made cheese sandwiches for dinner and took Mother's upstairs on a tray with a pot of tea, but when I opened the door, about to tell her she needed to eat something, she waved me away.

This morning, Mother tells me about the conversation she and the doctor had had with the greengrocer and his wife. She says they repeated what their impudent daughter, Clara, had told the doctor, which is that they have no idea where Violet is. Mother says the woman was quite rude and dismissive. She tried to make Mother believe that they didn't know Violet very well. She insisted they had only met her a handful of times. Mother accused her of telling lies. She accused the whole family of telling lies, Clara and Billy, too, and of harbouring a criminal. She told them that Violet had stolen money from them and she intended to inform the police and have her arrested. She warned them the police would search their shop and their home for any signs of the fugitive and they would be in big trouble if Violet was found on their premises.

Doctor Bradbury had pulled her out of the shop then, before she made any more of a scene. I suspect we are already the source of much gossip.

I am convinced that the greengrocers know where Violet is, of course they do, although I won't admit so to Mother. Violet could have been upstairs in their apartment at the very time Mother was venting her frustration and anger in their shop. But, considering their point of view, and considering what I would do in their position, I can't blame them. They are of the view that they are doing the right thing. They are protecting a vulnerable young mother and her baby. Keeping them together. Protecting her from the bad people who live in the big house. Protecting her from us.

Mother says she can never forgive them.

Doctor Bradbury, too, she says, isn't as innocent as he makes out. She says she won't find it so easy to forgive him, and neither will Father.

'He has been paid a substantial amount of money for his services, and for his discretion,' she says. 'And yet he still rejected any suggestion that he may have been at fault for not keeping an eye on Violet's movements.'

I persuade Mother that we should go back home. Lakeview Cottage in the winter is no fun. Even though I am closer to James here in Bowness, I desperately want to go home. We plan to set off at first light tomorrow, as long as the roads are free from ice.

*

James arrived this morning just before lunch and is now reading the newspaper on one of the sofas in the drawing room.

'I can't stop thinking about Violet' I say. 'Wondering where she is, and how she is.'

'My father doesn't know where she is,' says James.

'I know. That isn't what I mean.' I can feel tension building between us and part of me wishes he had stayed at home. 'It was such a horrible transaction. It should never have happened. A poor housemaid should never have been put in the position of having to give up her baby simply because she couldn't afford to keep it.'

James murmurs his agreement, but continues to read.

I wonder how Violet coped with living in here during the bitter winter months on her own, knowing that she was about to make the worst decision of her life at the end of her pregnancy. I don't know how she was able to bear it. Even though Clara is the person who undoubtedly now stands between us and Violet, I am glad that Violet found a friend who loves her enough to protect her. Secretly, although I will never admit it to anyone, I am proud of Violet for being brave enough to keep her baby.

'I think I'll go for a walk,' I say.

James has been reading quietly for the past hour. Nobody in the house feels like talking much. Lunch passed in silence, except for the occasional request to pass the salt or pour

255

more tea, but I cannot concentrate on reading. I walk over to the bookcase and slot my unread book back into its place.

'Are you sure you want to go in this rain?' he says.

'Yes, I've got a coat and a decent hat.'

'I'll come with you,' he says. He closes the newspaper and folds it in half.

'I'll be fine on my own,' I say. 'I just need some fresh air and a walk.'

'No. I'm coming with you. I know you're upset about Violet. Unless you would prefer to stay here and have a glass of wine, or a gin and tonic. What do you say?'

I smile at his attempt to cheer me. 'I'd say it's a little early for alcohol. I really would like to walk, if you don't mind.'

We put on our raincoats in the kitchen. I fasten a pink and red silk head scarf under my chin and top it with my hat, for double measure. James pushes a dark grey fedora hat on his head. As we set off walking, I slip my arm through his as he holds the umbrella over us both.

'Your mother seems upset by all of this, doesn't she? I'm shocked,' says James.

'Are you really?'

We reach the end of the driveway and James stops, one hand on the gate. He looks at me. 'Yes, I wouldn't have thought she would be so concerned about one of her servants.'

'Darling, that isn't why she's upset,' I tell him. 'She isn't worried about Violet's welfare. She's upset that she hasn't got her own way. This plan was her idea and it has fallen flat on its face. She feels humiliated, that's all.'

'Maybe you're right,' says James. He opens the gate. 'Come on, let's go to that nice cafe by the lake for a hot chocolate. I think we both need one.'

'In all honesty, I'd rather go and speak to Clara. It's only a short walk up the hill. I just want to ask her if Violet is all right and to pass on my best wishes.'

James agrees, and within fifteen minutes, we reach the greengrocers shop. James shakes the umbrella, closes it, and we both go inside. There is a small queue of three customers, so I pick up a basket, fill it with half a dozen apples, a few potatoes, and a large bunch of carrots, and wait behind them. When we reach the front of the queue, I put the basket on the counter.

'I know who you are. You're not welcome here,' says the man behind the counter. I presume this is Clara's dad.

'Can we speak to Clara? Please. Just for a moment,' I say.

The man shakes his head vehemently. 'No. Your mother has already been here, shouting and making demands. Clara doesn't want to speak to anybody,' he says. 'This business is nothing to do with us. Violet isn't here.'

'I just wanted to see how…'

'I suggest you leave now, while the shop is empty. Save yourself the embarrassment of being thrown out in front of other people.'

'I don't like your attitude, Mr…' James steps up towards the counter, but I put out my arm, holding him back. I can see that the older man is gripping the section of the counter that lifts up and within seconds, he could be beside us. I don't relish being manhandled out of the shop, into public disgrace, or worse. James doesn't appear to have noticed the way the man's fist is clenched, ready for action

257

'I don't care whether you like my attitude or not,' says the man. 'This is my shop...' The tinkle of the bell interrupts his tirade. 'Hello, Mrs Woodplumpton, and how are you today?'

'Very well thank you, dear.' An old lady wearing a long black raincoat and a broad-brimmed black hat enters the shop.

'Is it just your usual today?' asks the man.

'Yes please, dear,' she says. 'But you can serve your other customers first. I'm in no rush.' She takes her time untying the ribbon of her hat with arthritic fingers, removes it, and shakes off the excess rainwater. She sits down on a wooden chair near the counter and smiles at us.

'Don't worry, Mrs Woodplumpton, I will be with you in a moment. These kind people are just leaving.'

The man lifts the flap in the counter, marches over to the door, and pulls it open. A blast of rain shoots into the shop, soaking the floor around his feet.

James grabs me by the hand and leads me to the door. I trail after him, the groceries abandoned.

'Please tell Clara that we called,' I say. 'And could you please tell her to pass the message to Violet that I'm terribly sorry and that I would love to be able to talk to her?'

His frosty stare tells me that he will do no such thing.

'What an obnoxious man,' says James as soon as the door has closed behind us. He follows me along the narrow pavement. 'Wait for me, Mary. Don't you want the umbrella up?'

'I'm wet now, what does it matter?' I pull the collar of my coat tightly around my neck and shake drops of rain from the sodden collar. A burst of energy propels me down the hill. I no longer care if people see me walking ahead of James, with tears streaming down my face. The welcome rain allows me to cry. Months of anxiety and grief and hurt on behalf of my brother drip down my cheeks.

'We should have known that he would stop us from seeing her,' says James, as he jogs behind, using the pointed end of the umbrella as a walking stick with one hand while holding onto his hat with the other. 'Well, that's that then.'

I stop suddenly. 'That's that then, is that all you have to say on the matter?'

'Well, yes. I know Clara probably knows where Violet is, but now we seem to have lost the chance to speak to her, so what can we do?'

'So it's my fault we can't speak to her?'

'Mary, darling, keep your voice down.'

'I will not keep my voice down. How dare you blame me.'

'I'm not blaming you. I didn't say that I blame you, but...'

'But what?' I turn away from him and continue down the hill.

'I just think...'

'I don't care what you think, James. Let me tell you what *I* think.'

'Stop shouting, Mary, please.'

'I think that this whole sorry mess would not have happened but for your father. It's his fault. All of it.'

'My father?'

'Yes, that spineless, pathetic man could have done more. He should have done much more, and you know it, if you dared to admit it to yourself.'

'I had a feeling that you never liked my father, but isn't it a fraction too far to blame this on him? He wasn't the one who arranged the sale of the baby. Maybe the blame should be placed at the feet of your mother. It is her sorry mess, as you call it.'

'I'm not saying Mother isn't blameless in this, she certainly is not. But your father could have done more to find out where Violet was. Then we would at least have a chance of speaking to her and possibly reuniting her with Ernest.'

'That's utter hogwash. I'm sorry, Mary, but it is. How on earth would he have done that? He is a doctor, not a private detective.'

'He has a relationship with the greengrocer family. With all of them, but especially with the mother. He is their family doctor, isn't he?'

'Yes, he is, but…'

'So he should have done more to find out from them where Violet has run off to. How hard did he really try?'

'I don't know. Mary, slow down, please.'

'Why didn't he plead with her, the greengrocer, Clara's mother? He could have pleaded with her for more information.'

'I think he did everything he could.'

'How can you say that?' I increase my pace, determined to increase the gap between myself and James. I need to be alone. I should have insisted that James stayed behind with his book. I need some time by myself to calm my racing thoughts. It isn't like James and I to argue. He is my rock, my stalwart, the love of my life and I hate to argue with him. I shall tell him to go home. I will continue my walk around the lake until I feel calmer and then I can see him later. We can have a lovely dinner together when we have both calmed down.

'Mary, slow down! Mary! Wait!'

I can hear James' footsteps behind me as I approach the road. I am vaguely aware of fingers reaching out to grab the back of my coat. But I don't want to slow down. I need to walk, to expend my energy, so I shake him off.

As I step into the road, I hear the engine of the car, but I am not paying too much attention to it. The road is wet, visibility isn't good. I am not sure where the noise is coming from.

James lunges towards me. His fingers hook the belt of my coat.

'Mary! Stop!'

A screech of tyres. A blaring horn.

Someone screams.

A sickening crash.

I feel myself sprawling to the ground.

Then silence and darkness.

Chapter Thirty-Five
January 1909 – Violet

Clara's dad rushes into the living room where Clara and I are playing chess. Maggie is fast asleep in her basket at my feet, snuggled under the white blanket that Miss Mary sent for me last October (earlier, as I wrapped my baby daughter in the blanket for her sleep, I wondered whether Miss Mary envisaged that I would use it in this way). A welcoming fire crackles and spits and Clara and I are under strict instructions to throw as much coal onto it as we deem necessary. Clara's mum says that she doesn't want to be responsible for me catching a chill. Throughout the morning she has run breathlessly up the stairs at regular intervals from the shop to see that everything is all right, that we are warm enough, that Maggie is warm enough, that Clara is making sure I am taken care of, and my every whim is catered for.

'Dad, tell Mum that everything is fine, stop fussing,' says Clara, as the door crashes open.

'It's that Mary Compton,' he says.

'What, in the shop? Is she here?' I jump up and stand with my back to Maggie's basket, as though the Comptons are about to run up the stairs, pistols in hand, black masks over their eyes, and snatch her from me, like a highway robbery.

'No, no,' says Clara's dad. 'She's had an accident.'

He tells us that she came into the shop to see me no more than fifteen minutes ago with a young man, and he asked them to leave. Moments later, the news arrived, courtesy of a regular customer who likes to keep her finger on the pulse of the village, that Mary Compton had walked into the road and had been knocked down by a car.

'How is she? Don't tell me she's dead,' I say. I couldn't bear it if Ernest lost his sister. I know how close they are. He would be distraught.

'No, she's not dead. Mrs Goodman said that the young man was looking after her and someone had run for the doctor. She was knocked out at first, out cold, lying in the road like a wet lettuce, she said. But she soon came round and she was sitting up by the time Mrs Goodman came to the shop to relay the tale. Apparently, quite a crowd had gathered. I thought you'd like to know, is all. Now then, Clara, your mum says have you made sure Violet has had enough to eat?'

I pat my still-swollen stomach. 'I couldn't eat another thing, really, Clara is looking after me perfectly.' I turn away from Clara's concerned look and pretend to be fussing with Maggie's blanket so she doesn't see my tears. I don't know why I care. About Miss Mary. About Ernest. About any of them. None of the Comptons have served me well, but as I tuck the blanket around Maggie, I am filled with concern about the young woman only a year or so older than me. She hasn't been unkind. She didn't need to buy me a blanket or organise a cake to be made for me. She didn't need to give me one of her coats either. I could tell it was her way of helping when she knew I was trapped in an unfortunate situation, as her mother called it.

Despite everything, the Compton family remains the best thing to have happened to me. They have given me Maggie, so how can I possibly feel any bitterness towards them? I can't begin to fathom what Mrs Compton and her sister were thinking when they came up with the idea of making me an offer to buy my baby, but in all honesty, I can see that they thought they were doing the right thing. They have never been poor and they probably think it is the worst thing in the world. They see our tiny houses, packed with too many people and they probably shudder. What they don't see is the love that surrounds us. The evenings spent by the fire, chatting and laughing.

As I gaze at Maggie now, I wonder what life would be like for her if she was brought up by Mrs Comptons' sister and her husband. There is no doubt that she would have a privileged life. In the winter months, she would sleep comfortably in a warm bedroom with a roaring fire, rather than wrapped up like a cocoon, cold to the bone despite three or four blankets, sometimes waking to greet ice on the inside of the windows. In the spring, she would begin pony riding classes. Maybe she would have her own pony and later, as she grows taller, her own horse. She would choose a white mare, with black socks. Her nanny would stand and watch as the mare would carry Maggie effortlessly on her back around the field, and possibly around the grounds of Compton Hall when she was taken to visit.

'Violet, are you okay?'

I haven't realised that Clara's dad has left us, gone back to the shop, and we are alone again. 'Yes, I'm fine, thank you.'

'Lost in thoughts?' she says. She puts her arm around my waist and rests her head on my shoulders. 'Do you want to share them? Is it Mary Compton you're worried about? I don't think she dare come back.'

'No, it isn't that,' I say. 'I was just thinking about Maggie and wondering whether I have done the right thing.'

'What, by keeping her?' Clara looks appalled. 'Of course, you have done the right thing.'

'For me, yes. But for her?'

'Yes, yes, yes,' says Clara. 'And I don't ever want you to think otherwise ever again. Understand me?'

'Yes, yes, yes,' I say. I laugh. 'I just needed to hear a voice of reason. Sometimes I am guilty of allowing my thoughts to run amock.'

'She will be the luckiest girl in the world having you as her mum. She doesn't need all the wealth and trappings that the Comptons can give her.'

I nod. 'I had an amazingly happy childhood, and my sisters and my brother are happy. I just over-think and…'

'And you're doubting yourself? That's okay. But this little lady here will have the love of two resilient and self-sufficient women. She will be fine. More than fine, in fact.'

'Now I feel guilty for wondering what if,' I say.

Clara kisses me on the cheek and gathers the tea cups. I follow her into the kitchen as she piles them into the sink to wash. As the water fills the bowl, I remember watching my mother in the kitchen at home. She is a talented cook. At the weekend, on a cold and wet day, my mum and dad would sit at the kitchen table on a Sunday after church while a chicken or a piece of pork roasted in the oven, and they would chat for hours, while I sat next to them piecing together a jigsaw puzzle. 'All I want for Maggie is for her to have the same happy childhood memories that I have,' I say.

'And she will do,' says Clara.

'I'd like to go and see Miss Mary,' I say.

Clara shoots around. 'What? Why?'

I shrug. 'I'd like to talk to her, thank her for the blanket and the coat.'

'Don't be ridiculous.' Clara turns back to the sink and scrubs at one of the plates with more vigour than is necessary.

'Who's being ridiculous?' asks Clara's mum. 'I've come to check on you, everything all right here?'

'Yes, thank you,' I say. 'I was just saying that I'd like to go to Lakeview Cottage and speak to Miss Mary.'

'Mary,' says Clara. 'Just call her Mary. You don't work for them anymore and she's not your teacher.'

'Clara,' says her mum, with a warning edge to her voice. She moves her hand up and down as though patting the head of an invisible large dog and Clara seems to take this as a sign to be quiet. She looks at me. 'Why do you want to do that?' she asks.

'I think I'd like to return the money, the hundred pounds. Clara, I know what you're going to say.' Clara pinches her lips together, forcing her opinions to stay locked away. 'But I'm sitting here as though I'm a prisoner, like I've done something wrong, hiding from the Comptons, pretending I've run away, when all I want to do is go for a walk and sit by the lake with my baby.'

'You can do that when they've gone home,' says Clara.

'Maybe I can, but then what if Doctor Bradbury sees me and he tells them that I'm still here? Mrs Compton said she would get the police to come and arrest me. She would tell them that I had stolen the money.'

'Well you haven't stolen it,' says Clara.' She gave it to you.'

'In exchange for a child,' I say. 'And anyway, who would the police believe?' I take a deep breath. 'I've made up my mind, I want to give it back to her and tell her that Maggie is mine and I'm keeping her. I've got some money saved. I haven't spent anything while I've been here. Mrs Compton has paid for all my food and for the coal.'

'Well good for her,' says Clara.

'I agree, actually,' says Clara's mum. 'Free your conscience and then you don't have to run away. Would you like me to take the money to her? I can post it through the door, I won't speak to her. You can write them a note and explain who it's from.'

'Thank you, but I'd like to go up there myself. I can't take Maggie, obviously, so would you please look after her for me?'

'I'd be delighted,' says Clara's mum. 'But you can't walk. You had a baby less than a week ago. A dizzy spell could overcome you at any moment. Wait until the shop is closed and Clara's dad will take you up on the cart. He can wait for you and bring you back.'

I look at Clara and wait for her to smile at me and nod her agreement, but she busies herself wiping the pots with the tea towel and slamming them down on the dresser.

Chapter Thirty-Six
January 1909 – Violet

By the time we arrive at Lakeview Cottage, it is dark. Clara's dad is waiting for me on the road at the bottom of the drive. The old horse could do with a walk, he had told me as he helped me down from the cart. I am comforted by the fact that I know he will be nearby, leading the horse up and down and looking out for my return. He told me to take as long as I want, but now that I am here, I want the visit to be over. I want to run through the gates and beg him to take me back to their house, back to Maggie and Clara and young Billy. Maybe Clara was right. I don't owe the Comptons anything and I don't need to be here to give them an explanation.

I raise my hand to knock on the front door, but hesitate, my clenched fist in the air inches away from the huge brass knocker that I have polished so many times.

I can hear Clara's voice reminding me to be strong and reminding me that I am not their employee any longer and they have no right to talk to me as though I am. As I was getting ready to leave to come here, putting on my coat and boots in the living room, I could hear Clara in the kitchen muttering to her mum about how the Comptons have treated me badly, used me as a receptacle for a baby. Clara's mum speaks softly and I could not hear what she said without putting my ear to the door, but then I heard Clara tell her that they are horrible people and they have put their needs before mine and have taken advantage of the fact that I earn a low wage and have little prospects. Clara's mum's response was probably something along the lines of, 'Don't start getting political in front of your father. You know he doesn't like it.' I smiled as I listened to mother and daughter, and the love between them made my heart contract with love for my own daughter and for my mother.

I knock lightly on the front door and take a step back. I am beginning to sweat and I unbutton my coat, which is too tight over my stomach, thankful for the cold air that wraps around my neck. I am about to turn around and walk away, back down the driveway, when the door opens a crack. Philip's long shadow reaches for me along the ground, and I take another step back.

He laughs at me maniacally. 'Well, well, well, look what the cat dragged in.'

'That's not the right saying,' I say, feeling brave. 'There is no cat here and I'm not in.'

He scrunches up his eyes and grips the door frame with bony fingers. 'No, damn right you're not in. Clear off before you upset the mistress more than you already have.'

'Your fingernails need cutting,' I say.

'How dare you!'

'Philip, who is it?' I hear a male voice that I don't recognise.

'Just a peddler, sir,' says Philip. 'She'll be on her way now.'

'It's me, Violet,' I shout as loud as I can before Philip has time to close the door. I want Miss Mary to hear me and Mrs

Compton. I don't want my way to be blocked by Philip and the unknown man. I need to speak to them.

Suddenly the door is yanked from Philip's grasp and a man stands in the doorway. He is illuminated from behind by the light in the hallway, but I can clearly see from the likeness to Doctor Bradbury that he is his son. This must be James.

'Mr Bradbury, please can I have a word with the family?' He stares at me and looks behind me as if he checking who else is with me. Maybe he is searching for the baby. 'I am alone.' I tell him.

'Philip I can deal with this, thank you,' he says. Philip shoots me one last dagger before turning on his heel and walking towards the kitchen. 'Mrs Compton is resting upstairs, and so is Mary. She had rather a nasty accident this morning.'

'Yes, I heard. Is she all right?'

He nods. 'She will be covered in magnificent bruises by tomorrow and she sustained a bump to her head, but other than that, yes thank you.'

I glance up at the window to the master bedroom. I can see now that there is a pale light in the room and I imagine Mrs Compton propped up in bed, her head resting on the feather pillows. There is so much I want to say. Anger slowly rises inside me. No, it's not anger. It's injustice. What has caused Mrs Compton to take to her bed 'to rest'? She isn't tired. She is being self-indulgent. She has no idea what it is like to survive the daily grind of families like mine. Every day is a constant reminder of dreams deferred and opportunities missed. Men spend their last pennies in the local pub in an attempt to forget. Women don't allow

270

themselves the luxury, as they scrub and scrub until their fingers bleed. Yet here is Mrs Compton, in her second home, resting because she hasn't got her own way.

'Is Mrs Compton ill, too?' I ask. 'Has she caught a fever, or has she exerted herself with housework? I only ask because Philip answered the door, which means there is no maid to serve her.' I look over to the car which is parked at the side of the driveway. 'You would struggle to get four people plus luggage in that car all the way from Compton Hall.'

I can tell Mr Bradbury doesn't know how to respond. I am being impudent and I should be frogmarched from the premises, but he knows that Miss Mary wants to speak to me, Mrs Compton, too, if she could be bothered coming down the stairs.

'You had better come in,' he says. 'We are letting all the warm air out.' I step into the hallway and he closes the door behind me. 'Wait there.' He dashes up the stairs.

The door to the kitchen is ajar and I can see Philip eavesdropping. There is no light in the kitchen, so I cannot see his face, and I don't want to. I don't need to see his expression to know what he will be thinking. Within a minute, Mr Bradbury tiptoes back down the stairs.

'Mary would like to see you,' he whispers. 'But I am warning you, she mustn't be upset. Do you hear me?'

I nod and resist the urge to slap the finger pointing in my face. *You don't work for them anymore* I can hear Clara's voice in my head, giving me the courage I need to face this family for the last time. Mr Bradbury turns and walks back up the stairs and I follow him.

He turns left at the top and knocks gently on Miss Mary's bedroom door. I strain my eyes to see down the landing towards the master bedroom, but it is too dark. Mr Bradbury opens the bedroom door and then stands to the side to allow me in.

'You've got ten minutes,' he says.

'James, really,' says Miss Mary. 'It's all right. Bring Violet a drink will you, please? Violet, would you like a drink? Some tea? Water?'

'No, thank you, miss,' I say. My curtsy comes before I remember that Clara told me not to do it. *Don't you dare curtsy* were her exact words. It's an automatic response. But it's no matter. Miss Mary is one of the nice ones and she is worthy of some respect. 'I'm sorry to hear about your accident, miss.'

She touches the side of her head and winces. 'It was my own stupid fault. James and I were arguing and I didn't look. The poor driver, he was distraught. He thought he'd killed me.' She smiles but her face is so full of sadness that any mirth doesn't stand a chance. 'Sit down, please.' She points to a ladder back chair near the window. 'Pull it closer to the bed.' I drag the chair across the thick carpet and sit down. 'I am so glad you came,' she says.

The tears come unexpectedly and suddenly I am sobbing. Miss Mary clambers out of bed and grabs a facecloth from her dressing table. She hands it to me. I cover my face, resting my elbows on my knees, and sob and sob. She sits on the side of the bed and rubs my back, telling me that everything will be okay. Her tenderness creates more tears until eventually I sit up and take a deep breath.

'I'm sorry, miss,' I say. 'I didn't mean to cry like that. It's just been…'

'I know,' she says. There are tears in her eyes, too. 'It's been an emotional time.'

'You should be in bed, miss, after your accident. If Mr Bradbury comes back and sees you perched on the edge like this, he'll have my guts for garters.'

She laughs and says that she can deal with him and that I shouldn't worry. For a moment, we don't speak. The mantel clock ticks loudly.

'I can't stay long, miss,' I say. 'Clara's dad is waiting for me outside with the cart. He brought me here.' I fold the face cloth into a tiny square and place it on the bed in front of me.

'There is so much I wanted to say to you, Violet.' Miss Mary reaches for my hand and I allow her to take it. She holds it tight and I find my fingers wrapping around hers. 'But now that you're here, I don't know what to say. I presume you're keeping your baby?' I nod. 'And that's good, that's good, that's how it should be.'

'Really?'

'Yes, of course. A baby should be with its mother.'

'What about her father?'

Tears fall onto Miss Mary's cheek. She picks up the facecloth with her free hand and dabs at them. 'Ernest loves you, you know that, don't you? If things were different…'

'Yes, if things were different, I know. He doesn't love me enough though, does he?'

'Oh, but he does. He tells me everything, and he told me that he loves you.'

'But he loves Lucille, too?'

She shrugs. She drops my hand and rolls the facecloth into a tight ball. 'I need to get back into bed, in case James comes to check on me.' She walks around to the other side of the bed and climbs in. I resist the temptation to straighten the covers around her. She flops her head onto the pillow and closes her eyes. She is still crying, but I am not entirely sure why.

'Miss Mary, I want to give you something, to give to your mother if you wouldn't mind.'

'What is it?' She opens her eyes and sits up straight.

'I have the money that she gave me for the baby.' I pull out the envelope from my pocket and hold it out towards her.

'No, no.' She pushes it back. 'You keep it. You're going to need that money.'

'I'm not taking it,' I say. 'If you don't take it off me, I'll go and knock on your mother's bedroom door and give it to her myself.'

'But why?'

'Because she will tell the police that I stole it.'

'She wouldn't…'

'You know she would, miss. She told me she would. But apart from that, I want to be free. I don't want to look over my shoulder every minute of the day and live in fear that she would come and take Maggie from me, because she has paid for her.'

Miss Mary rests her right palm over her heart. 'You called her Maggie?'

'Yes, after my mother.'

'That's a lovely name.'

We both smile, but then I want to cry again. I leave the envelope on the bed. It sits there quietly judging us. The root of all evil in crisp pound notes.

'Where will you go?' she asks.

'I have two choices,' I say. 'Back to Manchester to live at home, or I can go to London and stay with Clara somewhere.'

'You're tempted to go to London, aren't you? I can see by the way your face lit up when you said it just then.'

'I am tempted, yes, but don't ever tell Clara. She'll be insufferable. I need a little time to think, that's all.' We both know that Miss Mary and Clara would never have a conversation, but she zips her mouth closed nevertheless.

'Is it all right if I tell Ernest that I've seen you? He will want to know that you're well and that the baby is well.'

'Yes, of course.'

'Can I tell him where to reach you?'

I shake my head. 'I would rather you didn't.'

'He might want to write, or…'

'I don't want to see him, miss.'

'You don't?'

'I never thought I would say it, but I don't love him anymore. I'm sorry, miss, I know he's your brother and everything, but he didn't treat me well and, well, I just don't love him. He left for Oxford without speaking to me and I don't care how much he insists he didn't have time, he did have time. He could have come to find me. He managed to find me plenty of times when he wanted me for other things before then.'

Miss Mary looks down and picks at the threads on the blanket. 'I am sorry, Violet, honestly, I am.'

'What do you have to be sorry for, miss?'

'I am sorry for the way you were treated by my parents. They should never have kept you and Ernest apart. Mother lied to Ernest and told him that you had run away, which is why he didn't try and find you.'

'Yes, he told me that, but if that was the case, why didn't he write to me at my parents' house, or get the train to Manchester and turn up on my doorstep with a bunch of daffs?'

'Roses, he could afford roses.' She laughs.

'Yes, roses. My home address would have been written down somewhere in your father's study. Surely he kept a list of all his staff. All he had to do was spend a little time searching for it. Anyway, it's all good now, so I'd better be on my way.' I stand up and straighten my coat. 'Thank you for this coat, miss. It served me well until my belly grew too big, and then I wore one of Clara's mum's.'

'Thank you for coming to see me,' she says. 'I can promise you, Mother won't be any trouble. I will talk to her tomorrow and tell her that she needs to leave you alone to get on with your life. Maggie is your baby and you shouldn't worry that she will be taken from you.'

'That's all I want, miss, that reassurance. Thank you.' I take the chair back to its original position under the window. I part the curtains an inch and peep through the window. The driveway is pitch black but I can see Clara's dad and the cart waiting for me under the orange glow of the street lamp. I feel sad that this will be the last time that I shall look through one of the windows of this beautiful house from the inside. I wish I had come during the day when I would be able to see the lake.

'Violet, before you go, please take this.' Miss Mary, having climbed out of bed whilst my back was turned, holds out a stack of pound notes. 'You will need some money to help with your move to London. Please take this, as my gift.'

'I can't take that, miss.' I look at the envelope on the bed.

'Oh no, this money isn't from that envelope,' she says. 'This is my money. From me to my niece. Please take it. Look.' She holds the envelope up with her other hand and I can see the money still inside. 'See, this money is mine and I'd like you to have it. I will give your money back to Mother and you don't ever have to think about it again.'

Chapter Thirty-Seven
July 1950 - Mary

On Sunday morning, I walk to St Martin's church in Bowness after breakfast for the Eucharist service. The vicar is waiting at the door, welcoming the parishioners as they arrive.

'Mary, how lovely to see you again,' he says. 'You're here for good now, I believe?'

'Yes, we're settled and unpacked,' I say.

'I'm delighted,' he says. 'It will be lovely to see you more often in church.'

I wander into the church, grateful for the cool shelter away from the summer sun. It is going to be a hot day today, I can tell. There are no clouds in the sky and no breeze. I left James in the garden with a full pot of tea and a bar of Kendal Mint Cake, together with strict instructions to keep Samson, our young labrador, out of the sun. He laughed and told me that it was as easy as keeping the waves from the shore, but he would do his best. Lucille is with him, visiting us for a week or so.

I collect a hymn book from the pile at the back of the church and I am about to sit down when I see Margaret, a young lady I met in The Lilac Tearoom last week. She is sitting in a full pew, so I simply wave at her, mouth hello, and settle in a pew on the other side of the church. After the service, I catch up with her in the doorway, just as she is leaving.

'Margaret, hello, how lovely to see you,' I say. 'Are you staying for a cup of tea?'

'Hello, Mary, isn't it?' she says. 'I wasn't planning to, but...'

'Oh, that's a shame.'

'Well, I suppose I can spare a few minutes,' she says.

'Wait there, I will go and get you one.' I rush to the back of the church and a few minutes later, return with a cup of steaming tea. Two biscuits are balanced on the saucer. 'I wasn't sure if you take sugar?'

'No, I don't,' says Margaret. 'But thank you for the biscuits. They are always welcome. Do you think we could take our drinks outside? It seems a shame to be in a dark church when it's so sunny.'

'Yes, that's a good idea,' I say. 'We have so little sunshine, we need to make the most of it.' I lead her outside to a wooden bench tucked away behind the front door of the church, overlooking the lake and we sit down.

'This landscape is so beautiful, isn't it? It is just waiting to be painted.'

'Oh, yes, I remember you said you liked to paint,' I say. 'You will have plenty of inspiration around here. Is that what you love to paint the most, landscapes and nature?'

'Yes I do, but at home I usually do portraits. They have become very popular in recent years and I have managed to make a small business for myself. I have been quite busy.'

'That's wonderful. What kind of people sit for you? Are they families, children?'

'Not necessarily,' says Margaret. 'I mean, asking a child to sit still for a couple of minutes is a challenge, never mind a couple of hours. I do mostly couples and sometimes people on their own.'

'That is fascinating. I would love to have a talent like that,' I say. 'I'm not creative at all. When artistic talent was given out in our family, my brother got my share, I'm afraid. He loved to paint and draw.'

Margaret smiles. 'I am extremely lucky,' she says. 'I have always loved painting and it was my dream to do it for a living. It all came about as a stroke of luck. My husband is a solicitor and one day, a client of his noticed a painting hanging on the wall in his office. He asked my husband who the artist was and couldn't believe it when Edward said that it was one of mine. The client happens to be an art dealer and the owner of a gallery in Camden. He said that he was always on the lookout for new talent, and well, one thing led to another. I did an exhibition of the paintings that I had already done and then people began asking me to paint for them and before I knew it, I had a waiting list of customers.'

'I am so impressed,' I say. 'I can't wait to tell my husband that I have met a real-life artist.'

A gentle blush sits on Margaret's cheeks and she tells me that beauty is in the eye of the beholder, especially in the art world. I tell her immediately that if she is trying to say her paintings are not beautiful, I won't hear of it. Being humble is one thing, but you also shouldn't hide your light under a bushel. As we sip our drinks, the conversation moves on to chit-chat about the local area, which shops sell the nicest dresses, which butcher has the best reputation, and which school might be the most suitable for Margaret's eleven-year-old son.

That flash of sadness that I spotted in the tearoom appears again around Margaret's eyes and I wonder whether, despite her protestations about loving Cumberland so much, Margaret's heart is still in London after all. Most likely with her husband, who she told me is still there while she spends a few weeks with her family.

'Will your husband be joining you?' I ask. 'You must miss him.'

Margaret nods. 'Yes, I do. They say absence makes the heart grow fonder, don't they?' she says. 'I have realised that I am missing my husband more and more, which is a good thing, I suppose. It hasn't been easy lately. I am afraid that this time apart might evolve into something more permanent. I'm sorry, I'm sorry, I shouldn't be telling you any of this.'

'No, it's me who should apologise. I didn't mean to pry when I asked about your husband.' I sip my tea.

'We're separated, you see,' she says suddenly. 'I think you would call it a trial separation, at least that's what I wanted to call it.'

'And is that what your husband would like to call it?' I ask.

'I'm not sure,' she says. 'I haven't spoken to him for two weeks now.'

'I'm sorry to hear that. If you need someone to talk to, I'm a good listener,' I say.

So, she tells me about the arguments between her and her husband, the silent dinners followed by frosty evenings when neither of them wanted to talk. Initially, neither of them would admit that there were cracks in their marriage.

When they eventually decided to face the problems, each one blamed the other. Margaret said that it was Edward's fault for not allowing her the freedom to be an artist. The busier she became, the more he resented it. Edward said that it was her fault for neglecting him and their son. The busier she became, the more time she spent away from them. Margaret told him that she had spent ten years being a housewife and a full-time mother and she wanted more from life. Their son was not a baby anymore. She didn't need to be at home all the time. But what about me? Edward had shouted. What about me? Margaret had shouted back. After another two weeks of stepping around each other's feelings, she decided to come to Cumberland for a break. She is staying with family, she tells me.

'I thought that when I told him I was coming up here, he would beg me not to,' she says. 'But he didn't. He barely looked up from the newspaper. He let me leave the house with hardly a goodbye. He didn't even carry my bags to the door.'

'Perhaps he was hurt,' I say.

'Yes, possibly. I hadn't actually thought of that. He is a gentle, caring soul. I suppose he could have been putting on a brave face, not showing his emotions.'

'Yes, men tend to do that, don't they?' I say.

'Oh, you're there, Mum. I've been looking for you. Uncle Billy will have lunch ready, remember, he asked us to be back by twelve-thirty?.'

'Okay, darling, I'm ready now. Mary, this is my son, Edward, named after his father. Everyone calls him Teddy.'

Standing in the churchyard is a handsome boy in a smart black suit, and a white shirt. The tie which he was previously wearing is tied around his wrist. I stare at him and take in his dark hair, the shape of his nose, his mischievous grin. There is something so very familiar about him, although we have only just met.

'Pleased to meet you,' says the boy politely. He holds out his right hand and I shake it. Then he turns and runs back inside the church.

*

The walk back to Lakeview Cottage takes just a few minutes. Samson gives me a warm welcome and I present him with a biscuit that I carefully wrapped in paper before I left this morning and kept in the top of my handbag. It's our little game. He seems to enjoy a biscuit from my handbag much more than one from the cupboard. James opens the back door and Samson takes his biscuit onto the lawn.

'Isn't this place beautiful in the summer?' says Lucille. 'The garden is just perfect.' She stands in the kitchen doorway and watches Samson devour his biscuit. When he runs back to her hoping that someone might have another one, she picks up his ball from where he had left it next to one of the plant pots and throws it onto the grass.

'Would you like tea, darling, or can I tempt either of you ladies with a gin and tonic?' asks James.

I look at the clock on the kitchen wall. 'It is technically afternoon now.'

'Then it would be rude not to,' says Lucille.

James goes into the dining room and prepares three large glasses of gin and tonic. By the time he carries them back to the kitchen, I have sliced a lemon. I add a sliver to each glass and we carry the drinks outside to the patio area and settle at a round wooden table. A faint scent of lavender envelops the garden. The bees add a gentle background hum. Lucille closes her eyes and breathes deeply.

'I fell in love with Ernest right here,' she says. 'Did you know that? December 1908.'

'Yes, I suspect you did,' I say. 'That first Christmas, I could tell you adored him, even though you hadn't known him long.'

Lucille smiles and sips her gin and tonic. I can feel emotion welling up inside me and swallow it down. For some reason, I am missing Ernest more than ever. Maybe it is because I can't tell him we have finally moved out of Compton Hall. He would have been happy for us and we could have reminisced over shared childhood memories of our beloved summer home. We clink our glasses together and sit in companionable silence for a few minutes, listening to the birdsong and watching the dog as he plays with his ball.

'I have arranged a surprise for us,' I say after a few moments.

'Oh how wonderful,' says Lucille. 'Are we going on a trip? On the ferry perhaps?'

'No,' I say. 'Although we can certainly do that one day. Do you remember the artist that I told you about last week, the one I chatted to in The Lilac Tearoom?'

'Yes, I do.'

'Well, I bumped into her at church. We had a nice chat outside after the service, and she said that she didn't have any plans for this week, so I have arranged for her to come to the cottage tomorrow afternoon and do a portrait for us. I thought it would be nice to have one of you and me in the garden, with the backdrop of the roses.'

'Yes, that would be lovely,' says Lucille. She gazes at the collection of rose bushes that have flourished at Lakeview Cottage for years. The various roses, baby pink, bright white, yellow, and blood red are at their best in July. 'The rose garden is in the sun though. You know how my shoulders burn if I'm not careful.'

'You don't need to worry about that,' I say. 'The artist can paint us right here in the shade, and then she can add the background around us. I have already discussed that with her. The other option would be to sit indoors and maybe have the fireplace as a background. Or somewhere else?'

'No, the rose garden would be perfect,' says Lucille. 'Thank you for organising that. It's such a thoughtful thing to do.'

I don't tell Lucille that I didn't organise the sitting solely for our benefit, but because I felt sorry for the artist. As we chatted in the churchyard, Margaret seemed to be shrouded with melancholy and I felt it would be good for her to do something that she loved. Something that would bring her joy. For an hour or so, she will have something to take her mind off her arguments with her husband.

I tell Lucille that she can sit by herself if she prefers, and then maybe she can give the portrait to her daughter, Beatrice, as a gift, but Lucille insists that she wants me in the painting too. Two sisters-in-law together, she tells me. She has the perfect place for it in her apartment at Compton Hall, she says, in the sitting room next to the window where she likes to sit and read. I agree that it will look beautiful

285

there. We begin to discuss whether we should ask the artist to paint all the roses the same colour, or whether they should be just as they are, naturally clashing.

James takes our glasses back inside to refill with more gin.

'Actually, I don't think you need to worry about your shoulders catching the sun,' he says on his return. 'Have you seen the rain clouds? It is certainly turning chilly.'

Lucille, equally anxious about getting her hair wet as she is about getting sunburned, hastily retreats indoors. I follow her inside.

Chapter Thirty-Eight
July 1950 - Mary

Margaret arrives at the house shortly after lunch. Once again, dark clouds have gathered and the threat of a sudden storm of torrential rain has kept us inside. We are settled in the bay window of the sitting room and watch as Margaret drives up the driveway and parks her car at the front of the house.

'That's a very expensive vehicle for a young woman,' says Lucille. 'Is her husband wealthy?'

'I suppose he is,' I say. 'She said he's a solicitor, so I presume he is well paid. That's not their car though. It belongs to her uncle.'

'How do you know that?'

'I asked her how she would get here and offered to go and collect her, but she said that her uncle had offered his car to her, to use whenever she wanted.'

'Well, still, it's a very nice car,' says Lucille. 'I wonder why her husband isn't with her. It seems strange to spend so much time apart, especially in the summer. It's the best time of the year.'

'Yes, I agree,' I say. 'But maybe it's just because he couldn't spare the time off work.' I don't want to tell Lucille about the private conversation I had with Margaret in the churchyard; she is such a gossip.

'I'll go and let her in, shall I?' says James.

'Oh thank you, James,' I say.

'Do you remember when we used to have a butler to answer the door at Compton Hall?' says Lucille.

'Yes, and maids everywhere,' I say, laughing. 'It's a wonder we grew up able to do anything for ourselves.'

Lucille is no longer listening. She is staring out of the window.

'Gosh, she has a look of Beatrice about her, don't you think?' says Lucille.

'Well, I don't know, they both have dark hair, if that's what you mean.' I watch as the artist climbs out of her car and is greeted by James. 'Although Margaret's is a little lighter and her eyes are blue,' I say. 'I remember thinking what a beautiful vivid colour they were. Almost violet.'

Lucille doesn't reply. A flash of lightning crackles through the sky and is closely followed by a rumble of thunder and large splashes of rain. James dashes back into the house and, seconds later, re-emerges with a large umbrella which he holds over Margaret's head as she lifts the boot of the car and takes out an easel and a wooden box. James passes her the umbrella, takes the easel and the box from her, and carries them to the house. Then he dashes back outside and holds the umbrella over her once again whilst she carries a large canvas to the house. They close the door as another flash of lightning strikes over the lake.

'Gosh, where has that rain come from?' Margaret's voice floats from the hallway. 'It was bright sunshine five minutes ago. I expected to be painting in the garden today. I feel all discombobulated.' James laughs and offers to take her coat and hang it up.

I watch Lucille as her frown develops. Her smile has disappeared. Lucille has quite obviously decided that Margaret is beautiful and she doesn't like it.

I stand as Margaret is led into the room. I hold out my hand for her to shake and am taken aback when Margaret gives me a warm hug instead.

'Mary, how lovely to see you again,' she says. 'Is this your beautiful sister-in-law who you have told me so much about?' Margaret reaches her hand out to Lucille, who shakes it without standing.

'Pleased to meet you,' says Lucille. 'I'm Lucille.'

'And I'm Margaret,' says Margaret. 'But please call me Maggie. That's what my friends call me.'

'Maggie?' I say.

'Yes, short for Margaret. I know I introduced myself as Margaret. I thought it would signify a fresh start, new beginnings and all that, but I just can't get used to it. I've always been known as Maggie. Named after my grandmother.' She laughs. 'Thank you so much for asking me to paint for you. I have been excited to start this project, but now that I've seen your hair, Lucille, I'm even more excited. That colour! It's so striking.'

Lucille smiles and thanks her politely. She takes compliments in her stride and I hope that now Maggie has offered her one, Lucille will be happy. But as Maggie crouches on the floor and begins to unpack paints and brushes from the wooden box, Lucille doesn't take her eyes off her, scrutinising her like a prowling cat watching a mouse.

James takes Samson upstairs to his study, out of the way of the delicate pots of paint and I take myself into the kitchen to make some tea, leaving the two women alone in the sitting room. By the time I return, a large dust sheet has been spread on the floor and the easel has been set up. The blank canvas patiently awaits. I put the tray of tea onto the wide windowsill and Maggie directs me and Lucille to sit exactly where we were before, with the light from the window behind us.

'Is this location all right?' I ask.

'Yes, it's perfect,' says Maggie. 'It would be better if we were in the garden, as natural light is always best, but I can make a start in here today and maybe we can move to the garden tomorrow. There's clearly a storm on its way, so we're better off staying here. There you go, if you could put your hand there, Mary. Lucille, face that way a little. Wonderful.'

'Mary tells me that you are just visiting Bowness and that you originate from London,' says Lucille.

A cloud passes over Maggie's face, but she smiles again and it is gone as quickly as it arrived. 'Yes, that's right,' she says. 'I'm staying just up the road, with family.'

'How long are you planning to stay?' asks Lucille. 'The whole summer?'

'I'm not sure exactly,' says Maggie. 'I might stay a while longer yet. If I'm still here in September, Mary said she would help me to decide which school is best for my son, didn't you, Mary?'

'Yes, I did. There are a couple of extremely good ones around here.'

I am anxious to direct the conversation away from Maggie's private life, so I tell her in detail about the two schools in Windermere. I explain that, having not had children of my own, I have no direct knowledge of them, but I am good friends with the headmistress at one of the schools and the vicar's children go to the other school, so whichever one Maggie prefers will be a good choice, I am sure.

Lucille continues to watch Maggie as she paints.

'You look very much like my daughter,' she says suddenly. 'You could be sisters. She has lovely dark hair, just like yours.'

'Oh really?' says Maggie, self-consciously touching her hair. 'I would have loved a sister. I am an only child, I'm afraid.' Maggie dips her paintbrush in a tiny pot of water and then swirls the tip in a pot of red paint.

'She is around your age,' says Lucille. 'She is thirty-five.'

Maggie nods. 'I turned forty-one this year,' she says.

'Born in 1909?' asks Lucille.

'Yes, that's right.' says Maggie. 'January. I'm impressed by your quick calculations. Maths was never my favourite subject.'

I scowl at Lucille, willing her to stop. I want to kick her ankle under the table. I know what she is thinking. Ever since Violet's baby was born, Lucille has been looking for her everywhere. Every summer when we returned to Lakeview Cottage, she was convinced that Violet and her child had returned to the area and were somewhere close by. Initially, she glared at young mothers and peered into prams, inspecting each baby and, as the years passed, she stared at dark-haired girls in cafes and shops and asked me whether I thought they could be Ernest's daughter. I have long ago given up telling her to stop.

When we last spoke about it, I told Lucille that if Violet's child wanted to come to Bowness looking for her dad, which was understandable, she would have done it years ago. I told her that she needed to forget about Violet and her child. We all had to forget about them. Lucille pouted like a child who wasn't being listened to and told me that I didn't understand what it was like, knowing that your husband had fathered a child who might appear out of nowhere and throw a hand grenade into the heart of your family. I conceded that no, I didn't understand, and then I held Lucille as she cried, and told her not to worry about something that might never happen.

But Lucille is a worrier. She likes the attention that worrying brings.

'My daughter gets her colouring from her father,' says Lucille. 'He was very handsome. He had black hair. Do you take after your father?'

'My mother actually,' says Maggie. 'I think there are hundreds, if not thousands of us, with this colouring, aren't there? Dark hair, pale skin, blue eyes. I don't know about your husband's family, but my family is from Irish ancestry. My mother's family came over to England at the end of the last century.'

'And what about your father, is he of Irish descent too?' asks Lucille.

'I'm not sure,' says Maggie. 'It isn't something I have ever asked. He died before I was born.'

Maggie, seemingly unperturbed by Lucille's interrogation, concentrates on painting, her eyes dotting between the canvas, her paints, and her subjects. I watch Lucille, who watches Maggie. The frown has returned to

Lucille's face. I want to tell her that, as far as I know, there is no Irish blood in our family. We have dark hair because of some other reason; maybe a distant relative was Spanish, or maybe our ancestry goes back as far as the Romans, who knows? In any event, I want to tell Lucille to leave Maggie alone, stop pestering her, relax, and enjoy the sitting. Maggie has confirmed that her father died before she was born, so the subject can be closed. Like the dozens of others that Lucille has worried about over the years, the lady before us isn't Ernest's daughter.

Instead, I talk about the sudden change in the weather and how this seems to be the worst summer storm we have had for a long time. I prattle about how it will be good for the roses, how it won't be so good for the lettuce growers; I chat about Samson's latest obsession with carrying things around the house, whatever he can find, shoes, newspapers, cushions, and about how the hymns at church are getting repetitive. Anything to keep Lucille from asking any further questions about Maggie's private life.

Chapter Thirty-Nine
July 1950 - Mary

Later, as the three of us sit down for dinner around the candlelit dinner table, despite my attempts to veer the subject away from Ernest's child, whoever she might be and wherever she might be, Lucille is determined to keep the subject open.

'I know that you think I'm being silly, and maybe a little paranoid, and you don't agree with me, but…'

'I know what you're going to say,' I say.

'Agree with what?' asks James. He pulls on a cork and it pops out of the wine bottle. 'Wine anyone?'

'Yes, please,' I say. 'Is this the new Cotes Du Rhone? Shouldn't we have a white wine with pork?'

'Stop trying to change the subject, Mary. It's infuriating. You've been doing it all afternoon.'

'Am I missing something here?' asks James. He pours wine into my glass, then into Lucille's, and then into his own. 'You two seem a bit tetchy with each other.'

'I am not tetchy at all,' says Lucille. 'I am simply frustrated because I have been trying to talk to Mary all afternoon about something that she clearly does not want to discuss.'

'Which is?' asks James.

'Ernest and Violet,' says Lucille. 'And more specifically, Ernest's child.'

'Oh that,' says James. He has known Lucille long enough to know that she refuses to be silenced when she has something to say, but he also knows that I am sensitive about Ernest. Sometimes the mere mention of my brother's name brings tears to my eyes. I have never got over his early death, which was a huge loss to all of the family, not only Lucille. But trying to explain that to Lucille, who has basked in the glory of being the chief mourner for so many years, is futile.

He was a young man, a mere twenty-six years old when a German soldier took his life during the Battle of Ypres. At that time, he didn't know that Lucille was pregnant with their first child. Their daughter, Beatrice, born at the beginning of the summer of 1915, is the image of him. Ernest would have loved her. She has inherited his deep brown eyes, black hair, and skin that tans quickly in the summer, giving her a Mediterranean look. Unlike her mother whose delicate skin has to be protected by shawls and wide-brimmed hats. Beatrice is a grown woman now, living at Compton Hall with her husband and two children of her own. Ernest would have been a grandfather.

Our family has had its fair share of tears and heartache over the years, but so have so many others. I know I am not unique, thanks to the two world wars that have taken so many young men before their time, leaving distraught families, mothers, wives, and children behind. But I can't help feeling angry that Ernest was one of them. He should have stayed at home and pleaded that he was a conscientious objector, rather than going off to fight a war that had nothing to do with him. He should have told the tribunal that he couldn't possibly go and fight because he believed that it was God's will that he should not kill. But I know it would never have worked. He hadn't been to church for years, since his wedding day in fact, so the tribunal would never have believed him. Apart from that, he wanted to join the Army and fight. He wanted to 'do what was right for his country', as he put it.

'I think that Maggie might be Ernest's child,' says Lucille, with a sigh.

'Maggie? The artist?' says James. 'Why would you think that?'

'Because…'

'Because, if you are being honest, you think that every young woman with dark hair might be Ernest's child,' I say.

'That isn't fair,' says Lucille. She slams her knife down on the table.

'Yes it is,' says Mary. 'It's the same every time you come to Lakeview Cottage, although…'

'Ladies, please,' says James.

I ignore him. 'Last year, do you remember, you made us follow that young woman and her husband all the way from the lake to the butchers at the top of the hill, just so you could get a proper look at her face. Then you decided that her nose was too big and she couldn't possibly be related to Ernest after all. You said she wasn't pretty enough.'

Lucille swirls her wine in her glass and takes a large mouthful. 'That was different,' she says. 'You can't deny that Maggie looks decidedly similar to Beatrice. James, what do you think?'

'But Maggie doesn't even have brown eyes,' I say. 'Her eyes are blue.'

'Fathers with brown eyes can have blued-eyed children,' says James.

I glower at my husband and he winks at me, as if to tell me to not take Lucille too seriously. Let her have her rant and get it out of her system. I know he is right and reluctantly I smile at him.

Lucille takes another mouthful of wine and then slams her glass on the table and runs from the room, tears streaming down her face.

'Leave her,' says James. He puts his hand on my arm. 'She'll be okay. You know what she's like sometimes. We should probably have had a week in a nice hotel somewhere with her. You know she gets too emotional when she comes here.'

'Yes, I know.' I take a deep breath. 'The thing is, James, this time, I hate to admit it, but she might be right.'

'What do you mean?'

'Maggie does look a bit like Beatrice, don't you think?'

'I suppose so.' James shrugs his shoulders. 'But not so much that I would assume they were sisters. I would have to see them side by side before I reached that conclusion.'

'I met her son.'

'Maggie's son?'

'Yes, at church. When we were talking outside, he came to look for her.' I wipe a tear with the corner of my napkin. 'He is the image of Ernest when he was that age.'

'What age?'

'He is eleven, I think Maggie said.'

'Can you honestly remember what Ernest looked like when he was eleven, all those years ago?'

'Now you're doing what Lucille accuses us of doing. You're not taking me seriously.'

'I'm sorry, darling. I didn't mean to come across as dismissive. I would just like some concrete evidence before I can conclude that a woman you have met a couple of times is a long-lost relative.'

'Yes, I can understand that,' I say. 'But women have intuition, and I have a feeling about her, too. On this occasion, I think that Lucille might be on to something.'

'Why is this occasion so different? You know that Lucille has seen many women over the years who she claimed looked like Ernest.'

'I know,' I say. 'I don't know why, but this time it feels different. That's all I can say. Maybe it's because I have seen her son and he reminded me of Ernest. I don't know. Now I feel like I'm being silly and over-dramatic.'

'Nobody can ever accuse you of that,' says James. He lifts my hand to his mouth and kisses each of my knuckles in turn. 'But, I thought you said that Maggie's father had died before she was born?'

'Yes, she did say that.'

'So if her father died in 1908 or 1909, he can't possibly be Ernest, can he?'

I shrug. 'If I was Violet and I didn't want my daughter to trace her father, I would probably have told her that her father had died. Lies are sometimes easier than the truth, aren't they? But, we can't ignore the fact that the woman is called Maggie, which is the name of Violet's daughter, and she was born in January 1909. How much more evidence do you need?'

Chapter Forty
July 1950 - Mary

'What I am struggling to understand, Mary, is why you don't want Maggie to be confirmed as Violet's daughter,' says Lucille the following day. 'After all this time, I thought you would be happy to meet her. It seems that you are scared to.'

I don't respond.

'Mary?'

'I'm sorry, Lucille. I don't know what to say. I'm as confused as you are. I thought my walk this morning would have cleared my head, but it hasn't. Obviously, nothing is confirmed yet, but I always thought that if I came across Ernest's child, I would be extraordinarily happy. To see my brother's face reflected in another's...'

'I know, I know,' says Lucille.

She leans across the kitchen table and grasps my hand. We are interrupted by the sound of the doorbell.

'That must be her,' I say.

'I'll get that,' shouts James.

I can hear his feet running down the stairs. As the front door is opened, a rush of cold wind blasts through the house. It sends a shiver down my back. I tighten my cardigan across my chest.

'Are you sure you want to question her?' I ask. 'We don't have to. We can talk about the unseasonal weather and enjoy having our portraits painted instead.'

'That's a great plan,' says Lucille. 'But I'd rather know the truth. It won't do us any harm. We have already experienced the worst.'

I nod. I know she is right. Losing Ernest was the worst thing to have happened to either of them.

'Are you ready, ladies?' asks James a few minutes later. 'Maggie is setting up in the sitting room.'

'Yes, we're ready,' says Lucille. She picks up the tea tray from the table and carries it out of the kitchen.

I walk into James' outstretched arms. 'Everything will be fine,' he whispers into my ear. 'Come on.' He takes hold of my arm and leads me into the sitting room.

When I see Maggie, I feel the negative emotions from last night gently dissipate, like dandelion seeds in the summer breeze. Maggie's infectious smile instantly warms the room as she greets us. At that moment, I make up my mind. I sincerely hope that Maggie is Ernest's daughter. I would be very happy indeed to have such a lovely woman as my niece. I give Maggie a welcome hug and settle myself into the same seat as yesterday, with the light of the bay window behind me. I ask Maggie about her journey and whether she has had a nice morning.

'I have had a wonderful morning, thank you,' says Maggie. 'Teddy has gone on a trip to Kendal with Uncle Billy, so he was in a better mood. He is very much an outside boy and yesterday's rain kept him indoors for most of the day.'

Lucille pours everyone a cup of tea.

'Did you say Uncle Billy?' asks Lucille. 'Is that the same Billy who owns the greengrocers?'

'Yes, that's right,' says Maggie. She takes a cup of tea from Lucille and places it on a side table next to the sofa.

'So your mother must be Clara?' asks Lucille.

Last night, I asked Lucille to be sensitive to the young woman's feelings and avoid bombarding her with questions. I had expected the conversation to be steered towards her family, but not so soon. However, Lucille seems determined and unstoppable.

'Clara? I didn't know that you knew her?' says Maggie.

'We just know that she is Billy's sister,' says Lucille. 'I don't know her personally.' Lucille passes a cup of tea to me before taking one herself from the tray. She sits in the chair next to mine. 'The family used to deliver groceries to Lakeview Cottage, many years ago,' continues Lucille. 'Isn't that right, Mary?'

'Yes, back when most people used to get groceries delivered. Now, I prefer to take a walk to the shop and choose them myself,' I say.

'Oh how lovely,' says Maggie.

I am not sure whether Maggie is referring to knowing Clara or enjoying a walk to the shop. I glance at Lucille who remains focused, looking straight ahead. Upright and still, her chin held high, Lucille resembles the stone lions at the park entrance—an ideal artist's subject. From the image she portrays, nobody would know the turmoil beneath the surface of her fixed smile.

Maggie holds a small pot of green paint in her left hand. It is dark and bold. The colour of a forest canopy. I presume she is painting Lucille's eyes. I watch as she glances between

Lucille and the canvas, her fingers working with confident speed.

'So, did you say that your mother is Clara?' Lucille repeats the question after a few moments of silence.

Maggie stops painting and peers around the canvas. 'Sorry, no. Clara isn't my mother. Although I suppose you could call her my second mother. My mother's name is Violet.'

My tea cup and saucer fall from my shaking fingers and crash to the floor. I run from the room. In the kitchen, I can hear Maggie asking Lucille whether I am upset because my favourite cup has broken. Did someone special buy it for me? Did it have sentimental value? Lucille tells her that I have had an emotional few days; family matters. I hear her apologising to Maggie for the disruption.

I run a clean tea towel under the cold water tap and dab it onto my face. I take deep breaths, breathing in the freshly washed smell. I sincerely wish that a broken cup was all I had to be upset about. Through the kitchen window, I watch James in the garden as he throws Samson's ball high into the air.

Lucille knocks on the open door. 'It's only me,' she says.

'I've made such a fool of myself,' I say. 'I am sorry for being such a baby and running out like that, but it was such a shock when she said Violet's name. After all these years, seeing Ernest's daughter…'

'I thought you would be happy,' says Lucille. 'We have found her, at long last.'

'I wasn't really looking for her,' I say.

'No, but I was. You can tell she is Beatrice's half-sister, can't you? They look so alike.'

'Yes, they do.' I pull out a chair and sit at the kitchen table, wringing the tea towel between my fingers.

Lucille sits opposite. 'You know what I've been like. Every time I came to Cumberland, I thought I could see her somewhere. I have enjoyed my summers here, honestly, I have. Your parents have been wonderful to me over the years, treating me like a daughter. But I found that I could only ever fully relax when I was back at Compton Hall.'

'Why there and not here?' I ask.

'I knew Violet would never go back there. She wouldn't dare, would she? Not after running to London with the baby, knowing that your aunt and Reverend Flynn were desperate for a child.'

'She was under no obligation to hand the baby over to them. She gave the money back, didn't she?'

'Yes, but your mother would have expected Violet to keep to her word. That's what servants did in those days.'

'It was a horrible time. I thought my parents would never speak to James' father ever again. I was petrified that they would force me to call it off with him.'

'They wouldn't do that to you, not after what they did to Ernest.'

'What makes you say that?'

'I think your mother knew that she was too harsh with Ernest. She should have let him and Violet marry.'

'No, not at all,' I say. I reach for Lucille's hand across the table. 'Times were different then. They would never have let him marry a housemaid. They weren't a suitable match at all. He was happy with you.'

'I hope he was. I did try to make him happy, Mary.'

'I know you did.'

I sense Maggie's presence before I see her. I leap up and dash to the kitchen door. Maggie is standing in the hallway, the pieces of broken crockery in her outstretched hand. Tears are streaming down her face.

'Maggie, I...'

Maggie drops the crockery onto the tiled floor and runs out of the front door.

Despite Lucille's protestations and the overwhelming feeling of terrible deja vue, of having to deal with the gatekeepers in the form of the greengrocer, Billy, and his wife, I know that I must go after Maggie. I must speak to her and explain. The poor woman will be distraught. I dash to the front door, but before I reach it, I can hear the car engine starting. All I can do is watch as a tearful Maggie climbs into her car and drives away.

I drag myself back to the kitchen. James has come in from the garden and is wondering why the session with the artist has ended so abruptly. Lucille is less than sympathetic. I had expected to find as much concern on Lucille's face as my own, but I found none. Lucille's quest of the past forty years had been to locate Ernest's daughter and now that she has completed it, she is happy. She need do no more. She can enjoy the rest of her holiday in Cumberland and return to Compton Hall content.

I explain to James what has happened and what I believe Maggie overheard.

'The truth will be a terrible shock to her,' I tell him. 'Imagine being told that your father had died before you were born, and then discovering that was a lie.'

'I don't see how that would have made the slightest bit of difference to her life,' says Lucille, coldly.

'What do you mean?' I say.

'Whether or not she knew who her father was, Violet would never have let her see Ernest, so he may as well have been dead to her.'

'No, I think you're wrong. If Clara's family had told us where they were living, he could have gone to see her and persuaded her to let him see Maggie. The poor child could have had a relationship with everyone from the Compton family, not just her father.'

Lucille shakes her head. I can't decipher what she is thinking and don't want to ask, fearing it might lead to an argument. However, I have a nagging suspicion that maybe she is right. An illegitimate child would not have been welcomed at Compton Hall, no matter how much I wanted her to be.

Chapter Forty-One
September 1951 – Maggie

I spend a minute or so trying to guess the sender of the letter until Edward begs me to put both of us out of our misery. I don't recognise the handwriting and I have exhausted the list of people it could possibly be from. I laugh as I begin to open the letter carefully, sliding the silver letter-opener through the top of the envelope.

'I have five minutes before I need to leave for work, so for the love of God, open the letter,' says Edward. 'The suspense is killing me.'

'I'm going to take my time on purpose, now,' I tease.

Edward reaches across the kitchen table, but I snatch the letter away before he grabs it. I blow him a kiss as I pull the folded letter out of the envelope. I love the way we are now, back together, both of us working on our marriage, making an effort to make the other one happy.

There are three pages and the writing is small. The author seems to have a lot to say. My eyes flick over the pages quickly. Before I read the content, I turn to the last page and scan down to the signature.

'It's from Lucille Compton,' I say.

'Lucille Compton? What does she want?' says Edward. 'You don't have to read it. I don't want you to be upset again.'

I nod. 'I want to read it,' I say. I begin to read aloud.

Dear Maggie,

I have started to write this letter many times, but the words have eluded me. It is so difficult to know where to begin.

I have thought about you almost every day since last summer. The first thing I need to say is that I am sorry. I am sorry that you heard Mary and I discussing your mother and that you found out about your father that way. I wish that things were different. I wish we could have talked to you before you left for London, but I fully understand that you were upset and you didn't want to see us.

Your father was a wonderful man and he would have loved you very much. Times were different when you were born and unfortunately, his parents wouldn't allow him and your mother to be together.

Ernest and I met in late September 1908. He was a friend of my brother, Frank, whom he met at Oxford University. I lived in Oxford at the time with my parents and they often invited Ernest over for dinner. The food at Oxford wasn't unpalatable by any means, but my mother took a shine to Ernest and wanted him to be surrounded by family at meal times.

Ernest and I began to walk together after dinner and sometimes on a Sunday afternoon and I quickly fell in love with him. I thought that his feelings for me were growing, and I was confident that I had found my future husband. At the end of the Michaelmas term when Ernest suggested that Frank and I should have a weekend at his parents' country house before Christmas, I was excited to spend more time with him and to cement our relationship. However, when we arrived at Lakeview Cottage, your mother was there. She was heavily pregnant with you.

She introduced herself to us as Mrs Compton's lady's maid and I had no reason to believe that there was anything between her and Ernest, although the way they looked at each other gave me more than a little cause for concern. That night, I saw Ernest coming out of your mother's bedroom after we had been out to dinner, and it was then that I knew the baby your mother was carrying was his.

I spent hours crying in my bedroom. I had only known him a short time, but I was so upset that I would lose him. In those days, I wasn't short of suitors, but I never had feelings for any of them the way I did for Ernest.

This leads me to my second apology. I am sorry that you never knew your father. He died in October 1914 in the Great War (some might say that was a blessing, as he only had to tolerate the horror of war for a short period of time), but even so, you could have had a father for five years. I am sorry that you didn't.

I feel responsible for that, as I did something terrible that played a large part in keeping your mother and father away from each other. Your mother wrote three letters to your father, which I found in her bedroom at Lakeview Cottage that weekend, and I am ashamed to say that I destroyed them before he had a chance to read them. I didn't read all the letters. All I can say is that your mother poured her heart and soul onto the paper, and had your father read them, he would have been in no doubt as to how your mother felt about him. I thought that because Violet was carrying his child, she was harder to resist than me. Despite my beauty as a young lady, I could not compete with her.

I was young and foolish and selfish, and I should never have done it.

Who knows whether the two of them would have married, with or without the blessings from the Comptons, but I did everything in my power to make sure that Ernest's attention remained on me, and me alone.

I am sorry that, because of my actions, you were denied your father's love.

I am also sorry you haven't had a relationship with your half-sister. I told you that day in Lakeview Cottage that Beatrice looks very much like you. You are undeniably sisters. Her character is like yours, too, from the little I know about you. She is kind and gentle. She is intelligent and quick-witted. She loves to paint, and she can see the beauty in everything. She would love to meet you, one day.

I hope you will take my apologies in the spirit that they are meant - with love.

I have thought long and hard about how to make reparations for my actions and I have a proposition for you.

I am not sure whether you know about the terrible death of Mary. She suffered a heart attack not long after I returned to Compton Hall in August. I would like you to know how concerned she was that you were hurt. Mary had a beautiful soul, just like her brother, and she would never have wanted to cause you any pain.

James was with her when she died. In the months that followed, James was a shell of his former self. It was as though life had left him too. Shortly after the New Year, he also died. He was staying with us at Compton Hall at the time and collapsed while out in the garden with Samson. The doctors said he also had a heart attack, but if this were a Jane Austen novel, she would have written that he died of a broken heart.

Our family solicitor had copies of Mary's and James' wills. As they had no children, I am now the new legal owner of Lakeview Cottage.

Maggie, I would like you to have it.

Had you been a part of your father's life and consequently a part of your Aunt Mary's life, I have no doubt that the cottage would have been bequeathed to you.

I will visit Bowness at a time to suit you, hopefully soon, and we can make arrangements for the Deed of Gift form to be witnessed. My solicitor has already drawn it up.

I understand that your life is in London and you may never want to live in Lakeview Cottage, but you can sell it and use the money to buy a house somewhere else. The place is yours to do with what you wish.

Your father would have wanted you to have it.

Please write back to me when you have had time to digest all this unexpected information.

Yours sincerely

Lucille.

'Edward, I don't understand. Why would she want to give Lakeview Cottage to me?' I pass him the letter so he can read the words, even though he has just heard them.

'Lakeview Cottage?' Teddy thunders down the stairs and into the kitchen. He is dressed in his school uniform. I glance at the clock. He should leave the house within the next few minutes, otherwise he will be late. 'That house in Bowness?'

'Yes. Your mother's a rich woman, Teddy,' says Edward.

'I am not. Don't listen to your father. Eat up your breakfast quickly. Have you packed your PT kit and your homework?'

'Yes, Mum, I have everything. My bag's in the hallway.' He grabs a slice of toast and takes a large bite. 'Why would someone give you Lakeview Cottage? Is it that old couple, have they died and left it to you in their will?'

'Teddy, don't talk with your mouth full, please,' I tell him. 'Well, yes, Mr and Mrs Bradbury have died, I'm afraid…'

'And they left the house to you? Well, so they should. You're family, aren't you?'

'It is Mrs Bradbury's sister-in-law, Lucille, who wants to give it to me. That's what that letter says.'

I am often amazed by my precocious son. I suppose the fact that he is an only child has contributed to him having an old head on young shoulders. Edward and I have never excluded him from our conversations, apart from our most private ones, of course. Sometimes I wonder whether we have done the right thing.

'The Comptons are millionaires, aren't they?' says Teddy. 'Aunt Clara says they are one of the richest families in the country. She hates them.'

'He says it so matter of fact, doesn't he?' laughs Edward.

'Edward, please. Families hating each other is not a laughing matter.'

311

'Why does she hate them so much?' asks Teddy.

Why does Clara hate the Comptons? How can I begin to answer that question? How can I begin to explain the relationship between my mother and Clara, and the Comptons? Teddy will know the whole truth eventually, but now isn't the time. He needs to go to school.

'Things were different in those days, darling. When your Granny Violet and Aunt Clara were young, many people, especially women, didn't have the opportunities they have today. Some were lucky to be born into a rich family…'

'Like the Comptons.'

'Yes, like the Comptons. Now, come on, time for school.'

I kiss Edward and Teddy and shoo them both out of the door.

'We'll talk about it tonight,' says Edward, as he kisses me gently on my mouth.

Despite our short separation last summer, our marriage is stronger than ever. I remember on the day of my wedding, Clara confessed to me that she loved my mum in the same way that I love Edward. She told me how lucky I was to have found a man that I could spend the rest of my life with. She told me to cherish each day with him, and from now on, I will.

I need to telephone her and tell her about this letter. I'm sure she will have plenty to say about it.

Chapter Forty-Two
Christmas Eve 1951 – Maggie

The house is finally quiet. Edward, Teddy, Mum, and Clara are all in bed. The Christmas tree sits in the corner of the room like a contented mother surrounded by all her children. The brightly coloured presents are in five piles, one for each of us, to be opened tomorrow morning after the church service.

Uncle Billy and all the family will be coming for Christmas lunch. Clara is looking forward to cooking turkey, pigs in blankets, roast potatoes, carrots, and sprouts. The whole lot. I'm so excited, I don't know how I will sleep tonight. It is going to be a magical day.

On the day we moved into Lakeview Cottage a few weeks ago, Clara held onto my hand tightly and led me upstairs to one of the bedrooms that looks out onto the front garden.

'That's where you were born,' she said, her eyes brimming with tears. 'My mum delivered you, with help from Edith, a lady I used to work with, the one who taught me how to cook. It was terrifying, but when you cried for the first time, there wasn't a dry eye in the room. We were all bawling.'

I laughed, but the tears followed very quickly. I clung to Clara and rested my head on her shoulders. I cried for the father I never knew, the grandparents who never had the chance to spoil me and feed me too much ice cream, and for my Aunt Mary, who never had the chance to talk to me after I ran out of the house last summer.

'Was Mum scared?' I asked.

Clara nodded. 'She was very brave. Of course, what she was scared of more than anything was that the Comptons would come and take you away from her.' Clara held my hand and bade me to sit on the edge of the bed with her. 'She loved you so much, even before you were born.'

'I know that,' I said. 'I felt the same way about Teddy.'

'So you can understand why she agreed to …?'

'Yes, of course,' I said. 'You don't need to explain. I understand.'

'She wanted you to have the best possible life.'

'I know, I know. I just wish that I knew my father. Mary was a lovely person, you know, and if my dad was half as lovely as she was…'

'Yes, Ernest was a wonderful man,' said Clara. 'From what your mum told me. She loved him very much. When your mum was a housemaid, he was the only one of the Comptons who treated her like a real person.'

'What are you two doing up here?' Edward peered around the door, holding onto the handle. 'It's no wonder I can't hear the kettle boiling. Who's making my tea if you two are both up here?'

'Cheeky bugger,' said Clara. 'I'm reminiscing. I'm just telling Maggie how brave her mother was when she was born.'

'Never mind all that mush, get the kettle on, woman.'

I jumped up from the bed and slapped him playfully on the arm as I left the room. Edward slapped my bottom in return.

'Now then, you can stop that,' said Clara. 'If I'm going to be in the room next door to you, I don't want to hear any shenanigans through the wall.'

'You should sleep in the other room then, the corner one. Out of harm's way,' said Edward.

But Mum has chosen the corner room, which I hoped she would. I can hear her gentle snores through the ceiling. She deserves a beautiful bedroom. It is decorated with pretty William Morris wallpaper. The delicate green and cream give a calming effect, and even on a winter's day like today, the room is light and welcoming, thanks to the two windows.

Lucille gave me a tiny ceramic vase with a delicate handle, which I put on her bedside cabinet. I have filled it with holly and eucalyptus leaves. Apparently, Mum used to love it. When she saw it, she burst into tears. She held the vase close to her chest and told me that it was the best gift she had ever had.

She's a silly old woman. But I love her dearly.

She will love living here with us in Lakeview Cottage.

THE END

Note from the Author

If anyone knows Bowness-on-Windermere, you will know the big white hotel that stands on a small hill overlooking the lake. I can imagine that when it was first built, it was built as a large house, rather than a hotel. I might be wrong, but one day on a visit to the town, which is one of my favourite in the Lake District, I began to imagine who might have lived there in the past.

I wanted to write a book from the point of view of a working-class woman because, contrary to popular belief, I am not related to aristocracy, but am in fact from working-class stock. A search of Ancestry.com showed me that my family on my dad's side (the Melody family) came over to England from Ireland in 1845 and settled in Manchester.

In the early twentieth century, they still lived in Manchester and most of them worked in the cotton mills.

Pearson, the name I have given to Violet, is my paternal grandmother's maiden name. I didn't come across any family members called Violet, but there were plenty of Margaret's – shortened to Maggie – and there is a Bridgett and a Thomas, which is also my son's name.

This book is dedicated to my female ancestors, who would have had an extremely difficult life in Manchester. From what I have read, although Ancoats is now called the Northern Quarter and is full of young professional people, artisan bakeries, and restaurants, in 1908 it was a very different place. Fictional Violet had it fairly easy, you might argue, escaping to live and work in Compton Hall, although I can't imagine how hard it must have been for women like her who discovered they were pregnant outside of marriage.

The tragedy of this story is that Ernest and Violet never married. He always loved her, but he didn't champion her to his parents as he should have done, and chose to marry Lucille instead. Societal expectations won in the end.

I hope you have enjoyed this story. This is the first historical novel I have written and I thoroughly enjoyed immersing myself in it.

I would like to thank Jane Rogers, an extremely talented writer and tutor at The Faber Academy who taught me so much and gave me invaluable feedback on my manuscript throughout the nine-month creative writing course that I finished in April 2024.

I would also like to thank my fellow students Nia, Ash, Asha, Clare, Mirte, Nick, and Ria for their feedback during the course and for their ongoing support in our WhatsApp group.

I can't wait for all of their books to be published. I have a space on my shelf waiting for them!

Printed in Great Britain
by Amazon

49069662R00179